52254

J F
WIL

Williams, Walter Jon

Rock of ages

$21.95 (5)

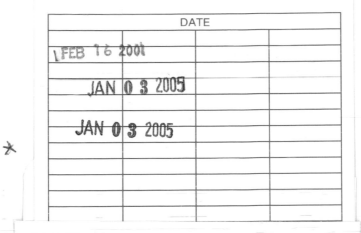

ROCK
OF
AGES

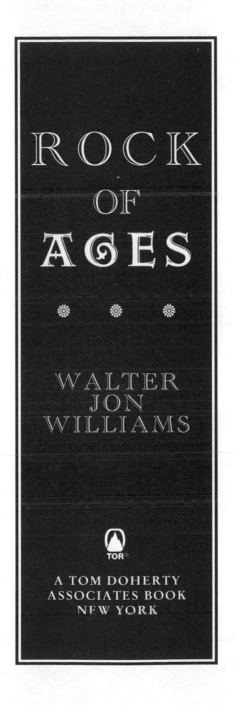

ROCK
OF
AGES

✻ ✻ ✻

WALTER
JON
WILLIAMS

TOR®

A TOM DOHERTY
ASSOCIATES BOOK
NEW YORK

For Rebecca, with thanks

This is a work of fiction. All the characters and events portrayed in this novel are either fictitious or are used fictitiously.

ROCK OF AGES

Copyright © 1995 by Walter Jon Williams

This book is printed on acid-free paper.

A Tor Book
Published by Tom Doherty Associates, Inc.
175 Fifth Avenue
New York, N.Y. 10010

Tor Books on the World-Wide Web:
http://www.tor.com

Tor® is a registered trademark of Tom Doherty Associates, Inc.

Design by Junie Lee

Library of Congress Cataloging-in-Publication Data

Williams, Walter Jon.
    Rock of ages / Walter Jon Williams.
        p.   cm.
    "A Tom Doherty Associates book."
    ISBN 0-312-85963-5
    I. Title.
    PS3573.I456213R63   1995
    813'.54—dc20   95-22694
                                                                  CIP

First edition: September 1995

Printed in the United States of America

0 9 8 7 6 5 4 3 2 1

"Tyrawley and I have been dead these
two years; but we don't choose to
have it known."
Boswell's *Johnson*, 3 April 1773

ONE

❋ ❋ ❋

It was a strange way to treat an Object of Desire.

The third wife of Francesco di Bartolommeo di Zanobi del Giocondo was centuries old but had lost none of her appeal. Admirers still came to extol her fine forehead and delicate hands—to offer her worship, to pay court, to covet. With lombardy poplar stiffening her spine, she received them all with the same temperate brown gaze, the same equable expression, the same intriguing smile.

Perhaps the smile was difficult on occasion to maintain, as some of her admirers were more extreme than others. More than once she had been abducted from her home; more than once she'd been rescued or ransomed or snatched from oblivion at the last second.

Today maintaining the smile must have been a struggle. In a semicircle around her were a squad of policemen, all in battle gear, all, with unforgivable rudeness, facing outward, their backs to her. She was surrounded by the invisible globe of a cold-field. Layered defenses, arrays of screamers and leapers, studded the floor, ceiling, and the walls to either side of her throne.

Facing her were two men. One was tall, white-haired, and gaunt. The other was of medium height—though, even facing the squad of police in battle array, he seemed taller. He wore his hair long, had buskins on his feet, a large diamond ring on one finger, and looked on the world with heavy-lidded green eyes that gave his face an indolent expression. He was in his late twenties.

"How do you like our La Gioconda?" the white-haired man asked. His voice was loud. Perhaps it was rude of him to say it within her earshot, but that was his way—he affected to be hard of hearing, and had a tendency to shout.

"I would like her better, Lord Huyghe, if I could get a little closer."

"Perhaps, Maijstral, if you asked *politely.*"

The line of police stiffened. Gloved fingers edged closer to weapons.

Drake Maijstral moved forward on silent feet and raised his hands. The guardians' trigger fingers vibrated with tension . . . and then Maijstral made a simple gesture as if to part waters.

"If you please—?" he said.

Reluctantly the line of guards parted and shuffled aside. An official—the lady's chief attendant, a Tanquer named Horving—seemed about to strangle himself with his own tail. Maijstral's lazy eyes, glowing with amusement, looked La Gioconda up and down. His ears twitched forward.

"I like her *sfumato,*" he said. "And it's a pleasant face, that should wear well. One could have it on one's wall and not tire of it easily."

At this ominous news Horving's breath began to wheeze through a constricted windpipe. It was difficult to tell if his pop eyes were a result of outrage or strangulation. Lord

Huyghe—he was an art historian—ambled forward and bent to peer at the lady's features.

"Mona Lisa is an old friend," he said. "We're on first-name terms."

"I congratulate you on the acquaintance. I know only her cousin—the *Lady with an Ermine.*"

"Ah. I don't believe I've had the pleasure."

Maijstral once had six days to make the acquaintance of *Lady with an Ermine,* the period between his theft of the painting and the time he sold it back to the owner's insurance company.

"In Prince Chan's collection, on Nana," he said. "The *Lady,* like Mona Lisa, is celebrated for the elusive quality of her smile. It makes one wonder if the artist had a way of amusing women."

"I believe history is silent on the matter," Huyghe said.

Horving, anoxic, collapsed to the floor with a hollow wooden boom. One of the policemen growled. Maijstral looked up.

"Don't look at *me,*" he said. "*I* didn't do it."

He gave La Gioconda a final, searching look, then withdrew. Huyghe followed and took his arm.

"Shall we go on to the Venetians, Maijstral?"

"Let's jump ahead to the Flemish. There's a Vermeer I have my eye on."

The two left the room and turned down the corridor. A squad of police anxiously trotted after. The guards had been expecting Maijstral to view the collection in order, Italians followed by Flemish. Maijstral's jumping about had destroyed their operational plan, and their officers were forced to improvise.

While flustered security men dashed from one place to another, Maijstral walked with perfect ease next to the historian. If one must view famous art treasures through a picket fence of policemen, he considered, the least one could do is tweak them from time to time.

"I heard from your father, incidentally," Huyghe said. His booming voice echoed in the corridor.

Maijstral frowned. "Recently?"

"Only a few days ago, through VPL. He asked me to look after you and make certain that you weren't associating with any—" He smiled. "Rude or unsuitable companions."

Maijstral sighed. No sooner had Gustav Maijstral been pronounced dead and laid to rest in his tomb on Nana than he took up a large correspondence, usually through the expensive Very Private Letter service—either complaints to his son about Maijstral's habits, demands for money to honor some old debt that he'd forgotten about for twenty years, notes to friends complaining about Maijstral's neglect, or suggestions to old creditors that they approach Maijstral and demand he pay up.

"Gustav said he hoped to see me soon," Huyghe boomed. "I don't suppose you permit him the funds to travel—?"

"He's quite safe in his tomb," Maijstral said. "He'd only get into trouble if he travelled." He looked at the older man. "I'm afraid his mind was wandering, Lord Huyghe. It happens so easily to the dead, you know."

"I quite understand," Huyghe said.

Maijstral found Vermeer's *Lacemaker* as splendid as advertisied, and he enjoyed the other Flemish works, although he wondered aloud why so many still lifes were the remnants of meals—dirty forks and smeared dishes hardly seemed the most cultivated subjects for fine art.

"If you were a starving artist," Huyghe asked, "would you let a meal stand for the amount of time it took to paint it?"

"Ah," Maijstral said. "I entirely take your point."

* * *

After viewing the collection, Huyghe and Maijstral strolled out of the Louvre toward where Huyghe's red Sportsman flyer waited on the old vintage concrete drive. Media globes, circling in a holding pattern over the car, spotted their quarry and zoomed in, jostling for the better shots, Maijstral framed by the Pei pyramid, the Khorkhinn carousel, the Floating Saucer of the Tuileries.

"May we expect a robbery at the Louvre anytime soon?" one asked.

"I'm here on vacation," Maijstral said. "I've never been to Earth before, and I have no intention of spoiling my pleasure here by indulging in my profession. I have too little time to properly appreciate my heritage: Paris, Edo, Tejas, Memphis . . ."

"Do you expect the recent recommendation of the Constellation Practices Authority, condemning burglary and urging that it be banned, to have any real effect on your occupation?"

Maijstral considered an answer. "Allowed Burglary is a custom that predates human civilization," he said. "One hopes that the various parliaments of the Constellation will have consideration for its antiquity."

"You think, then," a new voice, "that the Human Constellation should maintain inhuman customs even when they're contrary to traditional human civilization?"

Maijstral's green eyes glittered from behind heavy lids. The question was provocative, particularly the word *inhuman,* which had recently taken on a nasty edge. His own view was that the phrase "human civilization" had been something of a contradiction in terms until humanity had found itself annexed by an alien power; but he didn't want to make a reply as provocative as the question had been, so he temporized.

"I'm entirely in favor of human civilization," he said,

"but there's nothing civilized in change for its own sake. Why alter an institution that works, and that has been providing sport and entertainment for millennia?"

"Do you think you'll hold the championship as long as Geoff Fu George?"

Maijstral smiled. "Fu George is incomparable," he said. "I was lucky at Silverside Station, and if he hadn't retired, I'm certain he'd still hold first place."

"Nichole is onplanet," another globe said. "Do you plan to see *her*?"

At that point one alarm after another began to sing from the Louvre. Guards—massed near the entrance to see Maijstral off—jostled one another in confusion. Maijstral smiled in amusement: someone had decided to pull a job when the guards had their attention elsewhere. He turned to Huyghe.

"Let's be on our way," he said, "before they try to pin this one on *me.*"

The red Sportsman arrowed into the Parisian sky. Maijstral sighed as the media globes fell astern.

"How did Fu George put up with it all those years?" he asked.

"He had a more sizeable entourage than you," Huyghe said. "That time on Silverside Station, he was restricted in the number of people he could bring. Just two."

"Two and Vanessa Runciter," Maijstral said, "and she's worth an army." He shivered at a memory of staring down the barrel of Vanessa Runciter's rifle.

"Still, I'm afraid you'll need more people."

"I'm trying," Maijstral said, "but you'd be surprised at how hard it is to find promising young criminals these days."

A few minutes later the Sportsman set down on Huyghe's estate southwest of Krakow. Maijstral thanked his host for the tour of Earth's most renowned gallery, then made his way to his room to dress for dinner.

In his room Maijstral was met by his servant, Roman. Roman was tall even for a Khosalikh, and his family had been in the service of Maijstral's for more generations than Maijstral could, or for that matter cared, to count.

Maijstral handed Roman his pistols—he'd left his knife behind, as a courtesy to the museum's canvases—and then Roman began to unlace his jacket.

Roman's ears twitched forward. "I understand there was some difficulty at the museum, sir," he said.

"Not really. But just in case the police decide to doubt the evidence of their eyes and conclude it *was* me somehow, we might tidy things a bit—I don't know what the local regulations allow in the way of burglar gear."

"News flashes indicate the theft may have been successful, sir."

"Ah. In that case we may as well resign ourselves to a visit from the authorities."

A few weeks earlier, the Imperial Sporting Commission had, somewhat to Maijstral's dismay, rated him the top-ranked Allowed Burglar in all known space. Maijstral had never permitted himself to consider himself a serious candidate—during his entire professional career, Geoff Fu George had occupied the top spot, a position he'd secured during the Affaire of the Mirrorglass BellBox and in subsequent years made his own. But Fu George had just retired, two other leading candidates had the bad fortune to be sent to prison, and—Maijstral might as well admit it—he'd outdone himself on Silverside Station and come out of the business with a truly astounding array of swag. He'd managed to outscore the nearest rival by all of twenty points.

Roman finished unlacing Maijstral's jacket, and after picking off an offending piece of lint, carried the garment to the closet. Maijstral picked up a pair of binoculars and gazed out the window, trying to locate the detectives he knew were lurking on the fringes of the Huyghe estate.

Being first in the ratings, Maijstral had discovered, guaranteed the champion an unfortunate amount of attention from the local authorities.

There the police were, he discovered, behind some shrubs. The detectives were too dignified to actually crouch down behind the foliage, and were trying to act as if it were perfectly natural for some badly dressed, slightly seedy public servants to spend hours loitering behind the thorn bushes.

Maijstral couldn't help but hope they would fall into them.

Once Roman had finished dressing him, Maijstral glided silently into the study next door, where Drexler, a glass in his eye, was absorbed in the microscopic innards of a piece of burglar equipment, in this case a flax-jammer.

"The authorities should be here shortly," Maijstral said. "There's been a successful burglary at the Louvre."

Drexler turned in his chair and looked at Maijstral over his shoulder. He was a Khosalikh, having just reached maturity with his first molt. He was a little shorter than average—which made him about the size of a tall human—but was built very stoutly, as if for the long haul.

"Beg pardon, sir," he said, "but you shouldn't have done a job on a place like the Louvre without proper support."

"I didn't," Maijstral said. "Someone else timed a robbery to coincide with my visit."

Drexler's ears flattened. "I hope this doesn't turn into another Silverside Station situation," he said.

"I devoutly hope not," Maijstral said. "But if anything in your bag of tricks is illegal in Western Ukrania, or wherever it is we are, then please make it disappear for a bit."

"Absolutely," Drexler said. He put his work in a foam-lined case, put the case in a tough canvas drawstring bag, and tossed the bag in the air, where it stayed. At a (verbal) command, the window opened, and then at a (silent, electronic) command from the proximity wire in Drexler's collar, the drawstring bag flew out.

"I'll put it in a tree a few kilometers away, all right?" Drexler said, and his tongue lolled in a Khosalikh smile.

"Fine. Thank you."

"I didn't have anything actually illegal, but if the police confiscated it, it might be a while before it was returned, and then it might come back damaged."

"Very good."

"These things have been known to happen."

"Quite so. Thank you."

Maijstral returned to his dressing room, silently contemplating the problem of Drexler.

Drexler, like Maijstral, had experienced the madness of Silverside Station firsthand, but from an opposing vantage point. He'd furnished technical support for Geoff Fu George, and had been up to his muzzle in the mad contending scramble for loot that marked Silverside's social debut. Fu George's retirement had coincided with Maijstral's own tech leaving his employ, and Drexler had then offered his services to Maijstral. Maijstral hired him, albeit provisionally. Thus far the arrangement had worked well enough, though Maijstral hadn't precisely put Drexler's abilities to the test: he hadn't done any major jobs for the last few months.

But something, Maijstral thought, was missing. Maijstral had no complaints with Drexler's performance or abilities—Fu George wouldn't have hired anything but the best—but there was an intangible *something* that kept Maijstral from feeling entirely at home around Drexler.

It bothered him. It wasn't that he disliked Drexler, it was

just that he never found himself at ease around the Khosalikh, and he didn't know why. The fact that Drexler was a Khosalikh was not at issue, either, since Maijstral was perfectly comfortable around Roman.

Chemistry, he supposed. Regrettable, but there you are.

Maijstral finished dressing. Roman silently offered him his weapons, and Maijstral stowed them away. Distantly, Maijstral heard the booming of the dinner gong.

"Will you be needing anything else, sir?" Roman asked.

The room darkened as if a mass of ravens had flown beneath the sun. Maijstral looked out the window to see a phalanx of shiny black police fliers settling onto Lord Huyghe's lawn. Irritation crabbed at his nerves.

"What did I tell you?" he demanded. "They're not going to leave me alone for a blasted second on this blasted planet!"

He really *was* on vacation. He had come to Earth to attend the wedding of two acquaintances and sometime employers, Amalia Jensen and Pietro Quijano, and he was staying on as a tourist. He didn't want to steal anything on this trip, but it seemed as if no one was willing to take his word for it.

"Perhaps their visit will be brief," Roman comforted.

Maijstral took a few deep breaths and tried to dispel his pique.

"Stay in the room, will you," Maijstral said, "and make sure the cops don't steal anything."

Roman, ever the perfect servant, bowed.

"Very good, sir," he said.

Dinner was not delayed, though it was disturbed somewhat by the sound of heavy police boots tramping up and down the halls. The local police commissaire, a bushy-whiskered old soul named Przemysl, was invited to join Maijstral and Lord and Lady Huyghe, and sat down just in time for the soup course.

"Sorry about this," he apologized, speaking precisely in Khosali Standard. "Were it up to me, I wouldn't interrupt you till after dinnertime; but orders come from on high, you know. When they unified the police forces, I knew this sort of thing would happen." He brandished his spoon. " 'Listen,' I told them, 'those bureaucrats in Beijing won't care a stick about the feelings of the local gentry. They'll have me interrupting people at mealtimes, or dragging them out of their beds when you might just as well wait till after they've had breakfast.' And see if it hasn't happened." He turned his eyes piously to Heaven. "The Virtues only know what will happen if the Security and Sedition Act is passed. Then none of us will be safe."

"What exactly was taken from the Louvre?" Lord Huyghe asked.

Przemysl cast a knowing glance at Maijstral. "A painting undergoing cleaning and restoration," he said. "Titian's *Man with a Glove.*"

"Ah yes," Huyghe said. "I'd marked its absence."

Bootheels clicked on the dining room floor as a tall, frowning police officer stalked into the room. She was human, with blondish hair tucked, somewhat unsuccessfully, into a gleaming black-visored helmet more suitable to the Dread Squad of the Constellation Death Commandos than to a public servant approaching a person of distinction at his dinner. Her face was chiselled. Her manner was correct, but curt. Her uniform was of black leather and had many gleaming buttons. The others rose as she marched to Lord Huyghe's elbow. She saluted.

"Sir," she said, speaking Human Standard, "I am Colonel-General Denise Vandergilt. I would like to request permission for police to inspect the paintings in your gallery in order to make certain that the stolen picture is not hidden beneath them."

Lord Huyghe frowned and spoke in his normal—booming—conversational tones. Maijstral had to offer reluctant congratulations to Vandergilt for the fact she didn't leap back, flinch, or assume she was about to be assaulted and draw her pistol.

"What means do you intend to use?" Huyghe roared.

"For the inspection? Passive broadband fluorocameras. No injury to your canvases is possible."

"Ah. Very well." Huyghe waved his napkin, a signal for the other diners to resume their seats. "As you like, then."

Vandergilt's expression grew abstract for a moment as she pulsed silent commands to her troops through her in-the-helmet scrambler.

Lady Huyghe lowered her spoon and pricked her ears forward. She was a quiet woman, perhaps as a result of her husband shouting at her all these years, and when she spoke it was generally to the point.

"Colonel-General?" she said. "I don't believe that is a rank in the local constabulary, is it?"

"I am a member of the Constellation Special Services Corps, ma'am," Vandergilt said.

"The Colonel-General came here specially from Beijing," Przemysl said. His expression invited sympathy from the diners.

"And what precisely," Lady Huyghe asked, "does the Special Services Corps *do?*"

Vandergilt noticed that a disobedient strand of hair had drooped out from under her helmet. "We maintain the political security of the Human Constellation against foreign and domestic threats, ma'am," she said, stuffing hair into her helmet with one efficient black-gloved hand, "and investigate those deemed worthy of special interest to the Administration."

"Gracious," Lady Huyghe blinked. She turned to her husband. "Do you suppose there might be anyone of that description at our table?"

Vandergilt frowned. "If you won't mind an observation, ma'am, I am surprised that the owners of a select art collection such as yourself and, ah, Mr. Huyghe, would have as your houseguest a person whose profession it is to steal."

"Ha!" Lord Huyghe said abruptly. Vandergilt gave a little start, as if a pistol had just gone off near her ear. A strand of blond hair fell in her eyes.

"Maijstral's father and I were at school together," Huyghe said. "It's natural to offer hospitality to the son of an old friend."

"And of course I wouldn't steal from my host," Maijstral said. "That would be rude."

"And the name's Behrens, by the way," Huyghe added. "Anthony Behrens. Huyghe's just the title."

"Thank you, Mr. Behrens," Vandergilt said. She tried, and failed, to stuff the strand of hair back in her helmet. "I appreciate your reminding me that the title is, in the Constellation, only a courtesy."

Lady Huyghe frowned gently. "I believe," she said, "that *courtesy* is the operative word."

Vandergilt flushed. Her eyes narrowed as she looked at Lord and Lady Huyghe, and, watching her, Maijstral suspected she would be opening a file on them the second she returned to Beijing. Maijstral's father had been a notorious Imperialist, and now it seemed likely that Gustav Maijstral's school chum and his wife were about to suffer a case of dossier-by-association.

"Flattered as I am by the attention," Maijstral said, "I wonder how I merit it. How does being an Allowed Burglar— an occupation perfectly legal under Constellation law—somehow merit this, ah, *special interest* of nothing less than a full Colonel-General?"

"We do not believe," Vandergilt said, "that an inhuman sport like Allowed Burglary will be legal for long. And even

Allowed Burglary permits me to arrest you if I catch you in the act or shortly thereafter."

Maijstral's ears flattened. His green eyes glittered under his lazy eyelids. "I hope I shall be able to offer you and your people sufficient exercise," he said.

Przemysl beamed at him from across the table, and Maijstral sensed approval from Lord and Lady Huyghe. No doubt, he thought, they were anticipating Maijstral's leading this officious officer in a merry chase from vault to hideout and back again.

Maijstral knew he did not deserve the credit granted him by his fellow diners. He was damned if he was going to steal anything while a leather-clad fanatic like this was lurking about, just waiting to drag him off to Beijing and drop him in a lightless dungeon, no doubt one equipped with fetters, damp straw, rats, and other traditional paraphernalia. . . .

Vandergilt drew herself up. She knew a challenge when she heard one. "We have no intention, you see," she declaimed, "of allowing a notorious character such as yourself to plunder the heritage of the Human Constellation for his own aggrandizement." Her black-gloved hand rose, hesitated.

"Would you like a pin, dear?" Lady Huyghe asked.

"No. Thank you. If you'll excuse me, Mr. and Mrs. Behrens?"

She turned on her heel and stalked off. Lord Huyghe gave a sigh. "Thank the Virtues," he said, "she was only here for the soup course."

The police withdrew just as the meal got to its brandy-and-cigars stage, something that disappointed old Przemysl, who had only got halfway through his Monte Cristo before he had to leave.

"I like the fellow, you know," Huyghe said as he settled back into his chair, "but I'm rather glad he's gone. There are a few things I'd like to discuss with you, Drake, if you've no objection."

"None at all," Maijstral said. "By the way, is that a Jasper in the corner?"

Huyghe smiled. "It is indeed. An atypical piece—you have a good eye."

"I didn't know you collected moderns."

Lady Huyghe tapped ash from her Cohima and contemplated the brandy in her snifter. "My taste, actually," she said. "The piece struck my fancy years ago, and Tony bought it for my birthday."

"How thoughtful," Maijstral said.

"I was wondering, Drake," Huyghe said, "if you'd be interested in any commissions while you're here. There are some pieces in private collections that I'm itching to get a look at, but their owners are quite reclusive, and I'm afraid the only way I'll ever see them is if I arrange for them to . . ." He tapped cigar ash. "To appear in my own collection," he finished.

"I'd love to oblige," Maijstral said, "but my stay on Earth already suffers from an overfull programme. Perhaps I can give you an introduction to someone in the burglar line who will be able to accommodate you."

"I'd appreciate that very much." A light glowed in Huyghe's eyes. "I imagine you've got quite a few surprises planned for that Vandergilt character, eh?"

Maijstral smiled thinly. "Ye-es," he drawled. Not the least of which, he considered, was the fact he wouldn't be stealing anything at all while he was here.

Later that evening, Maijstral politely sniffed Lord Huyghe's ears and Lady Huyghe's wrist, then returned to his chambers determined to order Drexler and Roman to get rid of all the burglar equipment for the length of time they stayed on Earth. No point in getting arrested for carrying gear he had no intention of using, and which might be technically illegal in some jurisdiction or other.

Maijstral opened his door and told the room to turn on the lights. He looked up and his heart gave a leap of terror. He stared at his dresser and only managed to avoid gibbering because he was speechless with fear.

Atop his dresser, fresh from cleaning and restoration, was Titian's *Man with a Glove.*

TWO

Sweat prickled on Maijstral's scalp. He was being set up. He pictured Colonel-General Vandergilt kicking in the door with her heavy black boots, smiling an evil smile as she raised her mapper and squeezed the trigger. Caught red-handed, she'd say, too bad he tried to escape. . . .

Maijstral turned to the service plate, intending to summon Roman and have his servant somehow get the painting *away*.

"Hallo," said a voice. Maijstral spun around and winced as a brass doorknob punched his kidney. In an upper corner of the room, colors shifted as the holographic projectors of a darksuit turned themselves off to reveal a small woman, hand raised in a cheerful wave.

"Sorry if I startled you," she said. She floated to the floor a few feet in front of Maijstral. "I just wanted to show you my bag from the Louvre."

Maijstral made an effort to move his thrashing heart from his throat to a more conventional location. "You've shown it to me," Maijstral said. "Now please leave."

The woman held out her hand. "Conchita Sparrow," she said. "Pleased to meet you."

Her accent was uncouth and her hair was arranged in a kind of informal, outlandish dorsal fin on top of her head, perhaps in hope of making her seem taller. Her face was bright-eyed and pleasant, though not beautiful. Maijstral hesitantly reached out a hand, offered her a cautious one-fingered hand-clasp. She gave him two fingers in return, a presumption of a greater intimacy than Maijstral was willing, given the circumstances, to contemplate.

"Actually," she said, "I was looking for a tech designer job. I thought you might be more interested in looking at my recordings if I showed you how useful I could be."

Maijstral's eyes—wide open for once—moved to the Titian. "You may have proved far more useful to the police than to me," he said. "They were just here looking for that painting."

"I know," she grinned. "I saw them leave. Don't worry—they didn't see me. Especially not those two clots out in the thorn bushes—they couldn't skulk their way out of a dead people's convention. The only person who saw me was one of your people, the one in the darksuit, and he took off."

A cold finger touched Maijstral on the neck. "A darksuit?" he asked.

"Yeah. A good one—most detectors wouldn't have spotted it, but mine did. He flew in just after the cops left—he stopped at your window, looked in for a moment, then flew on. That's when he saw me and flew off."

"A moment, Miss Sparrow," Maijstral said. He reached to the wall by the door and touched the service plate. "Roman? Drexler? Were either of you just out on the grounds?"

The answers were negative. Maijstral turned to Conchita Sparrow.

"I'll look at your recordings if you like," he said, "but that person lurking around outside was probably a member of the Special Services Corps, and will be very happy to send me to prison for possession of that painting. So if you would oblige me by taking it *very far away,* I'll be in your debt."

"Only too," Conchita said, meaning *Only too happy.* Maijstral raised an eyebrow at this cheeky piece of cant. Conchita stepped toward the painting, took a bag out of her darksuit, and slipped it over the painting. Once bagged, the painting levitated as of its own free will, then followed Conchita to the window. Before she slipped through the drape she turned on the holo projectors of her darksuit, and blended almost indistinguishably with the background.

"The recordings are in your upper right drawer," she said. "Happy to've met you!"

The drapes parted, the window opened, and out she flew.

Maijstral went to his bureau drawer, saw a recording sphere lying there, and then marched to the service plate to summon Roman and Drexler.

They searched Maijstral's room for the next hour, but found no more surprises.

Next morning Maijstral bade farewell to Lord and Lady Huyghe and set off for North America. Once airborne, Maijstral put his car on autopilot and reviewed Conchita's recordings with Roman and Drexler. He understood why she was seeking employment as a tech. Though her equipment was first-rate—her black boxes always worked, and her darksuit's equipment wove an elegant path through a wide assortment of alarms—she was nevertheless a very poor thief. She was too nervous: she dropped things, or performed operations in the wrong order and had to start over, and once she forgot to tell her darksuit to neutralize a set of flaxes and had to fly in disarray when the alarms began to ring.

"She's a disaster," Drexler snickered, as he watched Conchita head for the horizon.

"Still," Roman said, "she would not be employed for her abilities as a thief. Her gear really is her strong point—it works flawlessly."

"When she remembers to use it," Drexler grinned, his tongue lolling. "She hasn't done anything I can't do. And besides, what happens if you need her to pinch something for you?"

"Quite," Maijstral said.

Drexler might lack a certain bonhomie, he reflected, but at least he didn't show up uninvited in one's bedroom with a stolen art treasure moments after irksomely fanatic police decided to search the place.

"Roman," he said, "put Sparrow in the file. We might hand her some contract work if Drexler is ever overburdened."

"I won't be overburdened at the rate we're going, Mr. Maijstral," Drexler said. "When are we going to steal something really big?"

"After vacation," Maijstral said, and was aware of Drexler's diaphragm pulsing in resignation.

Let it pulse, he thought. Drexler hadn't met Colonel-General Vandergilt.

"Maijstral," said Prince Joseph Bob, "I don't believe you've met my family."

"Haven't had the pleasure."

The young Lord Joseph Bob had been one of Maijstral's school friends at the Nnoivarl Academy. He hadn't changed much in the last twelve years—he was still tall and rangy and blond, and he still looked every bit the champion athlete he had been in school. The best pistol shot in the Academy, a top sabre man on the fencing team, a first-class swimmer, an excellent jumper and runner, first prize for debate . . . the list of accomplishments went on and on.

His huge house south of Fort Worth was situated on an estate that stretched as far as the hill country west of Austin. The drawing room, where Maijstral was meeting the Prince's family, seemed to range at least half that distance.

"This is my wife, Arlette," Joseph Bob said.

"Charmed."

The marriage was less than a year old, and it was clear to Maijstral that they would have beautiful children. Princess Arlette—the media called her "Lady Bob"—was almost as tall as her husband, with honey-colored hair and large dark eyes. Maijstral gave her two fingers in handclasp and sniffed her wrist and ears.

"Joe's told me a lot about you," Arlette said.

"Oh dear."

"He was *very* complimentary."

Maijstral smiled. "Of course, he never knew me well."

"And *this*," said Joseph Bob, "is my brother Will."

"Ah," Maijstral said, "the Bubber."

Just as the brother of King Louis always assumed the title of Monsieur, the brother of the Prince of Tejas was always the Bubber (the *r*, with genteel courtesy, is almost silent). Maijstral, acquainted only through his brother, sniffed his ears, offered him a modest two fingers, and received three informal digits in return.

"Do you still do card tricks?" the Bubber asked. He was neither as tall nor as rangy nor as blond as his brother, though his expression was more genial. He had come into the Nnoi-varl Academy the year Maijstral left, and Maijstral had never really known him.

"Of course," Maijstral said.

"Joe always said you were good."

"After supper, if you like."

"That would be delightful. Thank you."

Maijstral made a mental note to tell Roman to lay out the dinner jacket with the trick pockets. He turned to the Prince.

"I was wondering if I might ask a favor," he said.

"Of course."

"While I'm here, I'd like to learn to ride a horse."

"Really?" The Prince seemed faintly surprised. "Very well, if you like. Will can set you up—he's in charge of the stables."

"Sir." Joseph Bob's butler appeared in the doorway. "There is a slight disturbance at the front gate. Newton has apprehended a pair of interlopers who claim to be lost. They also claim to be police."

"Lost?" the Prince said. "On my property?"

Maijstral gave a sigh. "J.B.," he said, "I suppose I had better tell you about Colonel-General Vandergilt."

Later, as Maijstral went to his quarters to dress for supper, he turned a corner in the hallway and received a start. Coming toward him was a short, nondescript man in a green jacket.

"Mr. Kuusinen," Maijstral said, and offered two fingers.

"Your servant, sir. I'm pleased you remembered my name." Kuusinen gave two fingers in return and sniffed Maijstral's ears.

Maijstral was not likely to forget the name of Paavo Kuusinen anytime soon. The man had a habit of turning up. Twice now, on Peleng and again on Silverside Station, Kuusinen had been a part of adventures Maijstral would just as soon forget.

On those occasions Kuusinen had actually been of great assistance to Maijstral, but the very sight of the man made Maijstral uneasy. Call it ingratitude if you will.

"What brings you to Earth?" Maijstral asked.

"I'm still her grace's attorney, of course," Kuusinen said, "and she is here, as a guest."

"Roberta?" Maijstral said. "Here?"

"Indeed."

Roberta Altunin, the Duchess of Benn, was a famous amateur racer and the former owner of the Eltdown Shard, the fabulous gem which Maijstral had once had the pleasure and glory of stealing.

"Curious," Maijstral said, "that the Prince never mentioned she was here."

"You'll meet at supper at any case."

"Yes. I will. Your servant."

"And yours."

They sniffed ears again and parted, Maijstral frowning. He'd come to think of Kuusinen as a creature of omen—not necessarily *ill* omen, since after all the man had been of service—but at least a harbinger of unsettling times.

Once in his suite, Maijstral settled his unease by watching a Western till it was time to dress. This one, *The Long Night of Billy the Kid,* was an old-fashioned tragedy featuring the legendary rivalry between Billy and Elvis Presley for the affections of Katie Elder. Katie's heart belonged to Billy, but despite her tearful pleadings Billy rode the outlaw trail; and finally, brokenhearted Katie left Billy to go on tour with Elvis as a backup singer, while Billy rode on to his long-foreshadowed death at the hands of the greenhorn inventor-turned-lawman Nikola Tesla.

It was wonderful. Maijstral, transfixed by the ancient, fateful myth being brought to life, watched with an aching heart as the awesome story unfolded in its somber, tragic perfection.

And while he watched, he paid particular attention to the horses.

He was really looking forward to lessons.

Paavo Kuusinen, after leaving Maijstral in the hall, turned a corner and began counting doors. He counted the light fixtures and power outlets as well, but only because he was compulsive that way—counting the doors really had purpose.

When he came to the eighth door, he knocked. A servant opened the door and he entered.

"Your grace," he said.

The Duchess of Benn was a tall, graceful woman, eighteen years old, with short red hair and intense violet eyes. She held out a hand and Kuusinen took it, sniffed the wrist.

"Maijstral's arrived?" she asked.

"An hour ago or thereabouts."

"Good. And the, ah—the package?"

"It will be in place by tomorrow evening."

"Splendid. The Special Event goes forward." She smiled. "I will look forward to enjoying Maijstral's surprise."

Kuusinen bowed again. "As shall I, your grace. To be sure."

THREE

❋   ❋   ❋

His heart still brimming with the glory and tragedy of his Western, Maijstral glided down the balcony to join the others in the drawing room. Before making his entrance, he absently patted one of the hidden pockets in his jacket to make certain the stacked deck of cards was in its nesting place.

He had also prepared his ground by having Roman bribe one of the footmen serving dinner tonight. It was nothing, he reflected, that Houdini hadn't done.

Maijstral stepped into the drawing room. The Prince's string quartet played Haydn in one corner—among them Maijstral recognized Will, the Bubber, who puffed out his cheeks as he sawed away on his cello and stared intently at the music. The regular cellist, he observed, was standing out, absently fingering his own instrument in a corner of the room.

Standing with her back toward Maijstral was Roberta, the Duchess of Benn. She was speaking to an elderly Khosalikh female who stood shorter than Maijstral, which made her a miniature by Khosalikh standards. Roberta's gown was cut quite low in back and Maijstral approached slowly, the better able to appreciate the curve of Roberta's supple spine, the play of shadows beneath her scapulae.

"Your grace," he said, speaking in Khosali Standard.

Roberta gave a start, a larger one than Maijstral's usual silent approaches generally warranted. Maijstral confirmed an old suspicion that her grace of Benn was a bit too tightly wound.

"You startled me," she gasped, which was, Maijstral reflected, not only a fairly redundant remark for someone who's just jumped half a foot, but was what people *always* said in these situations.

"My apologies," Maijstral said. "I'm light-footed by profession, and sometimes I forget that I should shuffle a bit or clear my throat." Which is, more or less, what *he* always said in these situations.

Maijstral offered three fingers in handclasp—having once stolen her jewelry permitted him a certain intimacy—and was given three in return. They approached one another and sniffed one another's ears, and then Maijstral sniffed Roberta's wrist. The odor of Roberta's perfume sent a shimmer of pleasure up Maijstral's spine, something that caused him to reflect that the custom of shaking hands—recently revived by the Constellation Practices Authority as a "natural, human custom" to replace the refined ear-sniffing of the Khosali Empire—had a long way to travel before it could replace the voluptuous pleasure of approaching a beautiful woman's pulsing throat and taking a glorious whiff.

"It's an unexpected pleasure to see you," Maijstral said. "I ran into your Mr. Kuusinen, who informed me you were here."

"Allow me to introduce my Aunt Bathsheba," Roberta said. "She's my favorite member of the family. We call her Batty."

"Your servant," Maijstral said. Aunt Batty's soft dark fur was thinned with age, and she'd perched a pair of spectacles on her muzzle. Some lace hung from her pointed ears.

Maijstral was too familiar with the genealogies of aristocratic Imperial families, with their sibs-by-adoption and cousins-german and morganatic marriages and fostering-patterns, to wonder how a human duchess managed to have a Khosali aunt. He sniffed Aunt Batty's ears and offered her two fingers in handclasp, and she returned him three.

"Forgive the intimacy," she said, "but I feel as if I know you quite well. I'm writing a multivolume work about you, you see."

Maijstral blinked. He didn't know whether to believe this remark, or, if believed, to take it seriously.

"Are you indeed?" he managed.

"Two volumes so far. The first was rather twee, I think in retrospect, but the style of the second settled down nicely, so I have hopes for the third."

Maijstral sighed. Any number of hack biographies had appeared since he'd been ranked first in the burglar standings, and most were filled with a glittering scintillation of errors, some of which he'd cheerfully supplied himself.

"I hardly think myself worthy of the attention," he said.

"On the contrary," Batty said. "I've found you quite an interesting character, well worth the study. Of course I've had to make a few guesses concerning things not on the public record. And now that I've met you, I'll be most interested to discover whether my surmises are anywhere near the mark."

Maijstral laughed uncomfortably. "I hope I won't disappoint you."

"I'm sure you won't, however it turns out. Unlike so many of my species, I'm almost never disappointed in humans—even when someone does something that I can't entirely approve of, it's always for the most *interesting* reasons."

Maijstral was at a loss for a response to this. He couldn't tell whether she disapproved of him already, or planned to disapprove in the future, or if the remark wasn't directed to him at all, but rather to the general run of her biographical victims. . . . So he said the only thing available to him, which was, "Ah."

"And there are so many people here who have known you," Batty went on. "Roberta, of course, and the Prince, who knew you at school. And Mr. Kuusinen—well, he's a first-class observer, and I've already spoken to him."

Maijstral felt a chill of alarm at the mention of Kuusinen's name. The man was far *too* first-class an observer. There were certain things he hoped Kuusinen never guessed at—there was a little service he'd done the Empire, for one, that could get him killed if certain parties in the Human Constellation ever discovered it.

"Perhaps I could answer some of your questions," he said, "and spare you the trouble of researching me through acquaintances."

"That's very kind," Batty said, "but it's not my method. I do all the research first, then speak to the subject last."

Speak to the subject, Maijstral thought. He wondered if *corner the victim* might be more appropriate.

The Haydn quartet drew to a close, the Bubber sawing away with evident enjoyment. There was scattered applause, and then the sound of the dinner gong. With relief, Maijstral bowed toward Roberta.

"May I take you in to dinner?"

"I believe Will is taking me in," Roberta smiled. "But you may take in Aunt Batty, if you like."

"A pleasure," Maijstral said, and felt rather like the condemned man taking a stroll with his executioner.

Loud hosannas began to sound as Maijstral and Batty entered the dining room. Startled, Maijstral looked up to discover a music loft above the door, with an entire choir singing away.

"I'd no idea we were going to be so honored," Maijstral said. "A chorus *and* a quartet."

"Oh," Batty said, a bit offhand, "we hear this every night. His highness supports a full complement of musicians and singers."

That, Maijstral reflected, was where adroit politics would get you. Joseph Bob's family had gained their initial wealth and title through energetic support of the Khosali Empire; and their riches and renown had only increased in the last few generations, since they'd been early and distinguished supporters of the Great Rebellion.

Once Maijstral's family had commanded wealth and station nearly equal to that of the Princes of Tejas. Unfortunately Maijstral's grandfather had been a far more fanatic supporter of the Khosali Empire even than most Khosali, and the family fortune waned with the fortunes of the Empire. Until a few years ago Maijstral had spent his life scurrying from one hideaway to another, the bill collectors just behind.

Fortunately burglary, once you reached Maijstral's level, paid well. And now that Maijstral had signed a number of endorsement contracts, it looked as if he'd never lack for funds again.

Maijstral helped Aunt Batty to her chair and sat in his own, between Batty and Roberta, half-expecting at any second to hear the crash of doors and the tramp of jackboots as Colonel-General Vandergilt marched in with a warrant for his arrest for some crime he had neither committed nor even heard of. But nothing happened, so he turned to the Bubber, seated on the other side of Roberta, and said, "Perhaps, in thanks for your music, I might offer a little amusement of my own. Perhaps you could send a footman for a deck of cards."

*   *   *

Card tricks alternated with supper courses. Maijstral thought he performed well, though the sight of Roberta's bare shoulders next to him was a constant, if perfectly agreeable, distraction.

Maijstral squared his cards and paused in his patter while the dessert course was brought in—Tuscan-style leaping clouds, light and frothy, with warm jugs of coffee liqueur sauce. The Bubber poured sauce on his dessert and picked up his spoon.

"If you'll pardon me, your grace," Maijstral said, rose in his chair, and reached across Roberta's plate to plunge his fingers into the Bubber's dessert. Princess Arlette gasped. The Bubber seemed at a loss for a response. "Would this be your card?" Maijstral asked, and raised the three of crowns from the Bubber's plate. Little dessert-cloudlets rained from the card, but it was perfectly recognizable.

"Yes!" the Bubber gasped.

"Another dessert, if you please," Maijstral told the footman. "And another deck of cards—this one is soiled." He showed the card to the others, and there was a round of applause, feet tapping the floor in the pattern for "surprise and appreciation."

Maijstral wiped his fingers and the card with his napkin and left the card faceup on the table, a reminder of his prowess. He always possessed a certain sense of wonder himself at how the simplest effects produced the greatest reaction—the others assumed he'd performed some master sleight right in front of the Bubber's nose, whereas in fact he'd merely had Roman bribe the footman to put a prearranged card in the Bubber's dessert. Any actual skill lay in getting the Bubber to choose the three of crowns in the first place, but that was a fairly elementary "force," as the jargon had it, and hardly a challenge.

He'd worked for *years* on much more sophisticated

tricks that never made such an impression.

He turned to Roberta. "My apologies, once more, your grace, for reaching across you so rudely."

"You are entirely forgiven," Roberta said. There was a glow in her violet eyes.

"Still, by way of apology, I'd like to offer to perform a trick where you, not I, am in command. As soon as they clear away the last course."

She smiled. "One dessert on top of another, it would seem. I'll strive not to bolt the first so as to get to the other quicker."

"Let the first add savor to the second, your grace."

Roberta gave him a graceful nod. "You are a master *saucier*, Maijstral. I shall trust your taste in dessert courses."

After the last of the dishes were cleared away, Maijstral broke the seal on the new deck and shuffled it. It was a matter of little moment to switch the new deck for the deck of identical pattern that he'd been carrying in his pocket.

"Your grace," Maijstral said, "I would like, by way of example, to deal each of us a hand of court-imago."

"I thought you said *I* was to be in charge," Roberta said.

"But I want you to know *why* you shall be in charge, and to that end—six cards, so."

The cards sped across the table. Joseph Bob and Arlette leaned forward in their chairs to peer at the action. Kuusinen watched with an expressionless face and an intense narrowing of the eyes.

Roberta picked up her hand and sorted the cards.

"Is it a passable hand, your grace?"

"I would wager on it, were I playing court-imago."

"Please lay it down." It was a Little Prough. Maijstral turned his own cards over, showing a Big Prough.

"I win," he said. "But it was unfair, was it not?"

"Yes."

"Why?"

"Because you dealt the cards, and you are a card manipulator."

"True. Therefore, it would give you more of a chance if I were to shuffle, and you were to cut the cards, yes?"

Roberta considered this. "I suppose," she said.

Maijstral reinserted the used cards into the deck, seemingly at random (but not randomly at all), and shuffled the deck with a theatrical flourish that served artfully to disguise the fact that the order of the cards was not altered in any way whatever. He placed the cards on the table.

"Cut, if you please."

The Duchess obliged. Maijstral dealt her four tens and himself four princesses.

"Was that fair?" he asked.

"I think not."

"Why not?"

"Because . . ." Her eyes narrowed as she considered the possibilities, "you could have nullified the cut in some way. Or somehow forced me to cut where you wanted me to."

Maijstral smiled. "Very good, your grace. I could have done both, had I wanted." He swept up the cards and put them in his deck. "This time I will shuffle the cards, and then you will shuffle the cards. I will deal a hand to everyone here, and you may choose the best of them to go up against my hand."

The cards were shuffled and dealt. The others at the table compared hands, and Arlette's crown stairway was chosen as the best. "I'm afraid that isn't good enough," Maijstral said, and turned over his own hand, six major powers in a row, a full council.

Roberta's ears flattened. "You promised that I would be in charge, Maijstral. All I have been doing is following your lead."

"That is true," Maijstral said. "I've been most unfair—because it was I who dealt the cards, and I'm a card manipulator and might have arranged somehow to have the best hand." He pushed the deck toward Roberta. "Therefore, this time, *you* shuffle, *you* deal a hand to everyone here, *you* choose which of the other hands to match against mine. And we shall see what occurs."

Roberta smiled at the challenge, and reached for the cards. She shuffled and dealt. This time a pair of princesses was the best anyone could manage. Roberta gave Maijstral an apologetic look.

"Not very good, I'm afraid."

"No. I'm afraid not." Maijstral turned over his own cards, a full court from the rover to the emperor of ships, the highest possible hand in court-imago.

The Bubber, baffled, looked through his cards, then took the deck and fingered his way through it.

"It seems," Roberta said, "that I haven't been in charge at all."

Maijstral fingered his diamond ring. "I'm afraid not," he said. "My character, alas, is fatally flawed—I'm a liar. And a cheat. And, of course," he added, with an apologetic smile, "I steal."

Roberta gave a smile. "I believe I am personally acquainted with that last facet of your character, somewhat to my cost."

The Bubber took Maijstral's cards and looked at them in hopes of finding some clue to the mystery. "Maijstral," he said, "how did you *do* it?"

Maijstral's eyes gleamed beneath their lazy lids. "With great skill and a mischievous if refined sense of *diablerie*," he said. He reached for his glass of wine. "Perhaps we should let the servants clear the table."

The company adjourned for brandy, coffee, and tobacco

to the Colt Drawing Room, named after the antique firearms that Joseph Bob collected, and which were displayed in artistic array on the wall. One weapon, however, was under glass in a display case. "The first Colt revolving chugger," Joseph Bob said.

"The wood pattern seems an odd design choice," Kuusinen observed.

"That isn't ornamentation," Joseph Bob said. "The pistol's actually made of wood. It's a model that Colt carved on a sea voyage. Once he returned, he built a working chugger out of metal and patented his process."

"They built pistols out of *metal?*" Roberta said. "That seems as outlandish as a pistol of wood. Why would Mr. Colt use metal?"

"It wouldn't do to admit this in certain political circles," Joseph Bob said, "but here among friends, I believe I might observe that human technology was not always as advanced as it is at present."

Roberta briefly touched her tongue to the corner of her mouth, a simulacrum of Khosali mirth. Maijstral had noticed that the human residents of the Empire, where the Khosali were in the majority, more often used Khosali gestures than humans of the constellation.

"Here are a pair of chuggers you might recognize, Maijstral," Joseph Bob said, and indicated a matched pair of pistols on the wall.

Cold trickled up Maijstral's spine as he looked at the weapons. Years ago, when he was sixteen, he'd fought a duel with those pistols, and the horror he'd felt at the time had never left him.

"Oh yes," Maijstral said unenthusiastically. "I recognize them perfectly well."

"Back in our Academy days," Joseph Bob told the others, "Maijstral fought a duel with those pistols. I wasn't there—the seconds wouldn't allow witnesses—but everyone said Maijstral was the coolest fellow imaginable."

Maijstral looked at the assembled company and felt sweat gathering at his nape. What others mistook for coolness had been, in fact, a pure, horrified paralysis.

"I'm sure the others exaggerated," Maijstral said.

Joseph Bob put a hearty hand on Maijstral's shoulder. "Quite a feat, though, fighting a duel at that age—what were we? Sixteen? Seventeen?"

"Too young," Maijstral said.

"I've always envied you the experience. Here I am, a crack pistol shot and an exemplary swordsman, and I've never once had an encounter! I've always wanted a chance, but everyone's always been so *polite* to me."

Arlette looked a little nonplussed at this evidence of her husband's bloodthirstiness. Maijstral raised a thin smile. His ears pricked forward. "If I ever have another fight," he said, "you can substitute for me if you like."

Joseph Bob gave a hearty laugh. "Oh," he said, "I wish I could!"

"We youngsters were jealous of you," the Bubber offered. "And that girl of yours who was the cause of it all—we were jealous of her, too. Quite a pippin, that Zoe."

"Maijstral started quite a fad," Joseph Bob added. "There must have been a dozen challenges among the underclassmen before the term was out. We seniors had to suppress them all, of course."

Maijstral sincerely wished someone would act to suppress this topic of conversation. He didn't care for his youthful follies being the subject of quite this much speculation. He observed that Kuusinen was watching him with interest, and Maijstral liked neither the intrigued tilt to Aunt Batty's head nor the glitter in her eye. Probably she was planning on adding another note to her three-volume biography.

And Roberta, he noted, was looking at him with an admiration that made him thoroughly uneasy. On Silverside Station she had served as his second on a duel that, fortunately for him, had not actually come off. He didn't want to leave anyone with the impression he was a fire-eater happy to swashbuckle his way through life in search of deadly encounters. A reputation like that could attract more danger than it would keep away—just look at the career of Pearl Woman or Etienne, to name two among the Three Hundred who were constantly having to hack their way out of one lethal situation or another.

Perhaps, Maijstral considered, it was time for a bit of misdirection. "Say," he said, turning to an intriguing-looking shoulder weapon with Troxan markings, "what is *that* used for? Is that a *harpoon* of some sort?"

Annoyance flared in Maijstral as Joseph Bob clung to his reminiscence. "D'you know, Maijstral," he said, "after I got the pistols back, I couldn't hit a blessed thing with either one of 'em. Turned out the sights were out of true."

Maijstral suppressed a jolt of alarm, and instead said, "Perhaps the seconds were careless in handling them afterward. Asad and Zah were pretty excited by the whole business."

"I wonder—d'you suppose it was one of the masters bent on avoiding bloodshed?" Joseph Bob fingered his chin analytically. "Perhaps if word of the duel got out, one of our housemasters could have got into my room with his passkey and twitched the sights out of alignment."

It had been Maijstal, of course, far gone in the depths of terror, who had crept into Joseph Bob's room and tweaked the foresights with a handy pair of pliers. It had been his first successful breaking and entering, one of those painful, involuntary milestones on his path to the present. How many other people, one could well ask, have discovered their own utter cowardice and the silent joys of burglary at the same time?

Maijstral affected to consider Joseph Bob's theory. It occurred to him that the notion was far too close to the truth, and probably ought to be discredited altogether. "I think your theory probably gives the masters too much credit," he said. "It was never my impression that they knew anything we were doing, let alone anything we were *trying* to hide from them." His lazy lids closed over his eyes, leaving only slits. "I'm inclined to suspect it was just careless handling by the seconds. Julian and I held the pistols only for a moment or two, just long enough to shoot, but the seconds probably had them for hours."

"Mm," Joseph Bob conceded. "Very likely."

"Now what is this—*harpoon* sort of thing?" Maijstral asked, once more attempting his diversion.

As Joseph Bob went on to explain that the harpoon gun was intended to anchor the wandering, homicidal trees that lurched about one of the Troxan homeworlds, Maijstral viewed the other guests from beneath his slitted lids. Arlette, the Bubber, and Roberta seemed perfectly willing to be diverted by the harpoon gun. Kuusinen's polite expression, as ever, revealed little. But Aunt Batty's lace-covered ears were cocked forward, and her tongue lolled in a smug little smile as if, Maijstral concluded, some pet theory of hers had just been confirmed.

He wondered if there were some way he could read this biography.

Perhaps, it occurred to him, he could *steal* it.

The string quartet's rendition of a Frayng piece echoed up the hall as the company made their way to their rooms.

"I say—Maijstral?"

"Yes, Bubber?"

"Oh, call me Will, won't you? I don't care much for

meaningless titles, and I guess you don't, either, considering you don't use yours."

"Will. Yes. You may call me Drake, if you like. How may I help you?"

"I was wondering if we might do a trade. I'd be most happy to teach you to ride a horse tomorrow, and—well, what I want is—I, ah—could you teach me magic?"

A pause. "Well." Another pause. "I would be happy to teach you a few things, of course. But I won't be spending that much time here in Tejas, and I won't be able to give you anything but a few fundamentals."

"Oh, that would be fine. I understand your time is limited. But I'd like to find out if magic is something I could really master—you know, I've always lived with J.B., and he's a perfectly splendid person, but he's so *good* at everything. A better shot than me, a better fencer, a better rider . . . and probably a better lord, if it comes to that. And I can play the cello pretty well, but I'm not as good as the fellow who's normally got the job . . . so anyway, I thought if I could master something that J.B. isn't good at, then . . . well, I'd like to give it a try, anyway."

"I would be happy to teach you what I can."

"Thank you. Er—Drake?"

"Yes, Will?"

"Did I just say something—you know—pathetic?"

"Not at all, Will."

"Thank you." A sigh. "I'm relieved."

"Good night, Will."

"Good night. And thank you."

"Dear?" Strolling up the stairway a few moments later. "Did you really envy Maijstral his duel?"

"Oh, yes. Of course. It's a chance to find out what you're really made of, isn't it?"

"Don't you think you know what you're made of, Joe?"

"Well." A nervous laugh. "Not the way Maijstral does, I'm sure. I've done well, but then I started out with so many advantages that I would have had to work hard at doing badly in order to make a failure of myself. I certainly haven't been tested, not the way my grandfather was in the Great Rebellion, nor the way Maijstral was before he was twenty."

"You got *me* all on your own, Joe."

The sound of a kiss.

"Well," reflectively, "perhaps I haven't done so badly, after all."

The same stair. Another pair.

"Do things progress, Kuusinen?"

"Indeed, your grace. The mechanics of smuggling an object as large as a coffin into the house without Maijstral's knowledge presented some difficulties, but now that he's decided to go riding tomorrow, I believe we can use the window of opportunity afforded by his absence."

"And his servants?"

"His Highness's butler has been instructed to divert them. They, and your servants as well, will be taken on a special picnic tomorrow morning."

"Very good. Perhaps I will take exercise with Maijstral and make certain he'll be gone for a sufficient length of time."

"An admirable addition to the plan, your grace."

"I don't believe it will be any great sacrifice—it will be a perfectly pleasant morning, given good weather."

"Of course, your grace."

Another pause. "Is that Snail they're performing?"

"Frayng, your grace."

"Ah. I can never tell them apart."

"Hardly anyone ever can. I believe that's why they were provoked into their unfortunate duel—each thought the other was imitating him."

"They fought with bassoons, did they not?"

"Yes. Bassoons, your grace. Not the most graceful of weapons, but then they both died, so perhaps there is some hidden martial quality to the instrument of which we are unaware."

"Good grief!"

"Oh. Sorry, Mr. Maijstral. I really didn't mean to startle you."

Maijstral contemplated the jutting finlike pompadour sticking up above his rack of suits. "If you didn't mean to startle me," he said, "why did you hide in my closet?"

Conchita Sparrow's genial face worked its way out from between a pair of jackets. "One of your servants was in here a minute ago, and I didn't want him to see me, so I just nipped in for a second." She fondled a shoulder seam. "Nice suit, this green one. I like the cut."

"Thank you, Miss Sparrow. Would you care to step into the room now?"

"Only too." Conchita left the closet, took a breath, and grinned. "It was stuffy in there." She looked around the room. "Can you give me a drink or something?"

Maijstral, ignoring this last request, folded his arms and regarded the intruder. "The matter of your being in my closet is now explained, but we have yet to address the question of your being in my room in the first place. Have you dropped off another stolen art treasure?"

"Oh. No. I was just wondering if you'd had a chance to review my recordings."

"You needn't have come in person. You could have phoned. Or you could have knocked on the front door and asked for me."

"Well, yes," Conchita admitted. "But I wanted to show you how well I could neutralize the security in this place." Her eyes widened. "Oh. The closet. One moment."

She reached into the closet and removed the command override she'd placed on the closet's command systems. "Close the doors, please."

"I have been interfered with." The closet's tone was sulky.

"Close the doors, please."

The doors closed with a final grumble. Conchita turned to Maijstral and grinned.

"Your technical ability is without question," Maijstral said. "But I already employ a tech. The only work I could offer you is perhaps an occasional contract, and that only rarely."

Conchita's face fell. "Oh, come on, Mr. Maijstral," she said. "Your life would never be dull with me around!"

This, Maijstral considered, was becoming all too plain. "Perhaps that's so," he said, "but I can't fire a perfectly good employee just to relieve the tedium." At that point there was a knock at the door.

He and Conchita looked at each other for a moment, and then Conchita turned to the closet. "Open, please," she said.

"I won't," the closet said. "You interfered with my mechanisms."

"Open, closet," Maijstral said.

"Well," the closet said, "for *you.*"

The closet opened and Conchita ducked inside, jabbing her command override into the closet's systems as she did so. The doors shut smoothly, and Maijstral went to answer the knock.

Kuusinen's head was cocked slightly in an inquiring manner. "I hope I do not interrupt, sir," he said.

Maijstral unconsciously straightened his jacket. "Oh. Not at all. Would you come in?"

"Thank you, no. I had only a single question to ask you," Kuusinen said. "I hope you won't consider it impertinent, but I'm afraid I'm compulsive in certain ways, and I won't be able to sleep unless I know the answer."

"I will do my utmost to assume you rest, Mr. Kuusinen."

"What do you call the technique you used in the trick where the cards were hidden under the creamer? The one where you substituted one card on the very top of the deck for another?"

Maijstral blinked. "I must have performed the trick very poorly for you to have noticed."

"On the contrary," Kuusinen said, "your working of the trick was excellent, and I noticed nothing at the time. But, in thinking about the trick afterward, I realized how it had to be done, and—I apologize again—I was consumed with a desire for the information."

"I would be obliged if you refrained from sharing your line of reasoning with the others."

"I won't, I assure you. This is purely for my own satisfaction."

"The technique is called a top change."

Kuusinen closed his eyes and absorbed the bit of jargon with an expression akin to bliss. His eyes fluttered open. "Thank you, sir."

"I hope you sleep well."

"I'm sure I shall."

Maijstral closed the door and was on his way to the closet when he was interrupted by a gentle chime from the phone. He answered, and the visage of the Duchess of Benn appeared on the screen.

"If you're looking for Mr. Kuusinen," Maijstral said, "he just left."

"I wasn't, actually," Roberta said. "I was hoping that I might invite myself along on your riding trip tomorrow."

"You're most welcome," Maijstral said, "but I'm afraid I won't be a very challenging companion. I've never been on a horse in my life."

"Neither have I. We shall learn together."

"I shall look forward."

"Good night, Maijstral."

"Good night, your grace."

Maijstral turned from the phone to see the closet door gliding open. Conchita appeared. "Was that the Duchess of Benn?" she asked.

"It was."

"That's fingo all right!"

Maijstral raised his eyebrows at this piece of cant. "Sorry?" he said.

"I mean, I'm impressed. You stole the Eltdown Shard from her and she not only still speaks to you, she looks for ways to ride off into the sunset with you."

Maijstral blinked. There was a lot more to the Eltdown Shard story than ever reached the public, and he intended it stay that way. "I believe you were leaving," he said.

"Well." Conchita shrugged. "I suppose I was."

"Shall I open a window for you?"

"No thanks. I got in through the ventilation."

She popped a grill off the wall, floated up off the floor, entered feetfirst, and paused to give a wave before she disappeared into the ventilator shaft. Maijstral walked to the service plate and touched it.

"Roman. Would you come in here, if you please?"

It was Drexler's voice that answered. "Sorry, Mr. Maijstral. Roman left before dinner and hasn't returned. May I be of service?"

Maijstral paused. It was most unlike Roman to be absent at this hour, when he was usually required to unlace Maijstral from his jacket and trousers. Maijstral would have to summon a robot to do the job.

"Did Roman say where he was going?"

"No, sir. May I help you?"

First things first, Maijstral thought. "Yes," he said.

"Miss Sparrow has returned. I don't know if she left anything behind, but if she did, I want it found."

"I'll take care of that right away, sir."

"Thank you, Drexler."

Another long search of his own quarters, Maijstral thought wearily.

He hoped he wouldn't have to get used to this.

FOUR

Maijstral arrived for his ride dressed in what he believed to be the correct costume: wide Stetson hat, large bandanna, leather vest, fringed chaps, high-heeled proughskin boots with pointed toes, silver rowel spurs that gleamed in the sunlight, a stunner in the shape of one of Mr. Colt's revolvers on one hip and a waspish rapier on the other.

Will, the Bubber, regarded Maijstral with an expression of genial surprise as he stalked into the stables on his tall heels. "Very authentic," he said.

"Am I . . . overdressed?" Maijstral said. The Bubber's costume complemented his own only in the matter of boots.

"I don't *think* we're going to be attacked by outlaws," the Bubber said, "but I'm sure that if we are, we'll be thankful for the hardware. And I wasn't planning on riding through heavy brush, either, though the chaps will be useful if we do."

Roberta arrived, dressed casually, and looked at Maijstral in surprise. "I've seen that costume before," she offered. "You wore it on the night of the Grand Ball on Silverside, when you stole my necklace."

"I hope the associations aren't too unpleasant."

Roberta offered an ambiguous smile. "Quite the contrary. It was an exhilarating evening."

"Perhaps," said the Bubber, "I should introduce you to your horses. And, ah, Drake—I'd take off those spurs if I were you. There might be an accident."

Maijstral had fantasized himself flying along on a midnight steed, a lean animal, all clean streamlined angles and flying mane and surging muscle, but his horse turned out to be a gentle, middle-aged grey mare named Morganna, who jogged along the path without any apparent need for direction on Maijstral's part. Even so Maijstral found the sensation a bit alarming. The large beast moving beneath him gave him the sensation of being harnessed to a slow-motion earthquake, a natural force of sufficient power to cause injury if he made the wrong move. Still, he and the horse managed to get along well enough, and he found himself enjoying the experience.

Roberta was less successful. It became obvious from the first that she and her mount were engaged in a furious contest of wills from which, very possibly, there would be but one survivor.

"I can't understand it," the Bubber remarked, after they'd been riding about ten minutes. "Ringo's been a perfectly tractable animal till now."

"If this beast doesn't soon learn to obey," Roberta said through clenched teeth, "I'm going to break every single one of its ribs."

Roberta was a world-class racer, with the powerful legs necessary to negotiate the turns and leaps of the zero-gravity maze, and she might well have been capable of carrying out her threat.

"Just try to relax," the Bubber suggested.

Ringo regarded the Duchess from a red, rolling eye, ears flattened. *"Relax?"* Roberta cried. *"How?* With this *wretched animal* confounding my every . . ."

Roberta urged it forward, and instead, out of contrariness, it backed. Roberta's ears drew back in anger. She kicked the horse to get it moving, those powerful racer's legs driving into the animal's ribs . . . and Ringo took off with a bound, almost flinging Roberta over its tail, and raced top speed across country. Roberta hung on gamely, crouched over the horse's neck, and hurled abuse into its ear as it carried her off.

Maijstral watched in alarm at this development right out of one of his Westerns. The heroine's animal had run off with her, and it was clearly up to the hero to do something about it. If Elvis had been here, or Jesse James, the course of action would have been clear. But Maijstral, an equestrian tyro, was helpless to intervene. If he'd only worn an a-grav harness, he could have flown after the Duchess and plucked her from the saddle with ease.

Fortunately the Bubber was up to the challenge and raced off in pursuit. Maijstral peered anxiously after, but all he could see were two swiftly moving clouds of dust aiming for a convergence on the horizon. After a certain amount of negotiation with his animal he managed to work it up to a trot; and he jounced along in pursuit, feeling as if life had just handed him the sidekick role.

Eventually, emerging from the heat shimmer on the horizon came the Bubber on his horse, with Roberta mounted behind and a lathered Ringo following on a lead. The Bubber was grinning, and even Roberta had a smile tugging at her lips.

"I trust you're not injured?" Maijstral asked.

"Not at all," Roberta said. "Will was the perfect rescuer. Snatched me right out of the saddle and set me on his horse behind as if I were a child." She patted the Bubber on the shoulder. "You're stronger than you look."

The Bubber seemed pleased. "There's a trick to it. You just have to know how."

"And how do you know these tricks? Do you go plucking ladies off runaway horses every day of the week?"

The Bubber flushed a little. "I used to do a little acrobatic riding, but I haven't done anything like that in years. Surprising how the reflexes come back." He shaded his eyes and looked toward the sprawl of the Prince's residence, still looming on the horizon, then turned to Maijstral. "I'm sorry to cut your lesson short, Drake, but we'd best return to the stables."

Roberta looked firm. "I think not," she said. "You and Maijstral go on with your plans." She kicked one leg up over the Bubber's head—her athleticism was so effortless that it did not surprise—and slid off the saddle to the ground. "I shall *walk* Ringo back to the stables," she said. "And if the beast gives me trouble, I shall simply break the animal's knees."

The Bubber looked dubious. "We'll take you back," he said. "I'm sure Drake doesn't mind."

"Not at all," Maijstral said.

Roberta's violet eyes flashed. "*Maijstral,*" she said. "*Go for your ride.*"

Maijstral blinked. He had encountered Roberta's force of will before, and on consideration it amazed him that Ringo had managed to resist it for so long. "Your grace," he said, "if you insist."

"*I do.*" She turned to the Bubber, and her face assumed a less stern expression. "I'm perfectly capable of walking the couple of leagues to the stables. I'm a racer, after all."

"Well," frowning, "if you're sure . . ."

Roberta took her leave and began her walk, the exhausted, chastened horse following. Maijstral and the Bubber turned their horses and began a trot back to the road.

"Rather high-strung, ain't she?" the Bubber said.

"She has more reason for temperament than most," Maijstral said. "She is young, and has been to a strict school. No doubt she wishes to prove herself worthy of all the trust that has been placed in her. And of course she has to be constantly wary of people who want to take advantage of her—fortune hunters and so on."

The Bubber's ears reddened. "Well, yes," he said, "families can be a bother sometime. I find I'm glad I'm not the heir—I've much more freedom that way. I've got enough money to be comfortable, and J.B.'s kind enough to employ me at things I enjoy. Fortunately we get along."

"My titles came with no money or property," Maijstral said, "only debts. It was hard to think of them as an advantage."

They rode along pleasantly for a while, each with his own thoughts.

"Drake?" the Bubber said. "When do you think you might teach me a little magic?"

"Right now, if you like."

"*Now?*"

"A little theory, anyway."

"Oh. Well. To be sure."

"We have several varieties of effects to consider," Maijstral began. "All classic visual effects fall into one of a few categories—vanishing, production, transformation, transposition, restoration, penetration, and levitation."

"That seems rather a long list." Dubiously.

"Some effects are merely the reversal of another, vanishing and production for example. Allow me to give an example of each."

Discoursing thus, the two rode on companionably.

Behind them, out of sight of the two, a large transport craft descended onto the Prince's lawn to unload its cargo.

One large coffin.

After luncheon the Prince, his family, and his guests boarded a large flier and sped to the Grand Canyon, where, after a leisurely drift down the length of the Canyon at about medium altitude, with the Colorado still far below and the canyon walls looming high on either side, the flier soared effortlessly upward to a landing at Cape Solitude. There everyone disembarked to observe the Colorado stretching on down the length of Marble Canyon, and marvelled at the side canyon's grand, if inaccurately named, magnificence.

As the others absorbed the Canyon's splendor, Maijstral carefully watched Joseph Bob from beneath his lazy eyelids. He wanted to do a card trick that would astound everyone, but it required knowing the subject well. In the cant, it required "taking dead aim" at Joseph Bob.

But he wasn't certain if he knew Joseph Bob well enough. Maijstral had, during their school years in the Empire, known the young princeling as well as anyone, but he hadn't seen the man since graduation.

But Joseph Bob seemed not to have changed at all. Matured a bit, certainly, but in essence he seemed the same young human Maijstral had known at the Academy.

Well, Maijstral thought, he might as well find out. If this didn't work, he'd cover it with another trick.

The others were starting to drift back to the flier in preparation to moving to another vantage point. Maijstral approached Joseph Bob.

"Would you mind assisting me in a card trick?" he asked.

"Here?" Joseph Bob seemed surprised. "If you like."

"Perhaps we could use the table near that, ah, tree-ish thing."

"That's a Jasperian Sprout Vine."

"It is? So that's what a sprout vine looks like."

The others followed as Maijstral and Joseph Bob approached the table. They sat on opposite sides of the table, and Maijstral produced a deck of cards. He spread them expertly, faceup, in front of the Prince.

"If you could point to a card?"

Joseph Bob pointed to the four of ships. Triumph flooded Maijstral's blood. He swept up the cards, shuffled, handed the deck to Joseph Bob.

"Find your card, if you please."

Joseph Bob looked through the deck for the four of ships but failed to find it.

"Count them, please."

Joseph Bob counted the cards. Glancing around the table, Maijstral noted the little bobs of the spectators' heads as they counted along with him.

"There are only sixty-three," Joseph Bob said. "The four of ships is missing."

Maijstral's eyes glinted green from behind his heavy lids. "Perhaps," he said, "you might find the missing card in the inside left breast pocket of your jacket."

Joseph Bob reached into his jacket experimentally, and then his eyes widened. He withdrew his hand and in it, the four of ships.

"You were on the other side of the table from me the entire time," he said. "How did you *do* that?"

Taking dead aim, Maijstral thought, and gathered up the cards. He rose from his seat and looked out over the Canyon.

"Perhaps we might seek another point of advantage."

"I don't see why we should bother," Joseph Bob muttered, his ears pricking back in puzzlement, "since the advantage is all yours."

The afternoon was spent flitting from one part of the Canyon to the next, and ended with cocktails and a light buffet in the Redwall Cavern. Then the flier returned to the Prince's estate, where Roman helped lace Maijstral into his formal dinner dress.

Roman was feeling a warm, mild burning sensation precisely in the middle of his broad back, where he couldn't scratch it. All day he had felt mild fevers alternate with light chills. Phantom itches moved from place to place over his body, and wherever he scratched, his fine black fur flew.

As he'd experienced this twenty-odd times before, he knew perfectly well what was going to happen. He was about to enter molt.

Roman *hated* molt. He was an exceptionally bad molter, and his molts put him out of sorts for weeks. And the fact that the molt meant he was a year older did not improve his humor.

Another year, he might have thought, in service to Maijstral. Another year of being an assistant thief, occasional leg-breaker, and general voice of responsibility in a most irregular world.

Roman *might* have thought that . . . but he didn't. He was far too disciplined, too Khosali, ever to criticize his employer, even mentally. The most he would ever allow himself was an occasional diaphragm pulse of resignation.

"Did you have a pleasant afternoon, sir?" he asked as he did up the side-laces of Maijstral's jacket.

"Very satisfactory," Maijstral said. He looked at Roman over his shoulder. "A little looser in the armpit, please."

"Very good, sir." Roman pried at the laces.

"You were out last night," Maijstral said.

"I regret I wasn't back in time to unlace you," Roman said. "I lost track of time."

Maijstral tugged experimentally at his lapel, worked his arm in its socket. "I hope you had a pleasant time, wherever you were."

"I was at the library, sir."

"Oh." Maistral was surprised. "Well, I hope your reading was pleasant."

"I was reading history, sir," Roman said. "It was very fulfilling."

Which was a statement calculated to end Maijstral's questions. Roman, as well as the Duchess, had his own Special Project, one he had been working on for years, a project that involved Maijstral.

Last night, in the library in Rome, Roman had found the crucial bit of evidence that had brought the project to its climax. He just didn't want Maijstral knowing about it yet.

Roman handed Maijstral his pistol, which was promptly stowed in the armpit holster, and then Maijstral made his way downstairs to dinner.

Relieved to be left alone, Roman went straight to the service plate and called for a robot to come to the room and scratch the fiery itch in the center of his back.

Dinner featured pleasant conversation and no card tricks—Maijstral understood that to be consistently amazing is, in the long run, to risk becoming consistently predictable, if not consistently dull. Besides, Maijstral was very pleased with the one trick he'd performed that day, and had no desire to perform other tricks that weren't as spectacular.

After dinner, Joseph Bob, the Bubber, and Arlette played a three-sided game of puff-sticks in the drawing room, while Maijstral browsed along the bookshelves. There were a lot of histories and biographies, many of which concerned members of the Prince's family. Maijstral browsed the pages of one of these—it concerned the great Flax-Seed Scandal that rocked the Empire in the decade before the Rebellion, and the then-Bubber's ambiguous role therein—and discovered that the margins had been annotated in pencil. Most of the annotations were in the human alphabet, and consisted of the letter "L" or the letters "DL," sometimes followed by an exclamation mark.

Maijstral waited for an auspicious moment to interrupt the puff-sticks game, then asked Joseph Bob what the letters meant. The Prince gave the book a glance.

"Oh, that's my grandfather's notes," he said. "He annotated all the histories that way. L stands for 'lie,' and DL for 'damned lie.'"

Maijstral smiled. "I am enlightened," he said. "Thank

you." As he returned to the bookshelf the Duchess of Benn approached, rustling in a silk gown of imperial purple that admirably echoed her violet eyes.

"Maijstral," Roberta said, "I was wondering if you might join Kuusinen and me for a moment. There is something upstairs that might interest you."

"Of course, your grace." Maijstral closed the book and returned it to the shelves.

Feeling the sort of languid curiosity that is the best one can hope for after a large, well-prepared meal, Maijstral followed after Roberta. Little warning spikes of pain jumped along his thighs as he climbed up the stairs—the morning's riding, he thought. Roberta's gown plunged behind, and he found himself enjoying, once more, the supple play of muscle and shadow on the Duchess's back.

Roberta led Maijstral past her own suite, then opened a door into another room and stepped inside. Maijstral followed, saw what waited therein, and stopped dead. Kuusinen almost ran into him from behind.

Maijstral's first thought was that Conchita Sparrow had really outdone herself this time—not only stealing a huge cryocoffin from somewhere, but sneaking it past Joseph Bob's security and hiding it in the room—but then he began to recognize the coffin's sweeping bronze lines, turned into little classical scrolls on either end, and he frowned and stepped into the room, a song of warning keening in the back of his head.

Aunt Batty, he observed, had been keeping the coffin company: she was well established in a rocking chair in one corner, surrounded by a little thicket of manuscript on which she'd been working. Evidently the coffin's appearance was not a surprise to her, or to anyone in the Duchess's party.

Maijstral looked at the Imperial Arms and Lineage

etched into the coffin lid, and it only confirmed his worst suspicions. His heart sank.

"Hello, Dad," he said. "How did you get here?"

A plaintive voice came from the coffin.

"Is it time for my cocoa yet?" it asked.

FIVE

✽　✽　✽

Maijstral had believed that he had kept his late father
without enough funds to travel, and as his father's legal guard-
ian he'd forbade his father to borrow. Well, he thought, his
dad had got the funds from *somewhere*, probably a little account he'd been hiding all these years, or maybe an old friend
who'd been persuaded to make a loan; and Maijstral would
have to get the lawyers to start searching for the source . . .
after, Maijstral considered, the late Gustav Maijstral was
shipped home to his tomb and safely reinstalled in the home of
his ancestors.

"Drake?" the corpse inquired. "Is that you, Drake?"

"Yes, Dad," Maijstral sighed. "It's me."

"I came here for a very good reason," Gustav Maijstral
said firmly. "I want my cocoa!" And then added, ". . . I *think*.
I *think* that's why I'm here."

"Dad," Maijstral said patiently, "you can't have cocoa.
You're dead."

Maijstral gave an apologetic look to the others while his
father mulled this over.

"Oh yes," the corpse remarked. "You're right. I'm dead. I forgot."

It is impossible not to observe that the former Duke of Dornier, ex-Viscount Sing, onetime Prince-Bishop of Nana, and late Hereditary Captain-General of the Green Legion had not been a particularly astute man while alive, and that death had not improved him.

Kuusinen cleared his throat tactfully. Roberta took the hint and turned to Maijstral.

"Actually," she said, "it's my fault he's here."

"Oh yes!" the corpse added. "That's right!" He sighed, which came out of the coffin's speakers as a faint electronic sizzle. "I keep forgetting these things. . . ."

Maijstral turned his bewildered attention to Roberta. "He came to see *you?*" he asked.

"Not exactly," she said. "I arranged for him to be brought here to see you, but . . ."

"I remember! I remember!" the corpse cried triumphantly. "I remember why I'm here!" And then the voice trailed away. "I *thought* I remembered . . . just a moment . . . maybe it'll come back."

Roberta passed a hand over her brow. "This isn't working out the way I'd hoped," she said. "Kuusinen, can you help me?"

Kuusinen nodded and turned to Maijstral. "As you know, I am her grace's solicitor. Two years ago, her grace instructed me to undertake certain researches having to do with a Special Project she was undertaking in regard to her future. You and your family were among those to whom I devoted my efforts."

Maijstral's head was whirling, but he managed to put his finger on at least one important point. "That's why I keep running into you," he said. "On Peleng, and Silverside Station, and . . ."

"Just so," Kuusinen nodded.

"And what was the tenor of these researches?"

Kuusinen looked appropriately grave. "The contract of a matrimonial alliance," he said, "between Her Grace the Duchess of Benn and . . ."

Maijstral jumped as if stung. "*No!*" he said.

The others stared at him.

"Absolutely not," Maijstral said.

Roberta's eyes were wide. Her lower lip trembled. "But . . . why not?" she asked.

Maijstral folded his arms and looked stern. "I absolutely forbid you to marry my father. He's married already, for one thing, and for another he's dead, and I don't care what your demented relations told you would make a good dynastic alliance, you'd just be throwing your life away. . . ."

His words trickled away as Roberta's real intent slowly filtered its way into his mind.

"Oh," he said.

In Maijstral's defense it must be said that this really *was* a surprise. He'd been thrown off-balance by his father's arrival, and made slow by a good dinner, and wasn't operating at full speed.

All that said, he certainly proved a bit dense on this occasion. However, one should remember that this sort of thing happens to the best of us, and usually, alas, where personal matters are concerned.

"Well, yes," Roberta admitted. "It was you I was planning to marry, Drake."

Maijstral's head whirled, but even through all his inner confusion he couldn't help but admire Roberta's style . . . to have Kuusinen quietly case him for a year, to carry her valuable jewels to Silverside Station as a way of bringing herself together with Maijstral, and then to arrange for all the necessities of the formal betrothal as dictated by Khosali High Custom: a representative from each of the families (his father for the Maijstrals and, he presumed, Aunt Batty on the Duchess's side), a meeting on neutral ground (the estate of the Prince of Tejas), a neutral who had doubtless conspired with her to sneak Maijstral's father onto the premises while Maijstral was at the Grand Canyon or on his morning ride. He wouldn't be surprised if there was an Imperial Recorder stowed away in the next room, ready to transcribe all the niggling little details of noble lineage and so forth on a formal betrothal written with a jade pen on the tanned hide of a grookh, proper for transmission to the City of Seven Bright Rings, where the Khosali Emperor himself, Nnis CVI, would give his formal permission for the wedding. . . .

Permission in these cases was never denied, of course. Nnis CVI had retired to his cryocoffin long ago, and was probably in worse shape than Maijstral's father.

Roberta had acted brilliantly, and in so doing had displayed a surprising amount of subtlety for one so young. Maijstral was struck with awe.

He was also struck by the realization that he didn't know whether he wanted to marry Roberta or not. She was young, she was attractive, she was intelligent and interesting, she was staggeringly rich, and she was thoroughly worthy of admiration . . . but yet.

But yet. She was not, in his brief experience, an *easy* person. She was high-strung, she was quick-tempered, she was a fierce competitor who raced in the highest amateur league. Her force of will was prodigious. Maijstral admired her, but thus far he'd succeeded in admiring her only at a distance. Who knew what emotion might result from closer proximity?

Maijstral became aware that the others were watching him with their ears cocked forward in expectation. Clearly some manner of reply was required. He bowed toward the Duchess and placed a hand over his heart without quite knowing what he was going to say. Fortunately, his training came to the fore.

The Nnoivarl Academy, ridiculous though its curricu-

lum might be in any practical respect, is at least good for seeing its graduates through a crisis of style.

"I am astounded by your consideration," Maijstral said.
"I had never thought to look so high." As he rose from his
bow, he regarded Roberta carefully through half-closed lazy-
lidded eyes—was that a trace of disappointment he saw mir-
rored in her face? Had she expected, he wondered, for him to
throw himself into her arms?

If so, he considered, she shouldn't have surrounded herself with all these intermediaries.

Delay, he thought. He still had no idea what his response
would be—or, for that matter, *could* be.

"I should consult with my father to determine his
wishes," Maijstral said, then gave the coffin a dubious glance.
"Insofar as they *can* be determined," he added.

"Drake's going to marry the Duchess!" sang the corpse.
"*That's* why I'm here! Wonderful girl! Imperial family! Good
match! When the Emperor comes back, we'll all live like
kings!"

Well, Maijstral thought, *that* sounded like consent.

The impulse to delay was still uppermost in his thoughts.
He turned to Roberta, his ears flicking forward. "Your grace,"
he said, "may we speak to each other alone? Perhaps in the
next room?"

Roberta bit her lip. "There's an Imperial Recorder in the
next room," she said.

Knew it, Maijstral thought.

"But we can use my parlor," Roberta added. "It's only a
few doors away."

"The parlor will suit perfectly well." Maijstral turned to
Aunt Batty and bowed. "If you will excuse us."

He offered Roberta his arm and she took it. As he closed
the door behind them, she looked at him and bit her lip.

"You're not angry, are you?"

"Of course not. I'm . . . stunned."

"You didn't have any idea? Really?"

"I thought Kuusinen had been scouting me out on account of your jewels. I'd no idea you had any . . . other interest."

She opened the door to her parlor and passed inside. Maijstral sat down on a small settee, and Roberta sat next to him. His big diamond flashed as he reached to take her hand.

"How exactly . . . did this come about?" he asked.

Roberta looked at him with her violet eyes. "Well, the family were pressuring me to marry. And you can't imagine the sort of candidates they came up with. . . ."

"Indeed I can," Maijstral said. "Elderly bishops, and gawky schoolboys who can barely walk without falling down, middle-aged sportsmen gone to seed, a widowed duke looking for his fourth wife, lots of hopeful cousins who want your money, and an adopted human son of a Fifth-Degree Imperial Khosali Prince who is very fat and at least a hundred."

Roberta smiled. "I can see you've met them."

"On the contrary. I've met their sisters."

Roberta gave him a knowing look. "I see. Well, you know the situation, then. All the candidates were so *hopeless* . . . and, of course, *safe*, in the purely dynastic sense, of course. So I decided that, if I had to marry, I would at least find a candidate who suited me better."

"And I was chosen? Out of all our busy galaxy?"

Her ears reddened a bit. "I had a short list of about a dozen," she confessed. "Paavo Kuusinen met all of them, over the course of a few years, and sent in his reports, and I arranged to meet some of the more promising candidates myself, and . . . well, I made my choice on Silverside Station, when I met you. Since then I had to travel back to the Empire to inform my family, and, well, to inform yours. Such as he is."

"You could have done far worse," Maijstral said. "You could have contacted my mother."

Roberta bit her lip. "We don't have to invite her to the wedding, do we?"

"Don't ask her for my sake. But if we don't invite her, she'll probably crash the reception anyway, with an escort of His Majesty's Secret Dragoons."

"We'll try to contain her somehow."

They looked at each other for a moment, then self-consciously looked away. "I still don't know how you fastened upon *me*," Maijstral said. "You made your decision years ago, apparently, before I was very well-known to the public."

"I knew a few things about you," Roberta said. "I knew you would inherit an old title, which removed any objection on account of birth. I knew your parents were dedicated Imperialists, and your grandfather old Dornier was the most famous human Imperialist of all, so that removed any objections on account of politics and your citizenship in the Constellation. You were poor, of course, but I've got so much money that I certainly don't need to marry it, and anyway you've eliminated that objection yourself by earning a fortune in the last year. . . ."

"But why me? There must be a thousand poor, virtuous, titled Imperialists out there."

"Well." A little smile crept onto her face. "If you stand to inherit a fabulous gem like the Eltdown Shard, you spend a lot of your girlhood trying to imagine who's going to try to steal it from you. Trying to picture the romantic stranger who's going to fly in the window some night. And, of course, your family security people keep a list of all the top burglars, and you get dossiers . . . your face crossed my desk when you took out your burglar's license, and I remember thinking, Well, *there's* one I wouldn't mind meeting some dark night . . ."

"I took out my ticket ages ago. You must have been just a girl."

"Oh yes. Red hair and freckles and a school uniform that wouldn't fit. I'm glad you didn't know me then."

"I'm pleased to know you now."

"Are you?" Her eyes sparkled with interest. "Had you considered me a marriage candidate?"

"Frankly, no. I hadn't thought of myself as suitable." Maijstral touched his chin thoughtfully with a forefinger and regarded her, absorbing the creamy shoulders, the intriguing shadows about her clavicles, the gems that sparkled about her neck.

"I *had* thought about trying to get you into bed," he said, "but on Silverside we were both busy, and we had a business relationship besides, and since I've arrived here there hasn't been time."

She flushed becomingly. "Well," she said. "At least you noticed I was trying to make myself attractive."

"Your grace," Maijstral said, "I would have had to be as inhuman as a Drawmiikh *not* to notice."

Roberta smiled a little. "That inhuman, eh?"

There was a moment of silence as the two shared a memory. A Drawmiikh, they had once discovered, was more unforgettable, and inhuman, than either anticipated.

"Your grace," Maijstral finally said, "this whole marriage situation seems impossibly complex. Couldn't you just be my mistress for a while?"

She gave a little smile. "I *could*," she conceded, "but they'd probably make me marry someone else first."

"I suspected as much," Maijstral said. There was another little pause. "You saved my life," he added, apropos perhaps of nothing. "When that madwoman attacked me."

"Yes. I did, didn't I?"

He looked at her. "Have I ever thanked you properly?"

Kissing Roberta, Maijstral discovered, was very pleasant, and he prolonged this pleasure for some little while. When there was a pause, Roberta said, "What do we tell everyone?"

"Tell them," Maijstral said, "that negotiations are on-going."

Negotiations onwent a while longer, and then Maijstral and Roberta returned to his father's room holding hands. Kuusinen and Aunt Batty looked up expectantly.

"We have more talking to do," Maijstral said.

"What's the problem?" Gustav Maijstral demanded. "Is the girl ugly or something?"

"No, Dad," Maijstral said. "Her grace is very beautiful."

"I order you to marry her whether she's ugly or not!" the corpse said. "Gad, son, the girl is rich! Think of all the money for the Cause!"

Maijstral offered the Duchess an apologetic glance. Money and the Cause were two of his father's favorite topics, and once the old man had broached either subject it was difficult to keep him from enlarging upon it. Maijstral spoke up quickly.

"Time for your cocoa, Dad," he said.

An hour or so later Maijstral returned to his own room and called for Roman to unlace him. The tall Khosalikh arrived with a thick leather tube under one arm.

Maijstral looked at the tube, then at Roman, and then at the bare patch of pink flesh on the underside of Roman's muzzle. He thought he recognized the dangerous red-rimmed look smouldering in Roman's eyes, and ventured a cautious question.

"Are you molting again, Roman?"

"It *has* been a year since the last molt, sir." Roman put the tube on a table and turned to attend Maijstral.

"That long, eh?"

Maijstral made a mental note not to overstress Roman in the next week or so, and not to send Roman on one of the errands that sometimes proved necessary in his line of work—breaking the odd leg, say—not, anyway, unless Maijstral wanted the leg well and truly broken. Roman was not a good molter, and during the height of molt his normally moderate temper tended to veer unpredictably toward the savage.

"Sorry," Maijstral said. "If you want to just take a week off, I can get along with Drexler and a few robots to handle the lacing and unlacing."

Roman's ears flattened. "I am perfectly capable of discharging my duties, sir," he said.

Maijstral recognized the finality in Roman's tone. "Of course," Maijstral said. "I never had any doubts on that score whatever, I merely wished to make you as comfortable as possible."

He raised his arms to give Roman access to the side-laces. Roman picked at the lace-points expertly. "Was the evening enjoyable, sir?" he said.

"It was eventful, at least," Maijstral said, and gave his servant a sly, sidelong look. "Her Grace the Duchess of Benn made me an offer of marriage."

Roman's ears stood straight up, as did the surprised hair on top of his head. "Indeed, sir?" he said.

Maijstral smiled. He hardly ever saw Roman nonplussed. "She even arranged for my father to come here to Tejas to put his blessing on the union."

"His late grace is here?"

"Yes. You should probably pay your respects tomorrow."

"I will not fail to do so, sir." Roman smoothed down his top-hair, and a swatch of it came away in his fingers. His father had served the late Duke with the same resigned, half-despairing dedication with which Roman served Maijstral, and his grandfather had served Maijstral's grandfather, and so on back to the first Baron Drago, the Viceroy of Greater Italia in the early days of Imperial conquest.

Roman looked at the tuft of hair in his fingers with distaste and, rather than let it fall to the carpet, stowed it in his pocket. He returned to picking at Maijstral's laces.

"May I inquire as to the nature of the reply with which you favored her grace, sir?" he asked, his feigned casualness so studied that Maijstral was forced to turn away with a smile.

"Her grace and I," he said airily, "are still discussing the matter."

Well might Roman's diaphragm pulse in resignation at this answer. Despite the familiarity brought on by years of association, despite all the adventures shared and obstacles overcome, when all was said and done Maijstral was, quite simply, incomprehensible.

"Very good, sir," Roman said. Dutiful, as always.

Roman was all too familiar with the defects of Maijstral's situation. They could be summed up as follows:

Money. For most of his life, Maijstral had been desperately short of money. This situation was not, Roman knew, Maijstral's doing, but that of his father, who had spent such of the family money as survived the Rebellion in crackpot Imperialist political schemes and who on his death had left Maijstral with nothing but debt.

Maijstral's response to his fiscal dilemma was reflected in Defect Number Two, to wit:

Profession. What better way to get money than to steal it? Allowed Burglary was legal—though barely, in the Human Constellation—and it was, thanks to its regulation by the Imperial Sporting Commission, a profession that a gentleman could adopt without danger of losing his position in society.

But some respectable professions were still more respectable than others. Allowed Burglary was lumped in with various other wayward callings, like drunkenness, banking, and the composition of satires, that were permitted but not precisely overwhelmed by the honors and distinctions given more respectable characters like civil servants, courtiers, great actors, military officers, or Elvis impersonators.

If one was a burglar, one was compelled to associate with many of the wrong sort: fences, enforcers, people willing to sell their employers' secrets, the agents of insurance companies (parasites of parasites, in Roman's view). Allowed Burglary required an irregular life, and constant travel both to avoid the police and to find new objects to steal. Often burglary was dangerous. It was irregular. Sometimes it was sordid.

But, Roman was willing to concede, it was necessary in Maijstral's case. It was where his master's talents lay, and his master, alas, needed to earn a living. His attempts to do so, and to live in the social stratum to which he was born, involved Defect Number Three:

Position. Though he preferred not to use his title, Maijstral's theoretical social position was perfectly on a par with the Duchess of Benn's, if not slightly better: he was descended from one of the oldest human families ennobled by the Imperium—which wasn't much compared with an old Khosali title that might go back tens of thousands of years, but it was pretty good as humans go.

But, due to the misfortunes of his recent ancestors, the titles were empty of anything save honor and debt. Someone of the exalted rank of the Duke of Dornier should move effortlessly in the highest society (without, needless to say, having to steal), should grace government ministries with his talents, should endow foundations and pioneer planets—and, if the political situation should call for his employment as the Hereditary Captain-General of the Green Legion, he should occasionally go out and conquer something.

But none of this was possible without money. It cost a lot to live in the highest reaches of society, and Maijstral had no sources of income not connected with burglary—even the Green Legion was mothballed, its existence memorialized only by a few ancient battle flags hung in a side chapel in the City of Seven Bright Rings. Thanks to a devoted attention to his profession and the fame this had brought him, Maijstral was only now beginning to enjoy the pleasant and civilized mode of life which should have been his from the beginning. But Allowed Burglary was a precarious existence at best, with arrest always a possibility, and though Maijstral's income was now a comfortable one, it wasn't anywhere near the state that would have permitted him to live as effortlessly and gloriously as the Duke of Dornier, in Roman's estimation, ought.

Marriage with the Duchess of Benn solved every single one of Maijstral's problems. He would have access to as much money as anyone would desire. He would no longer have to earn a living as a burglar. And he would be able to live fully up to his position.

It was, in Roman's view, nothing less than Maijstral's *duty* to marry the Duchess. Personalities and the complications of human character didn't enter into it—as far as Roman could tell, they were unintelligible anyway, even to humans.

Roman finished Maijstral's side-laces and deftly pulled off Maijstral's jacket and put it in the closet. Maijstral began working at the side-laces of his trousers.

"I would like, on this auspicious occasion, to make a small presentation," Roman said. He shifted his shoulders in his jacket. That itch between his shoulder blades was back.

Maijstral's ears pricked back in surprise. He looked at the leather tube, then back to Roman.

"Pray go ahead," he said.

Roman retrieved the tube, uncapped it, and drew forth a

scroll. The scroll had been made of grookh hide of the finest quality, thinner than paper and more resilient than steel, suitable in fact for a Memorial to the Throne.

But whereas a Memorial would be written with a jade-tipped pen in large, florid handwriting—emperors and their advisors have to read a *lot* of documents, and they appreciate large print—the writing on Roman's scroll was quite literally microscopic. There was a device in the lid of the scroll case that enabled one to read it.

Roman felt his heart swelling with pride as he laid the scroll out on a table. "This is the culmination of years of research," he said. "A kind of hobby of mine."

This was Roman's Special Project. Many long hours in the composition, he hoped it would prove decisive in this business of marriage. Reminding of the awesome weight and majesty of his ancestors might inspire Maijstral to prove worthy of them.

The itch burned in the center of Roman's back. Inwardly he snarled in annoyance.

Maijstral looked at the endless lines of tiny print in bewilderment. His trousers were unlaced and he had to hold them up with one hand. "There's certainly a lot here," he said.

"I have taken the liberty of tracing the history of the Maijstral family," Roman said.

Maijstral's ears cocked forward. "Really? *My* family?"

"Indeed, sir. You will observe—"

"Why not your own family?" Maijstral asked.

Roman's ears flicked in annoyance. The itch brought a growl to his lips. "My family's history has already been very well documented, sir," he said. Like most Khosali, his ancestry could be traced many thousands of years past the Khosali conquest of Earth . . . though, also like most Khosali, he was too polite to mention it.

"If you will observe, sir," Roman began, and deployed

the reading mechanism, "I have made some rather interesting discoveries. Your ancestors are far more distinguished than either of us had any reason to suspect."

"Yes? That Crusader fellow you always talk about—you confirmed him?"

"Jean Parisot de La Valette," Roman said. "Indisputably. My library researches took me, last night, to Rome, where I had the honor of personally inspecting the records of the Knights of St. John. I found undisputable confirmation, which you will observe . . ." He placed the reader. "Here."

"Most interesting." Maijstral manipulated the reader with one hand and hitched up his pants with the other. "The wrong side of the blanket, of course," he noted. "Typical of my family, I suppose."

Roman's diaphragm throbbed. He wished Maijstral wouldn't disparage his ancestors in that fashion.

One of Roman's hands crept around behind his back and covertly began to scratch. No good—Khosali spines are somewhat less flexible than those of humans, and he didn't come anywhere near the itch.

"You will also observe Edmund Beaufort I, Earl and Marquess of Dorset," Roman said. "His fourth son married a Matilda of Denmark, who was descended from Henry the Lion. You are thus a descendant not only of the Welfs, but Frederick Barbarossa, the Plantagenets, the Tudors, and all the ruling houses of Europe."

"You don't say," Maijstral murmured.

"And on the Asian side," scratching furiously, "there is Altan Khan and the Vietnamese emperor Gia-Long, not to mention—"

Maijstral was peering at the top of the list. "Who's this Wotan person?" he asked. "He seems to be right at the head of the list, but he doesn't have any dates."

"Ah." Roman's diaphragm pulsed again, and he gave up the scratching. "Allow me to explain, sir."

* * *

"Thank you, Roman," Maijstral said. "It is a wonderful treasure."

"Thank you, sir."

"It must have taken you many hours. I'm impressed, as always, by your dedication."

Roman's black fur rippled with pride. A few little tufts drifted toward the floor. "Thank you," he said. "It was a privilege to work on such a project."

"My trousers," Maijstral said, and handed over his pants. Roman hung them in the closet and retrieved Maijstral's dressing gown. Maijstral shrugged into the gown and sealed it.

"That will be all, Roman, I think," Maijstral said.

"Very good, sir. Shall I leave the genealogy on the table?"

"Please do. I may wish to look at it."

"Very good, sir."

"Thank you very much for the gift," Maijstral said.

"It was entirely my pleasure, sir."

Roman bowed and left the room. Maijstral walked to the table and sighed as he looked at the scroll.

As if he didn't have enough to do with ancestors today, he thought. Not only was his father here to urge him to do the right thing, but now Roman had brought in the kinfolk all the way back to Wotan.

Maijstral had really done his best to ignore the fact that he was heir to a dynasty, and now the whole business had dropped right on his head like a sandbag flung from Heaven.

It wasn't that he disliked the Duchess. It wasn't that he disliked the thought of marriage. But somehow it was all too pat, all too . . . foreordained.

Oh well, he thought glumly, maybe it *was* time to marry and settle down and produce more Maijstrals. Though why the universe needed more Maijstrals was beyond his capacity to explain.

Idly, he glanced at the genealogy—there was a complicated bit of business involving a Prince Boris of Gleb, who
apparently married his aunt, and Maijstral couldn't help but
wonder what the family had said about *that*.

He very carefully rolled up the scroll and stowed it away
in its tube. There was all too much to think about without
worrying about Prince Boris's problems.

He took a casual stroll about the room, making certain
that neither Conchita Sparrow nor Colonel-General Vandergilt was hiding in the closet or under the bed, and then climbed
into bed and told the lights to extinguish themselves.

The situation revolved slowly in his mind. He would
probably not sleep tonight.

There was a gentle knock at the door. *Now* what? Maijstral thought.

He put on his dressing gown and approached the door.
Wary force of habit made him keep well to one side as he said,
"Who is it?"

"Roberta. May I come in?"

Maijstral opened the door and revealed Roberta silhouetted in the hall light. She wore a dressing gown and a somewhat
furtive expression. She stepped in, and Maijstral closed the
door behind her.

"Well," she said.

Maijstral regarded her in the dim light. She was standing
very close, and he could feel her body's warmth.

"Well," he echoed.

"I was just in my room thinking—" she began, and then
stopped. "Look, Drake," she finally said, "would you mind
kissing me again?"

"No. Not at all."

Maijstral put his arms around her and performed as re-
quested. The kiss was a pleasantly lengthy one.

"Oh good," the Duchess murmured. "That helps."

"I am happy to oblige."

Her eyes, dark in the unlit room, looked up at his. "Do you remember earlier this evening," she said, "when we were alone, and you asked if I could just be your mistress for a while?"

Maijstral smiled. "I believe I recall that remark, yes."

"Well . . ." she drawled, and gave a little laugh. "Here's your chance."

Maijstral's ears flickered in surprise. "I see," he said.

"This one's free, you know," Roberta added. "It has nothing to do with whether you should to marry me or not."

"You are . . ." Maijstral searched for words, "remarkably direct, your grace."

"Roberta."

"Roberta."

"Bobbie, if you like," she said. "But only Aunt Batty calls me that anymore."

"I think I prefer Roberta."

"So do I."

Maijstral contemplated the woman in his arms. Roberta kissed his chin.

"Can we go to bed now?" she asked.

"Certainly."

Well, Maijstral thought, no doubt Prince Boris and Altan Khan would approve.

He drew her bedward. "I've had a very active life, you know," she remarked. "Going to school, and racing, and running all the planets I've inherited . . ."

"No doubt," Maijstral murmured. He kissed the juncture between clavicle and neck, and Roberta shivered.

"And of course I've been very thoroughly chaperoned," she went on.

"How frustrating."

"Yes. So what I'm trying to say is—*Wow!*" Maijstral's

researches had encountered a particularly sensitive point. "What I'm trying to say," she repeated, "is that I'm not very practiced at this."

"I will bear that in mind."

"I'm not practiced at all, in fact."

"Oh." Maijstral halted in surprise and looked at Roberta.

"I have a very good imagination," she added. "I hope that will help to make up for any lack of genuine experience."

"No doubt," Maijstral said, half to himself. And then, "Your grace, are you absolutely certain you want to do this?"

"Oh good grief yes," Roberta said quickly. "It's about time, don't you think?" She laughed. "If we're to be married, it'll make the long engagement go more quickly. And if we're not, at least I'll have had the man of my dreams."

Maijstral nodded. A glittering midnight gleam entered his lazy eyes.

"Well," he said finally, "I hope I prove worthy of that imagination of yours."

Maijstral was awakened by an authoritative knock on his door. The situation—loud banging on door, girl next to him in the bed—awakened a long-standing reflex of many years' duration. He made a smooth vault from the bed, snatched dressing gown and pistol, and was halfway to the window before he was brought up short by a bolt of pain that seized his nether regions in a grip of iron.

Staggered, he leaned on a table for support and looked about him. Roberta was blinking at him lazily from her pillow, and the knocking continued.

He took a step toward the door and the pain clutched him again. What, he tried to remember, had he and Roberta *done* last night?

And then he realized that the pain probably had a lot

more to do with his first horseback ride than anything he and Roberta had got up to in bed.

"Just a moment," Maijstral called, and put on his dressing gown. He found Roberta's gown and gallantly held it out for her. She rose gracefully from bed and slipped her arms into the silk-lined sleeves.

"This way," Maijstral said, and turned to the closet. "Closet," he said, "open."

The closet obliged. Maijstral escorted the Duchess inside, and observed that Conchita Sparrow's command override, which she had left behind, was still in place, a fortunate accident in that it would allow the closet door to close with someone inside. He kissed Roberta, who looked up at him with amusement glittering in her eyes, and then he told the closet to close.

The hammering on the door recommenced. Maijstral looked down at the gun in his hand and wondered how it had come there.

Perhaps, however, it was best to be cautious.

"Who is it?" he demanded.

"Joseph Bob," came the answer.

There was a knock on the inner door that led to his sitting room, and Drexler stepped in, his ears cocked grimly forward. "Trouble, boss," he said. "There's a fleet of police fliers dropping on the lawn."

"Ah," Maijstral said. "I see. Someone must have stolen something, somewhere, and the cops are trying to pin it on us."

"Roman's making sure the rooms are clean," Drexler said.

The hammering started again. Maijstral hobbled toward the door and opened it. Joseph Bob, Arlette, and the Bubber were outside, each looking hastily dressed, and each wearing a grim expression.

"What's the problem?" Maijstral asked.

"There's an item missing," Joseph Bob said. "And though we're quite sure you have nothing to do with its disappearance . . ." Words, or perhaps tact, failed him, and he looked around for support.

"We're sure you will want to demonstrate your innocence," Arlette filled in, "and won't mind if we search your rooms."

Behind Maijstral the window darkened as a pair of police in a-grav harness took up position. Maijstral turned to the window and cocked an eyebrow.

"Did you *have* to invite the cops?" he asked.

Joseph Bob frowned. "I didn't," he said. "One of the servants must have called them."

"Well," Maijstral said, "I'm sorry, but neither you nor they can search my rooms. I stand on my rights as a citizen of the Human Constellation. Good morning."

He shut the door in Joseph Bob's surprised face, then hobbled toward a chair and sat down. Pain shot through his thighs.

"Maijstral," came a muffled voice. "Be reasonable, now. Open the blasted door."

"Citizens of the Human Constellation can be unreasonable if they want," Maijstral said, and adjusted his position to an attitude that only caused pain if he happened to move or breathe. He turned to Drexler. "I don't suppose you can produce some coffee?" he asked.

Drexler look at him in surprise. "I'll see what I can do."

Drexler headed for the sitting room. There was a pounding on the door, followed by Joseph Bob's voice. "Maijstral!" he said. "Open the door! Damn it, I *own* this door!"

"I'd advise you not to dent it, then," Maijstral said.

He could hear the tramp of boots out in the corridor, and then a muffled conversation. "We're getting a warrant!" Joseph Bob called.

"I hardly think you've got grounds," Maijstral said. "Somebody stole something. You've got no reason to think it was me."

"We'll *find* grounds," promised another voice, and Maijstral was not surprised to recognize that of Colonel-General Vandergilt.

"If you can get a warrant on these grounds," Maijstral said, "it won't stand up in court, and you know it."

Pure bluff of course, but he *hoped* it was true.

Maijstral had dressed—a painful operation—moved to the sitting room, and finished half his coffee by the time the warrant arrived. Drexler and Roman had joined him. Roman wasn't looking his best, with patches of grey skin where his fur had fallen out and a dangerous red-rimmed look to his eyes.

Those in the corridor pushed the warrant under the door. Maijstral nodded to Roman, who picked the warrant up and looked at it. He looked at Maijstral and snarled.

Maijstral was not accustomed to seeing his servant snarl—Roman was fairly mild-mannered, and broke legs and arms only with reluctance. It took Maijstral a half second or so to overcome his surprise, and then he shrugged. He'd done his best to preserve decorum.

"May as well open the door," he said.

Joseph Bob and his family entered on a flood of uniformed constabulary. The Prince of Tejas looked apoplectic as he stalked toward Maijstral's chair. The police deployed weapons and detectors.

"Blast it, Maijstral!" he said.

"You might have given me time for coffee," Maijstral said. He put down his cup and managed to rise to his feet without more than a wince of pain crossing his features.

There was a crash as a policewoman knocked over a small table and dropped a six-hundred-year-old Pendjalli vase to the floor.

"I'll assume responsibility for the damage, sir," said Colonel-General Vandergilt as she marched into the room. "My department will pay."

"I didn't know your department had *that much money,*" Maijstral said. Vandergilt looked doubtful for a moment. Maijstral began to lurch toward the bedroom. He wished to be present when Roberta was discovered, and offer such moral support as was possible.

"Not so fast, Maijstral," said Colonel-General Vandergilt. She stepped forward in her black uniform, silver buttons shining. "You'll have to be searched." So eager was she to get about the searching that no less than three separate strands of hair had escaped her helmet and were dangling in her eyes.

"You can search me in the bedroom as well as anywhere," Maijstral said, and kept moving.

"Life-form in the closet!" called a policeman from the bedroom, and suddenly there was the businesslike clacking of weapons being readied, and the cops began to deploy into attack formations.

Alarm flashed through Maijstral. "Put the guns down!" he said hastily. He had arrived in the bedroom door and was acutely aware that anyone firing would probably have to shoot right through him. He gingerly stepped to one side.

"Closet," he said. "Open."

Roberta looked quite cool as she stepped into full view, wearing her dressing gown as if she were making her grand entrance at a ball, and if Maijstral hadn't been quite so concerned about all the guns levelled at his spleen, he might have spared a moment or two for admiration.

No guns crackled, and Maijstral breathed a fervent sigh of relief. "Ah," he said, and stepped into the bedroom. "Ladies and gentlemen, allow me to introduce my alibi, Her Grace the Duchess of Benn. Your grace, this is Colonel-General Denise Vandergilt, Constellation Special Services."

Colonel-General Vandergilt stuffed stray hair into her helmet and stalked into the center of the room, followed by Joseph Bob and his family. Vandergilt looked coldly at the Duchess while the Prince and his family looked in surprise at each other.

"What's your real name?" Vandergilt said. "I don't use titles."

"No titles?" Roberta said. Her eyebrows rose. "Fine with me—*Denise*. My name is Roberta Altunin."

Vandergilt looked as if she was adding the name to some mental dossier, which she probably was.

Maijstral turned to Joseph Bob, who was beginning to look abashed. "I would have let you in earlier," he said, "but there are certain things a gentleman—"

"*Object in the ventilator!*" called a policeman.

Maijstral threw up his hands. This was going to be a long morning.

"It's the right wave pattern," the policeman added, peering at his detectors.

The ventilator was pulled away, and Colonel-General Vandergilt produced a "fingerprint handkerchief," which, despite its name, was a handkerchief guaranteed not to remove fingerprints, and which could be used for holding and transporting evidence. She reached into the ventilator and took out the object therein. When she showed it to the assembled company, there was a triumphant glow in her eyes.

"Is this your property, sir?" she asked the Prince.

The room reeled about Maijstral. He wanted to clutch his heart, fall to his knees, and (were ashes only available) pour ashes on his head.

Displayed on the white handkerchief was the prototype wooden revolver of Colonel Samuel Colt.

"I didn't do it!" Maijstral said.

Colonel-General Vandergilt smiled thinly. "That's what

they all say." She handed the pistol to an underling. "Have that checked for fingerprints," she said.

Had not Maijstral been preoccupied by visions of the fate that awaited him—red-robed judges, unfriendly prison wardens, overly friendly fellow inmates, fetters, thumbscrews, and so on—he would have noticed Joseph Bob turning a dangerous shade of red.

Vandergilt puffed her cheeks and blew a strand of hair out of her face—she didn't want to spoil her big moment—and then looked stern and dropped a black-gauntleted hand on Maijstral's shoulder.

"Drake Maijstral, you're under arrest!" she proclaimed, then turned to Roberta. "And so are your accomplices," she added, and smiled.

"*Accomplices!*" Roberta said, outraged.

"Accomplices," Vandergilt repeated, and then she turned to Joseph Bob. "Sir, if you will accompany us to the police station, you can make a formal identification of your property and sign a complaint."

"I didn't do it," Maijstral said again, but no one seemed to be listening to him.

"Complaint?" Joseph Bob muttered. He was bright scarlet. "Complaint? Damned if I'll sign a complaint! A guest in my home!"

Maijstral looked at Joseph Bob in sudden hope. Joseph Bob was going to save him! he thought. His old school chum! Good old J.B.!

The Colonel-General looked puzzled. "Sir," she said, "if you don't sign the complaint, I won't be able to arrest Maijstral and his gang."

"I'll be signing no complaints!" Joseph Bob said, and then he turned to Maijstral, and Maijstral's heart stopped at the fury in the Prince's eyes. Joseph Bob shook a finger in Maijstral's face. "A guest in my home, and you steal from me!"

"I didn't do it," Maijstral pointed out.

Joseph Bob socked him in the jaw. It was a clean, professional punch, one that would make any pom boxer proud, and it knocked Maijstral sprawling.

Joseph Bob had a number of intentions at this point, all of which were fated to go sadly awry. His first intention was to stand commandingly over Maijstral's prone body while denouncing him, a dramatic pose recommended by any number of precedents derived from the theater. Unfortunately Joseph Bob had just broken two knuckles on Maijstral's head and spoiled his intended effect by hopping around the room while clutching his wounded hand.

"Maijstral!" he yelped, turning white. "I'll have satisfaction on the field of honor! My brother will speak for me!"

Joseph Bob's second intention, likewise derived from the theater, was to stalk dramatically from the room and leave behind an awed silence, an intention that was frustrated, in the first instance, by the rather crabbed, hunched-over stance his wound was compelling him to adopt, and in the second, by the well-delivered power kick that Roman planted in his face.

Roman, as it happens, *was* a pom boxer, and in the course of avenging his employer against a dastardly surprise attack, he knew better than to risk fragile hand bones battering away at the solid bone of someone's skull, not when a better weapon was at hand—in this case, a foot encased in a sturdy boot.

Joseph Bob's nose exploded like an overripe kibble fruit, and the Prince de Tejas sailed backward into Maijstral's room and joined him on the carpet.

Arlette flung herself down on her husband, either to assure herself as to his well-being or to protect him against further assault.

His remaining fur bristling, Roman advanced, a huge, alarming, red-eyed menace, but was brought up short by the weapons of a dozen or so police that were suddenly thrust up under his muzzle.

"Roman," Roberta warned. *"Don't."*

Roman fell back, but the snarl remained on his face.

He really *was* a bad molter.

Maijstral, to this point, had been too stunned by Joseph Bob's punch to be able to react to any of the subsequent events. He tried to sit up, then decided that remaining prone might prove a course easier to sustain. Roberta dropped to his side and cradled his head in her hands. "Are you all right?" she asked.

"No," Maijstral said, and felt a certain pride at retaining his grip on both speech and reality.

"Shall I stand as your second?" Roberta asked. "I've had practice at it, after all."

Maijstral, who didn't at this point wish to attempt more syllables than absolutely necessary, nodded his answer. She turned to the Bubber.

"Will," she said, "I'll talk to you later." She looked at the others. "I believe the rest of you no longer have any business here."

Joseph Bob was unable to regain his feet, and he was carried from the room by the police. When Roman kicked someone, the someone stayed kicked.

Maijstral, the chimes in his head subsiding, realized that he'd been saved from the prison by virtue of the fact that he was about to die in a duel with the finest swordsman and pistol shot in the Principality of Tejas.

SIX

❀ ❀ ❀

Roman, Drexler," Maijstral said, "I want Conchita Sparrow brought to me. I confess I do not care how this is accomplished. But as I intend that she confess to framing me, I would prefer her conscious, or at least capable of consciousness, by the time she actually arrives."

"Very good, sir," said Roman.

"Take any recordings you may find. When she stole the pistol, she may have recorded her mission to sell on the market."

"Yes, sir."

"Go at once."

"Very good, sir."

Drexler and Roman bowed and, after stuffing their clothing with weapons, made their exit, Roman trailing a fine cloud of black hair as he left. Maijstral fingered the large semi-life patch that was extending its anaesthetic tendrils into his damaged flesh and considered that, if he were Conchita Sparrow and saw Roman in his current state coming toward her with evil intent, he'd confess on the spot.

He rose stiffly from his chair and lurched toward the service plate, where he summoned robots to carry his belongings to his rented flier. It was now impossible to stay at Joseph Bob's estate. He would be moving to the next place on his itinerary, the Underwater Palace of Quintana Roo, where he had been invited for a weekend. He would be arriving a few days early, but fortunately that was all right with Prince Hunac, his host, who already had many guests in residence.

There was a knock on the door, and Roberta stepped in without waiting for a reply. She kissed Maijstral's cheek, thoughtfully choosing the undamaged one. "I've been talking to the Bubber," she said. "I thought he and I had best establish a few protocols at the start."

"Very sensible," Maijstral said. He was all in favor of protocols and technicalities, anything that would delay or complicate the situation long enough so that Maijstral could either find the real culprit and get the duel called off, or alternatively somehow fix the encounter's outcome. Either way, as far as Maijstral was concerned, would prove satisfactory.

He hobbled to the sofa and sat down with a sigh of pain. Roberta joined him. The latest-model Windsong robots entered the room on silent repellers, and on Maijstral's instructions picked up his luggage in their invisible grapplers and carried it off.

"Will doesn't think you did it, either," Roberta said. "He ventured the opinion that you're a sufficiently good magician that, if you'd *known* the pistol was there, you could have kept anyone from finding it. So he's inclined to help Joseph Bob see reason."

"And Joseph Bob?"

"Disinclined to see any reason whatever, I'm afraid. And Roman's knocking him silly didn't help matters."

"Hmm."

"He insists that you're at fault for 'permitting your servant to attack him,' as I believe he phrased it."

Indignation flamed in Maijstral. "I don't know how I could have stopped Roman, since I'd just been floored by His Highness's sneaky punch," he said. And then he realized he was being indignant and made an effort to suppress it. People torn by indignation didn't wriggle out of duels, and *that,* he reminded himself, was what he was after.

"It occurred to me to point this out," Roberta said, "but I decided it wouldn't improve matters, so I didn't."

"Quite rightly," Maijstral said.

Roberta smiled. "Thank you," she said. "Now, I suppose, we ought to discuss weapons."

Oh, why bring *them* into it, Maijstral thought.

Still, best to get it clear. The array of duelling weapons permitted by Khosali High Custom was truly staggering, and there had to be *some* that would give Maijstral an advantage.

"Joseph Bob is an expert pistol shot, and a fine swordsman," he said. "I would prefer to leave those out of the picture entirely."

"Very well."

"I'd also like to delay the whole business," Maijstral said. "Give tempers a chance to cool, and give me a chance to find the real culprit and prove it was she who stole the pistol."

"*She?*" Roberta's eyebrows lifted. "Do you know who did it?"

"A licensed burglar named Conchita Sparrow. She's been trying to get herself hired as my tech, and I turned her down. By way of demonstrating her abilities, she broke in here two nights ago, interestingly enough by way of the same ventilator shaft in which Colonel Colt's pistol was found."

Roberta cocked her head to one side as she considered this. "It sounds plausible, at least. You don't have any other idea who might have been responsible?"

"So far as I know, I don't have an enemy in the world.

Unless it's one of your beaux," he added, "mad with jealousy." He tried to smile, but pain stabbed his jaw, and he winced instead.

"Poor Drake." She patted his uninjured cheek again. "What, by the way, do we tell the family?"

"Tell them the whole thing's a misunderstanding."

"No." She smiled patiently. "I mean about *us.*"

"Oh." Maijstral blinked. Preoccupied with his own problem, he'd quite forgotten the whole matter of his betrothal.

"Well," he said, "it seems to me that it would be unfair of me to make you a widow before we're even engaged. Why don't we tell the family that we're postponing any announcement until my business with Joseph Bob is resolved?"

A shadow of disappointment crossed Roberta's face. "Very well," she said, and rose. "I'll go tell them now."

She walked toward the door. "Roberta?" he said.

She turned. "Yes?"

"Thank you."

She smiled. "You're very welcome."

"And will you do me another favor?"

"If I can."

"Will you ship my father down to Quintana Roo for me? I'll look after him from there."

"Of course," she said, and made her exit.

"*I didn't do it!*" Conchita Sparrow yelped.

Drexler advanced menacingly, a hi-stick dangling from his muzzle. "Pull the other one," he said, demonstrating a surprising grasp of Human Standard vernacular. (In Khosali it would have come out "Drag the remaining unity," which would have lacked the colloquial verve of the original.)

In any language it was purely a figure of speech, since Conchita Sparrow was in no position to pull anything.

Roman, by contrast, was in a position to pull all the legs required, as he was holding her by one ankle over the edge of Kanab, one of the Grand Canyon's more impressive side canyons.

"Honest!" Conchita said. "I didn't do it!"

"I bet Roman is getting tired," Drexler said. "Aren't you, Roman?"

"I could lose my grip at any moment," Roman warned. He loosened his grasp slightly, just enough for Conchita to fall a few inches, and then caught her again. Conchita gave a strangled shriek.

Drexler took a languid draw on his hi-stick. "Careful, Roman," he said, relishing the opportunity once again to demonstrate his grasp of slang, "you might do the lady a mischief."

Maijstral contemplated this picture with pleasure. Roman, a menacing piebald giant big even for a Khosalikh, held Conchita, small even for a human, at arm's length, with rather more ease than Maijstral could hold a child. Media globes, controlled by the proximity wire in Maijstral's collar, circled the pair like orbiting satellites, ready to record any revelations that might drop from Conchita's lips.

"Give a moment to your surroundings, Miss Sparrow," Maijstral said. Walking bowlegged to minimize his pain, he approached the edge and regarded the deep canyon below. He took a deep, appreciative breath. "Consider the eons that must have gone into the creation of this magnificent sight into which, at any instant, you may take flight. Consider the work of millennia, as erosion, as vast landslides, as the uplift of the local geology all did their work. Consider its glory in comparison with the alteration in the local formation you will make when you strike the ground below. Which is to say—" He looked at her meaningfully. "*None at all.*"

Maijstral threw out his arms to glory in the Canyon's

vastness. "Consider the gorgeousness that will be your last living vision—will you appreciate it as you fall, I wonder?"

"I'll be too busy screaming my head off," Conchita said.

"Tell us what we want to hear," Maijstral said, "and there will be no need for screaming at all."

"*I didn't do it!*" she screamed. Which was followed by a somewhat less coherent scream, abruptly cut off, as Roman's grip relaxed, then firmed again.

"I can prove it!" she said. "I was out stealing last night! I recorded everything—it's in those spheres your goons captured!"

"His *what?*" Drexler growled, his bristling.

"Assistants! Associates! Whatever!"

Annoyance crackled along Maijstral's nerves. He really didn't want to credit the notion that Conchita actually had an alibi.

"Stealing where?" he asked. "And what?"

"In Australia. An entire consignment of rare pink and green Australian diamonds from the Nokh & Nokh depository. No style points, but I needed the cash."

Maijstral frowned. Conchita's story had the discouraging ring of truth.

It must be admitted that sometimes even Allowed Burglars—whose calling glorified, nay demanded, the search for and acquisition of the rare, the wonderful, and the celebrated—sometimes even Allowed Burglars demonstrated a regrettable lack of regard for the possibilities of their profession and merely stole things for the money. Usually, it must be said, in bulk, Conchita's vaultful of diamonds being a good example. Because these jobs were rarely granted anything like the full ten points awarded for style, many were never submitted to the Imperial Sporting Commission for rating, but merely went to support the burglar in maintaining the high style with which he floated from place to place, looking for rarer forms of plunder.

Maijstral, particularly in his early days as a burglar, had been known to plunder the odd diamond vault himself. And even Ralph Adverse, the most legendary burglar of all, Ralph Adverse of the Losey Portrait, the Manchester Apollo, and the Eltdown Shard itself, was said to have knocked over a bank or two when the opportunity presented.

"Drexler," Maijstral said, "go to the flier and check the news bulletins. Find out if Nokh & Nokh had a robbery in the last day or so."

Drexler snapped his hi-stick in two and tossed the broken bits into the Canyon. "Whether she's telling the truth or not," he said, "she still called me a goon. *I* think we should chuck her in just for that."

"Sir," Roman said, as Drexler walked toward the flier, "it would have been daylight in Australia when the pistol was stolen. Hardly an ideal time to break into a vault."

Maijstral brightened. "Daylight, eh?" he said cheerfully. He turned to Conchita. "What do you say to that, Miss Sparrow?"

"It was William Bligh Day," Conchita said. "A holiday. I had the whole day to plunder the vault."

Maijstral scowled. He was vexed with William Bligh, and he didn't even know who Bligh was.

This was unfortunate, for had Maijstral only known it, Bligh had much in common with Maijstral's family, specifically Maijstral's grandfather. Both Bligh and Governor His Grace Robert, Duke of Dornier, had the misfortune to suffer mutinies and handle them badly. Bligh suffered no less than two mutinies during his naval career, and then suffered the final martyrdom when the entire continent of Australia mutinied against his administration. Duke Robert had only one mutiny to deal with, but he mishandled it so spectacularly that his name, and that of his descendants, were blighted forevermore.

It is instructive to observe how the Khosali dealt with

each of these unfortunate officers. With their passion for law, discipline, and regularity, the Khosali were sympathetic to Bligh, viewed him as a martyr to Order, and created a holiday for him. Statues were built to him throughout Oceania. Duke Robert, by contrast, had acquired such an infamous reputation that the Khosali preferred to treat him gingerly, when they treated him at all. No mention was made of him, no statues built, no holidays declared. No posthumous decorations were ordered. The Green Legion was mothballed, and any mentions in the official histories were as terse and uninformative as possible.

Even the Khosali quest for Order has its limits.

"Bad news, boss," Drexler said from the flier. "Nokh & Nokh got knocked over."

Maijstral took the bad news stoically. He turned to Roman. "You might as well let Miss Sparrow down, and she can show us her recordings of the happy event."

"Do I have to?" Conchita said, rising and dusting herself off. "I didn't exactly cover myself with glory on this one."

Which proved to be an understatement. The burglary had begun quite well, with Conchita's black boxes successfully overcoming the vault's alarm systems, defense robots, and locking mechanism. She walked into the vault looking very pleased with herself, and then carefully closed the vault door behind her so that no passing guard might see that the huge round door was open.

At this point Drexler's tongue flopped from his mouth in uncontrollable mirth. Maijstral turned away so that Conchita wouldn't see his smile. Only Roman managed to maintain his previous demeanor—which was not in his case difficult, considering that he was nearly psychotic with surging hormones, continual itching, and persistent shedding.

For Conchita had just locked herself in the vault. With all her vault-springing mechanisms left *outside*.

The video-Conchita, however, took some time to realize this. She emptied the vault of its contents, packed everything neatly into the levitating luggage she'd brought with her. She was looking quite relieved that she hadn't bungled anything for a change . . . and then she turned to leave.

She looked at the door. Frowned. Frowned some more. Drexler began massaging his diaphragm, which was cramping with pleasure. "I can't look," he moaned.

"All my black boxes worked," Conchita said defensively. "That's my specialty."

"How did you get out?" Maijstral asked.

"Vaults aren't constructed so as to prevent people from breaking *out*," Conchita said. "I had to improvise some tools from bits of my luggage and some things I'd found in the vaults."

"And how long did this take you?" Maijstral asked.

"Nine hours," Conchita said in a small voice.

"I think," Maijstral said as he turned off the display, "that we may spare ourselves the next nine hours of video."

"Perhaps we could just skip to the end," Drexler suggested cheerfully.

Maijstral turned to Conchita. "I apologize for the hasty assumptions that led me to bring you here. My associates will return you to your home."

"Thank you." She gazed at the surrounding countryside through the flier's transparent top. "It was nice to get a chance to see the Grand Canyon. Even though I've lived on Earth all my life, I'd never come here."

"And you were favored with a unique perspective of the Canyon that few others will ever have experienced."

She giggled. "True." Her brow furrowed. "What is it all about, anyway? What exactly was I supposed to have done?"

"Well," Maijstral sighed, "I suppose after all this I might well owe you an explanation."

He told her, briefly, the facts of the case. She whistled.

"You're in the soup, all right. And that explains how you came to have a semilife patch on your face. But how did you figure it was me that did it?"

"I'd turned you down when you applied for a job."

"What—you don't have any worse enemies?"

Maijstral frowned thoughtfully. "It would appear that I do."

"Any idea who they are?"

Maijstral flattened his ears in perplexity. "No one really comes to mind," he said. "Colonel-General Vandergilt, of course, but I don't know whether she's fanatic enough to plant evidence, or for that matter whether she or her associates have the skill to do it. Putting the pistol in the ventilator of the room I was sleeping in would have taken no small ability."

"But Vandergilt's a member of the Special Services Corps, right?" Conchita said. "Then she's a spy, or at least knows spies. That pistol might have been planted by a government burglar, not one of us stylish amateurs."

Maijstral considered this and felt a nebulous, creeping sort of gloom float into his mind, like a low cloud casting cold shadows on his thoughts.

"Or possibly the burglar was one who'd been arrested, and was given special consideration if he agreed to set you up," Conchita added. "Maybe you should check to see which burglars have been arrested lately and then let loose. Drexler"—smiling over her shoulder—"can you spare a histick?"

Drexler scowled as he forked over the intoxicant.

"Roman . . ." Maijstral began.

"Very good, sir. I'll check the arrest records as soon as I take the young lady home."

Conchita turned to Maijstral. Her eyes sparkled. "Maybe I could help," she said. "I have some contacts among Earth burglars. I'll make a few calls and see if I pick up any rumors."

"I would appreciate that," Maijstral said.

"I *told* you I could prove useful."

"So you did." Maijstral opened the flier and stepped out. "I thank you in advance for any information you may discover."

"I say we still chuck her in," Drexler growled. "She called me a goon."

Conchita stuck out her tongue at him, but Maijstral gave no sign that he had heard. He hadn't.

An image was repeating itself in his mind over and over again: Joseph Bob pointing a pistol at him, squeezing the trigger, and firing. The image recurred with minor variations, all of which involved the pistol's muzzle getting larger and larger.

Cold sweat trickled down Maijstral's neck.

He was going to have to think of something fast.

SEVEN

❊ ❊ ❊

There were a lot of colorful stories about Prince Hunac, and for the most part he did a good job of living up to them. He was, for starters, the direct descendant of the Kings of Palenque, whose descent and lineage had been carefully hidden away during the Spanish and Ladino occupation, but which were nevertheless fully documented by records immaculately kept in their original Mayan script. When the Khosali had conquered the Ladinos, and for that matter everyone else, and when subsequently the black-furred conquerors had proved to be such thoroughgoing legitimists as to restore to at least some of their former glory various Habsburgs and Bourbons and Wittelsbachs and all the other smug, dreary royalty from which humanity had after bloody centuries finally unsaddled itself, the lords of Palenque had emerged from seclusion to present their credentials. The City of Seven Bright Rings had been pleased to recognize their legitimacy and made them Dukes of Palenque and later Princes of Quintana Roo.

During the Great Rebellion, Prince Hunac's family had

sensibly taken both sides, some fighting with the Emperor, others with the rebellious humans. After the Rebellion's success, Prince Hunac's grandmother, a rebel leader, had been appointed heir, and the family thus retained its land and wealth after the establishment of the Human Constellation.

Though Maijstral had never met Prince Hunac, he'd naturally heard of him. Leaving behind a fine record as a dashing eccentric and sportsman, Hunac had graduated ten years ahead of Maijstral at the Nnoivarl Academy. (Just because Hunac's ancestor had fought for the Rebellion was no reason for the family to turn up its noses at the social advantages of a thoroughgoing Imperialist education.) Hunac had become something of a legend at the school because of his adoption of the stylish dress of the Khosali Al-Ashi Dynasty, which involved elaborate feathered cloaks and headdresses similar to what Hunac's royal ancestors might have worn on formal occasions. He had kept quetzal birds in his rooms, and was alleged to conduct elaborate religious rituals in secret, not only to maintain his own status among his subjects but, it was said, to maintain the integrity of the universe.

Since leaving the Academy, Hunac had sponsored hundreds of archaeological expeditions in his native Yucatán. He had donated tens of thousands of items to museums, kept thousands of others in his collection, and contributed greatly to the understanding of the native cultures of the area. He had also made a name for himself as an oceanographer, in which role he charted any number of obscure ocean depths, restored fish populations, and, of course, built the fabulous Underwater Palace on, or rather in, the reefs of Cozumel.

But Hunac was most famous as a host. His week-long theme parties rolled on for half the weeks of the year, and to those with anxieties over their status in the *ton,* it was a comforting confirmation of one's social arrival to receive one of Hunac's invitations.

Celebrated and renowned though the Prince was, Maijstral hadn't been prepared for one aspect—the Prince's size. Hunac was *short*. Shorter even than Conchita. Almost as short as a Troxan.

Short. Hunac was very, very short. Maijstral had not been prepared.

Maijstral advanced, clasped hands—two friendly fingers each—and then Maijstral bent a surprising distance to sniff the Prince's ears. Hunac smiled up at him and spoke in Khosali Standard. "The Show Business Party is still under way," he said. "The Glorious Achievers' Party, which was to be yours, won't be on for a few days, but I imagine you'll find people to talk to in the meantime. The fellow who plays you on video, for one."

Maijstral looked around at people drifting through the reception area. "Anaya's here?" he said.

"That's the *old* video Maijstral. Laurence is the new one. Don't you keep up with your own exploits?"

"I'm afraid I haven't seen either one."

Hunac cocked an eyebrow. "Really? How modest of you."

It wasn't modesty, Maijstral wanted to explain, but pure lack of interest. After living with Nichole for several years, he'd had all he needed of actors and their concerns. And he knew that though the thefts in the videos themselves were based on his own professional recordings, with his image electronically altered, the fictional dramas surrounding the thefts were so contrived and awful he didn't want to be caught watching them.

But it didn't seem the sort of thing to admit at a show business party. Where there were celebrities, there were reporters, and where there were reporters, there were usually hovering media globes recording conversations and replaying them for Empire-wide audiences.

Maijstral hadn't seen any so far, but that didn't mean they weren't there.

"Please have a drink," Hunac said hospitably, "and meet some people. If you want to go out and tour the reefs, we can equip you with a submarine or diving gear—whichever is to your taste."

Maijstral gazed out at the reefs surrounding him. "Thank you," he said. "I'd like that."

Celebrated though Prince Hunac was, the majesty of his person was somewhat overwhelmed by the aquatic glory of his surroundings. Cozumel's reefs—huge coral castles, honey-combed with tunnels and alive with blazing color—loomed on either side, visible through the reception room's transparent dome. Mayan steles from the Prince's collection stood in a circle around the reception area, looking like an underwater homage to Stonehenge. Ideograms for "ocean world" and "palace of the lord" floated holographically in the air.

Hunac took Maijstral's arm and began strolling toward the bar. "I was wondering if you might give me some advice regarding security matters," he said. "I have so many rare and valuable things, and it's only a matter of time before a real first-rate burglar takes a crack at them."

"Your palace is secure by its very nature," Maijstral said. "It's accessible only through the tunnel from the mainland or by submarine. I would hate to try to steal anything here—getting away would be a challenge."

"It's a complication, admittedly—have some of this Rhenish, it's splendid—but for someone as inventive as yourself, surely it's only a matter of false credentials or flummoxing an airlock. Child's play, I'm sure."

Maijstral sipped his wine. "Hardly that." He gave the matter thought. "A place like this would be a major operation. One would need many assistants, which multiplies the number of misunderstandings or mistakes that could occur. If one went in by submarine, one would have to take immense trouble to keep your underwater sensors from seeing it—I take it you *have* underwater sensors?"

"Oh yes."

"Well, the cost of preparing the submarine would be high, which would necessitate stealing a whole submarineful of artifacts in order to make a profit, and the sheer size of the operation would make it dangerous."

"Profit isn't always the motive for Allowed Burglary, is it?" Hunac said. "Sometimes you steal for the sheer glory of it, or to publicly surmount an obstacle, or because there's simply something you want to possess. Ralph Adverse, for example—he stole the most beautiful objects, but he died bankrupt, because he wanted them for their beauty alone, and not for the wealth they could bring him."

"You won't find many Ralph Adverses in the burglary business these days," Maijstral said.

"You disappoint me, Maijstral."

Maijstral thoughtfully sipped at his drink. "I would say," he said, "that your chief danger comes, as you say, from someone entering under false credentials, stealing something valuable but fairly portable, and then just riding the train to the surface through the tunnel."

"Or," Hunac smiled, "I could invite someone into my home who *is* a burglar, simply because I thought he would make an interesting guest. And he could take something, thinking that my hospitality would extend to such a thing. In this assumption, of course, he would be wrong."

He had shifted to High Khosali, unmatched for both difficulty of parsing and precision of communication, as each word commented on the word before it, thus adding cumulative impact to the entire statement.

A cold current wafted up Maijstral's spine at the whiteness of Hunac's smile.

"Naturally the burglar would be wrong," Maijstral said, responding after a moment's hesitation in the same difficult parsing. He added a commonplace aphorism of the sort that was frequently found in High Khosali, because it saved the trouble of constructing something original.

"Hospitality should at all points be respected," he said.

Hunac's smile whitened. "I have heard something of your problem with Joseph Bob."

Maijstral felt himself stiffening. "It is a misunderstanding," he said.

"I am pleased to hear it. I mention the matter only to make certain that no such misunderstandings ever plague our friendship."

"I am certain they will not."

Hunac shifted back to Khosali Standard. "Very good." He patted Maijstral's arm, then turned to an approaching guest. The guest looked remarkably like Elvis Presley, white suit, jeweled wrestler's belt, and all.

"Maijstral, have you met Major Ruth Song?"

"I have not had the pleasure. Charmed."

Maijstral offered Major Song two fingers in the handclasp—everyone knows Elvis, after all—and received a single formal finger in reply. She stiffened a bit as he sniffed her ears. Perhaps, he thought, she did not wish him to inspect her cosmetic job at such close range. No need to be so nervous, Maijstral thought: the work was very good, and had turned her into a remarkably successful facsimile Elvis.

"I hope to persuade Major Song to perform tonight," Hunac remarked.

"I will look forward with pleasure," Maijstral said.

"Thank you," Song said. "I need to stay in practice, with the Memphis Olympiad coming up."

She replied, oddly, in Human Standard, not Khosali, and Maijstral and Hunac obliged her by switching languages.

"Major Song is ranked very high by the cognoscenti," Hunac said. "She stands a very good chance of winning."

"I hope to attend the Olympiad myself," Maijstral said. "I wish you the very best of luck in the competition."

"Thank you. If you'll excuse me?"

Major Song made her congé, swirled her cape, and left. Hunac frowned. "How odd."

"Sir?" Maijstral said.

"She obviously intended to order a drink. But now she's left without one."

Maijstral flicked his ears. "Perhaps she forgot. Or remembered an errand."

"Perhaps."

"I see the riding lights of a new submarine arriving at the port—red, white, green, I'm afraid I don't know it offhand. Still, whoever's inside, I should offer my greetings—Maijstral, I hope you will have a pleasant stay."

Hunac made his way toward the airlock. Maijstral resisted the impulse to gulp his drink—the reminder of his trouble with Joseph Bob had not been pleasant—and then drifted through the reception area, looking for someone he knew. A lot of the faces looked familiar, and he knew he'd seen them on video, but he couldn't remember precisely where, and he couldn't remember their names.

There was one young man, unfamiliar to Maijstral and dressed rather dramatically in black, who was looking at him as if he were undecided whether to approach and introduce himself. Maijstral assumed he was some sort of burglary fan, and, as he didn't feel like talking to fans at the moment, he turned away and wandered on, and then recognized someone and approached to sniff her ears.

"Hello, Alice. Congratulations on obtaining your freedom."

Each gave the other two fingers: they were professional acquaintances, but not intimates.

Alice Manderley was a woman of middle years, dark-haired and slender. She was also one of the best burglars in the galaxy, a consistent high performer who always outpointed Maijstral in the ratings. She had been rated third, and was a contender to succeed Geoff Fu George as first in the ratings, until she encountered ill luck while attempting to steal the famous Zenith Blue.

"I hope prison was not too bad," Maijstral said.

"It was *prison,*" Alice said. "Of *course* it was bad. Even the *nicest conceivable* prison is bad." Her brow furrowed and her voice grew harsh. "And to think I was put there by an *amateur.* She was on her way to school, saw the shimmer of my darksuit, and hit me with a briefcase full of study materials. Knocked me unconscious. I can't *believe* my luck." She scowled. "They gave her the Qwarism Order of Public Service (Second Class). *Second class!* What kind of insult was *that,* I ask you!"

Alice seemed likely to continue in this vein for some time, and Maijstral thought it a good idea to change the subject. "It is a surprise to see you here among the actors," he said, "though of course a delightful one."

"I'm with Kenny. There's a producer here he wants to talk to."

"Oh. Of course."

Kenny Chang was Alice's husband, a notably unsuccessful actor whose personal charm seemed unable to translate properly to video or the stage.

Maijstral was nearly as disinclined to talk about Kenny's career as he was to chat about the features of Alice's prison.

"Are you going to get your ticket renewed?" he asked.

Alice sighed. "I already have. I must admit that burglary has lost much of its appeal, but while I was in stir Kenny took a flier on Forthright bonds, and now I need to get us out of debt."

Maijstral had been offered the same bonds less than a

year ago, and had walked away with a loathly shudder. The Forthright Company had been such an obvious swindle (the company's chairman, Xovalkh, was ranked near the top of the Imperial Sporting Commission's ratings for confidence men) that the only investors likely to actually turn over their funds were either the brain-damaged or those who purchased bonds solely for their entertainment value—Xovalkh was quite a performer, for those who appreciated that sort of thing.

Maijstral suspected that Kenny did not, however, belong to this latter category of investor.

"Well," he said, "if you have any plans for the near future, I could offer you logistical support. I'm on vacation, and I don't want my crew to get rusty."

Alice looked at him with a peculiar expression. "That's kind of you, Maijstral," she said.

"Drexler in particular has been complaining I don't give him enough to do."

"I have my people already picked out. But thank you."

"Ah well. If I can give help of that sort, let me know."

"Thanks." She looked over Maijstral's shoulder. "There's a young man who keeps staring at us."

"Dressed in black? I noticed him earlier."

"He looks familiar, but I can't place him."

"I hope he is not a connoisseur of burglary statistics."

Alice made a face. "I will make a point of avoiding him."

Maijstral glanced to his right, and was surprised to see Aunt Batty making her way toward him. He sniffed her lace-covered ears and touched his tongue to his lips in a subdued Khosali smile.

"That was your submarine that just arrived?"

"Yes, indeed."

"Is her grace with you?"

"No, I'm afraid she's still in negotiation with the Bubber. It's just me and your father."

"Your *father* is here?" Alice asked. "Didn't I hear he'd died?"

"Yes, on both counts," Maijstral said. "We're having a sort of a family conference. Alice Manderley, may I present—" He looked at Aunt Batty and blinked. "I'm afraid I only know you as Bathsheba."

Batty took Alice's hand and sniffed her ears. "I'm the Honorable Bathsheba sar Altunin," she said, indicating her adoptive family, "but you can call me Batty."

"How do you do?"

"I am sorry to have saddled you with my father," Maijstral said. "But I'm afraid my life has been more disorganized than usual—"

"No need to apologize. Gustav and I have been having a perfectly fine time, just chatting away."

Maijstral's ears pricked forward in surprise. "Indeed? And what do you chat about?"

"You, mostly."

"Ah. For your work."

Batty lapped daintily at her drink. "Yes. I think the third volume is shaping up in a most interesting fashion."

When all this was over, Maijstral thought, he *would* steal those manuscripts.

"I'm not certain I would trust this particular source overmuch," Maijstral said, "given the state of his memory. He keeps forgetting he's dead, for one thing."

Aunt Batty's tongue lolled in a smile. "I *have* noticed that, dear, yes. But I do try in my best historian's fashion to confirm everything with another source."

"Very good."

"For example, was your stuffed bear's name really Peter Pajamas?"

Maijstral blinked. "Do you know, I believe it was. This is the first time I've thought of that in—well, decades, I suppose."

Alice had been watching this dialogue with little indication of interest, but smiled at this last. "I perceive my own stuffed bear approaching," she said. "Batty, may I present my husband, Kenny."

"Hi," Kenny said.

He was a handsome man with long, fashionably careless hair. He had, to a discerning eye, rather overdone the fashionable carelessness, with his falling bands partially undone, his collar turned up, his day's growth of beard, *and* his hands in his pockets, but perhaps this was a matter of taste.

Maijstral, considering for a moment Kenny as stuffed bear, concluded that Peter Pajamas had a decided advantage in brains.

"I talked to Winky," Kenny informed Alice, "and he said I'd fit the part hand in glove, but it's not up to him, it's up to the people with the money, so who knows? He says he'll call."

"Perhaps he will," Alice said.

Probably, Maijstral thought, he wouldn't, even though Kenny seemed to be on nickname terms with him five minutes after acquaintance.

He really didn't know anyone who'd call Kenny voluntarily.

"There's such a lot of deal-making going on here," Kenny said. "I've really got to stay on the jump. Have you met that Elvis? Major Song?"

Alice's ears flattened. "Yes," she said shortly.

"Loathsome little weasel, but there's money there. Maybe if I just sing the praises of the Security and Sedition Act, and pretend to hate the rats long enough—"

Alice put a hand on his arm. "Stay away from her, dear. She's not an association that would do you any good. Not in the long run."

Kenny considered this, scratching his day's beard. "Well,

if you say so. Plenty of other mammals in this terrarium." He grinned. "Hey, that was pretty good, wasn't it? 'Cause we're in a kind of a reverse fishbowl here, right? And it's the fish that are looking in. Get it?"

"Very good, Ken," Alice said.

"Well, I'm off to corner myself a—" He started to leave, then seemed to notice Maijstral for the first time. "Say, Drake," he said, "you know Nichole's going to be here?"

"So I understand," Maijstral said.

"You and she are still friends, right? I mean, no hard feelings or anything."

"No."

"Not after she took up with you on that what's-its-name planet, Peleng, and then dumped you for that fellow she's living with now."

"It didn't happen," Maijstral said.

"Hm?" Kenny looked surprised. "No, really. She's living with him. It was in the news and everything. He's her set designer or something."

"I mean," Maijstral said patiently, "that Nichole and I were not involved on Peleng, and, insofar as we weren't involved, she didn't jettison me when she took up with Lieutenant Navarre."

"Oh." Kenny took a moment to process this—the thought that something reported in the media might be a falsehood was obviously a difficult one for him—and then he brightened. "Well, good. You're still friends, then. You wouldn't mind introducing me to her, would you? I'd love a chance to work with Nichole if I could. Associating with the Diadem never hurts a fellow's career."

Poor Nichole, Maijstral thought. Still, celebrity was something she had chosen, along with all the little annoyances that went with it. Annoyances with names like Kenny or Winky or Vang-Thokk.

"Should the opportunity present itself," Maijstral said, "I will make the introduction, yes."

Kenny looked over Maijstral's shoulder and frowned. "There's a fellow in black keeps staring at me. He probably wants an autograph or something, the vermin. I'll just roll away, then, and keep out of his way."

"Bye," Maijstral said.

When he'd been living with Nicole, he'd had *many* conversations just like this one.

"I believe I'll accompany Kenny," Alice said, and made her congé.

Batty and Maijstral looked at one another.

"What a . . . *forceful* young man," Batty said.

"It could be worse," Maijstral said. "He could drink."

"Your father," said Batty, "has been put in my room."

"That's exceedingly good of you," Maijstral said. "We can move him to my suite later, and I can engage someone to look after him."

"As you like, dear, but that really won't be necessary. I'm growing accustomed to him, and as it was our family that brought him here in the first place, I have no objections to looking after him until you get over your trouble with Joseph Bob."

At the expense, Maijstral considered, of having Batty dig farther into his life history. Still and all, his father didn't really know anything likely to prove too embarrassing—since he'd reached the age of reason, Maijstral had kept his family strictly away from anything important—and so all the little gems Batty was likely to discover would be of the Peter Pajamas variety, domestic and perhaps even endearing.

Besides, sharing digs with a dead man, even a father, was hardly to his taste.

"If you truly don't mind," Maijstral said.

"That young man is still staring at us," Batty observed.

A silver sphere descended from somewhere near the ceiling and swooped closer to Maijstral. Following it, on foot, came a young woman with an unusually sculptured hair arrangement and a peculiar bell-shaped skirt.

"Mr. Maijstral?" she said, in Human Standard. "I'm Mangula Arish from the Talon News Service."

The appearance of such a person was inevitable, of course. Maijstral's lazy-lidded eyes half closed as they regarded the journalist.

"How do you do?" Replying in the same language.

A second media globe joined the first, recording the subject from another angle. "Has your journey to Earth been productive?" Mangula asked.

"No," Maijstral said, "but then I had not intended to produce anything while I was here."

"I meant," patiently, "will we see the disappearance of any of Earth's finer artworks or gemstones while you are on-planet?"

Maijstral sighed and once again told the truth, perfectly aware that no one would ever believe him. "I am here on vacation, and to attend the wedding of some acquaintances. If anything disappears, it won't be my fault."

"Is this restraint motivated by any regard for Earth's great history and its priceless collection of treasures?"

Maijstral's eyes narrowed to slits. "It is motivated by the fact I am on vacation."

"Do you intend to offer an apology to the people of Earth while you are here?"

Maijstral's eyes opened in surprise. "Apologize?" he said. "What have I to apologize for?"

"It was on Earth that your grandfather, the Imperial official better known as Robert the Butcher, committed the great majority of his crimes against his own people."

Maijstral's ears cocked forward as he feigned puzzlement. "And therefore?"

"And therefore," the journalist went on, "you, as his descendent, might be expected to apologize for his behavior."

"I was not even alive at the time, miss," Maijstral said, "and had nothing whatever to do with my grandfather's decisions, the actions that resulted from them, or any of the consequent suffering. But if anyone can receive comfort by an apology from someone who had nothing to do with the acts being apologized for, then I will happily offer mine, for whatever good they will do."

He was tempted to apologize as well for the acts of other bad eggs such as Jesse James and Mad Julius, considering that he had about equally to do with those, but some lingering sense of diplomacy kept his mouth shut.

As for Mangula, it took her a moment or two to disentangle the grammatical complexities of Maijstral's last statement. She blinked. "So you *do* apologize?" she asked.

"I thought I already had."

Mangula blinked again. The whole apology question had been one she'd raised herself on the assumption that, however Maijstral answered, she'd be able to turn it into something provocative, but it hadn't turned out quite the way she'd wished, and so she plunged ahead, hoping to be able to provoke a bit of sensation out of the jumble.

"Do you disavow the Cause for which your grandfather fought?"

Maijstral thoughtfully fingered the semilife patch along his jawline.

"Miss Arish, I believe history has disavowed my grandfather's Cause more than I ever could. I wish everyone well, and I desire peace for all, regardless of their politics, and really, what more can I say?"

It would require a fair degree of context removal—"editing," in the journalistic sense—to make anything remotely sensational out of this, and Mangula decided to end the interview and let her news director decide what to do with the results.

As a consequence, she completely forgot to inquire as to the significance of Maijstral's semilife patch, which by now had become rather prominent in view of the swelling its rooted tendrils were sopping up—and that inquiry would have given her a scoop indeed.

"Thank you, Mr. Maijstral," she said, and made her exit, silver globes swooping after her.

"Does that sort of thing happen *all the time?*" Batty asked.

"Oh yes," Maijstral said. "More now than ever."

"What a strange life you must lead, I'm sure."

"One must be sure to always make one's answers to the media as complex and laden of context as possible. They can never make a simple, sensational story out of it that way. Not without a good deal of effort, anyway."

Batty's eyes shifted over Maijstral's shoulder again. "That young man in black is approaching. And he's got a friend with him."

Maijstral sighed—the last two people who spoke to him had been rather a trial, and there was no guarantee that this one would be any different. Still, he turned to face the newcomers with as civil a face as possible.

The young man in black had long hair styled similarly to Maijstral's, and Maijstral observed he wore a large diamond on one finger—the same finger as Maijstral's own diamond, and a very similar diamond at that. The man's friend wore a bottle green coat and gold jewelry.

"Maijstral," the man in black said, offering Maijstral three fingers in the handclasp to Maijstral's one, "I'm Laurence."

Maijstral sniffed the actor's ears. "Pleased to meet you," he said. "I'm told you do me rather well."

The actor stepped back with a look of surprise. "It sounds as if you haven't seen me."

Maijstral probably should have assured the young man

that he'd seen him scads of times, and thought him very good, not that his opinion really counted, but fortunately it was shared by all the very best critics, and Laurence must surely be pleased—after which Laurence would have gone off a happy man. But events had thrown off Maijstral's social timing, and he'd already had to deal with one actor today and his patience was probably shorter than usual, and so he did the worst thing possible, which was (once again) to tell the truth.

"I'm sorry to say I haven't," he said. "My life is rather pressing and I have little time for video. But I'm told that many people prefer you to that, ah, other fellow."

"Anaya."

"Quite so. My apologies, anyway, for not recognizing you." Laurence frowned, and his ears were pinned back, but he turned to his friend and made the introduction.

"This is Deco, my companion."

"Pleased to meet you," Maijstral said. He had discerned by this point that he'd made a gaffe, and in amends gave two fingers to Deco's one, then mentally sighed at how it did not seem possible to achieve social attunement this afternoon no matter how hard he tried.

Maijstral introduced Aunt Batty, and then the four stared at each other for a long, uncomfortable moment.

"It is a most-attractive dwelling, is it not?" Batty finally said. "Most underwater environments give one such a sense of confinement, but Prince Hunac has made everything here so spacious that one's sense of claustrophobia is quite underwhelmed."

"True," Deco said.

"Very," said Laurence.

Silence reigned once more. Aunt Batty concluded that she'd done her best.

Laurence, it should be observed, did not actually play Maijstral on video. He played a character superficially similar to Maijstral, or at least similar to who Maijstral might have been if he were the hero of a video series—brave, stalwart, chivalrous, handy with his fists, and staggeringly successful with women. The company that made the series had (after the Imperial Sporting Commission) first call on the videos Maijstral made while stealing, and mixed Maijstral's videos with their own, altering Maijstral's image to that of Laurence. It was *understood* that Laurence was playing Maijstral, even if the character had a different name, and it was suggested that all the video adventures, preposterous though they were, were in some sense true, that they all offered details of Maijstral's life that had not been made public. And since Maijstral could never commit as many burglaries as a character in a weekly series, the producers bought videos from other burglars who were unlucky enough not to have series characters designed after them, and likewise altered the image to that of Laurence—and in the end Maijstral got the credit for a lot of spectacular capers that he had never actually performed.

"I see you wear a diamond ring," Maijstral observed.

"Yes." Laurence brightened. "It's just like yours. I use it as a focus, when I'm acting—I look at the ring, and I say to myself, *I'm Drake Maijstral, I'm the greatest burglar ever.* And then I do my scene."

"But you wear the ring when you're not acting," Maijstral said. "Doesn't that cause confusion? When you look down at your plate at luncheon, for example, and see the ring, don't you say to yourself, *I'm a burglar,* and then have to fight away a crisis of identity along with an impulse to slip the silverware up your sleeve?"

"But Laurence *is* a terrific burglar," Deco said. "He's had lots of practice."

Maijstral looked at Laurence in surprise. "Do you actually steal?" he said.

Laurence flushed. "Well, no. My contract doesn't permit—it wouldn't do for the star of a series to end up in prison. But I've done everything *but* steal."

"He's got a very good darksuit," Deco said. "I made it myself—I've studied how all the tech is done. Sometimes he flies out at night, just *being a burglar,* you know."

"It's really helped my interpretation of the role," Laurence said.

Maijstral looked from one to the other and decided that, yes, he was intended to be impressed by this. He was trying to decide how to respond when one of Hunac's servants approached.

"Sir, a message for you. Miss Nichole. There is a privacy booth in the corner."

Maijstral manufactured an apologetic look. "My apologies, gentlemen," he said, and moved away.

"Umm," Laurence called after him. "You know—I really wanted to talk to you about Nichole. . . ."

Maijstral escaped to the privacy booth and activated the field that sealed him off from any eavesdroppers and lip-readers. At a command Nichole's face appeared before him.

She was a tall blond woman located ambiguously on the cusp between mid and late thirties, and she was one of the Three Hundred who were so famous they bore only a forename. She was, technically speaking, an actress, but her real profession was so far above a mere *actress,* above *celebrity,* even above *star,* that only a place in some fairly all-embracing pantheon could probably do justice to her standing.

When she spoke, entire planets hushed to hear her words. People she had never heard of, and never *would* hear of, committed suicide at the thought they were unworthy to share the universe with her. Obscure alien races knelt at her image and spit up, with appropriate ritual obeisance, offerings of the very best regurgitated fish-liver wine.

She was, so to speak, colossal. Even for a member of the Diadem she was big.

Maijstral had once turned down a chance to join the Human Diadem and live on the same plateau as Nichole. The refusal had made him, briefly, more famous than if he had accepted, but the industry that was Nichole rolled on without him, generating more fame, more glory, more worship, while the comparatively small enterprise that was Maijstral, denied the constant barrage of publicity and glory granted members of the Diadem, was compelled to sneak up on success and win it by stratagem rather than bag it in one grand rush.

But when Nichole's image appeared before Maijstral, it was not that of a distant goddess, but rather that of an old friend. It did Maijstral's heart good to see her. In this crisis, it was good to know who one could trust, and Nichole was a true and tested comrade in adversity.

"Hello, Nichole," he said.

Nichole's superb eyes glittered with concern. "Drake," she said, "what's this I hear about a duel between you and the Prince of Tejas?"

"I see that I can spare you a certain degree of exposition," Maijstral said. "How did you hear about it?"

"Diadem security, of course," Nichole said. "Background checks on everyone at the party."

"Of course," Maijstral agreed.

Members of the Diadem floated through existence in their own perfect world, with no stray locks out of place, no buttons unfastened, and certainly no rude interlopers trying to crash the party. Diadem security, smooth, efficient, and all-embracing, was the envy of all people of prominence, including the Constellation's President. His own security problems were never dealt with in such a seamless way.

Of course, he didn't pay his own guards nearly as much. And for that matter he wasn't nearly as famous as Nichole, something he found just as galling as the difference in service.

"What in heaven's name provoked this?" Nichole asked.

Maijstral told her. Her look softened.

"Oh, Drake," she sighed, "and I thought, when we met, that I was going to unburden my problems on *you*."

"This may be your last chance," Maijstral muttered darkly.

"Who's acting for you?" Nichole asked.

Maijstral told her. Nichole frowned. "Isn't she awfully young?"

"She's quite mature for her years."

"Still, it's your *life* that's at stake."

Maijstral winced. He did not need reminding.

"You have no idea who provoked this?" Nichole went on.

"No. I've been racking my brains, but I can't think of anyone who would really want to—"

"I will have Diadem security begin an in-depth survey of everyone you know."

Gratification sprang warmly to life in Maijstral's heart. "Thank you." A cold little icicle of suspicion touched his thoughts. "Your people keep track of burglars, yes?"

"More or less automatically, yes."

"You might have them concentrate on Alice Manderley. Check the status of her bank accounts."

Nichole nodded. "Right away. And I'll advance my schedule and arrive tomorrow morning, so that we can confer," Nichole said. "I'd come sooner, but there's a reception this evening I can't escape—the King of Libya." A frown crossed her face. "I *think* it's Libya. I haven't had my briefing yet."

"I'm sure he will be pleasant, whatever he's the king of," Maijstral said. "Kings have every reason to be pleased with their lot. And in the meantime, I will be very pleased to see you tomorrow."

Doubt entered Nichole's voice. "Drake?" she said. "What if they do it again?"

Maijstral stared, his blood running chill.

He would have thought of this himself if he'd not been so completely distracted.

"Why would they?" he asked in desperation.

Nichole's ears flickered. "Why did they do it *once?*"

"I will arrange for security."

"That would be advisable." She smiled. "Please give my best to Roman, by the way."

Maijstral fled to his chambers as soon as the conversation ended, striding past Laurence and his companion, who seemed to want to converse again.

When Maijstral arrived, the room was empty save for the reef fish under the room's bubble aquarium dome. Maijstral went to the service place and touched the ideogram for "service."

"Roman?"

"At once, sir."

When Roman arrived, Maijstral was shocked at the transformation. Roman was bald, grey-skinned, red-eyed, and he scratched continually, his hands moving, void of volition, from one bodily torment to the next. Maijstral had never seen Roman this bad.

"It has occurred to me," Maijstral said, "that whoever planted the pistol on us might well try again."

Roman growled, a long, ominous sound. Maijstral smoothed down the hairs that had just risen on his neck.

"I want maximum security on our rooms," Maijstral said. "Every alarm and detector we can acquire. Every nasty little surprise that we wouldn't want to encounter ourselves in the course of our business. Plant them *all.*"

A grim light of satisfaction entered Roman's agate eyes. "Very good, sir," he said.

Another cold suspicion lodged in Maijstral's breast. "You might check all the alarms personally," he added. "I'd rather you arranged things, rather than Drexler."

Roman stiffened. Another low growl rolled from his throat. "Am I to understand that we are no longer trusting Mr. Drexler, sir?"

"We are trusting no one, Roman. Drexler was working for Fu George on Silverside Station, remember, against our interests. It's possible, if unlikely, that he may have conceived an elaborate plan of revenge. Or someone may have conceived it for him."

"Vanessa Runciter, sir?"

Maijstral's brow darkened. Now *there* was someone for Nichole's people to look into. "I wouldn't put it past her," he said. "So when you have no other duties, you might simply make it your business to keep tabs on Drexler."

"Very good, sir."

"One other thing," Maijstral said. "Nichole sends her love."

Roman's ears flattened in pleasure. He and Nichole had always had a most sympathetic relationship.

"I hope we are still trusting Miss Nichole," he ventured.

"Of course we are."

Roman's tongue lolled in a smile. "Very *good,* sir."

Maijstral had just finished dressing for dinner when Roberta called. His insides quailed as he saw the grim expression in her violet eyes.

"What news?" he said, and hoped his voice didn't quaver.

"Joseph Bob continues to insist on the fight, and continues to insist that it be soon. There's no getting around it, and he's got the right. Unless you'd rather he called in the cops, of course."

Maijstral sat down and suppressed an instinct to swab away the sweat that had just appeared on his brow.

"How soon?" he asked.

"The day after tomorrow. The meeting is on an island in the Dry Tortugas. The Prince wanted pistols, then swords, and I said no to both."

"Very good."

"So we've settled on a weapon with which neither of you have any experience. It's called a *dire staff*."

Maijstral quailed at the very name. He tugged at his throat lace. "I don't believe I'm familiar with that weapon. . . ." he managed.

Roberta's hands waved near the phone's service panel, and next to her image appeared the staff, a long steel pole with a complicated knot of interwoven steel blades on one end and a blunt protrusion on the other.

"It was used in ritual combat by the Hennese," Roberta said. "It has blades at one end and a low-level stunner at the other. The combatants are placed within reach of one another right at the start, so that anyone attempting to use the stunner exposes himself to a possible attack from the bladed end. And the stunner is, as I said, low-level, so it will only slow the target down, not actually drop them."

"So the point of combat with this weapon is to slow the enemy with the stunner, then butcher him with the other end once he can't defend himself."

"Apparently."

"How charming." Maijstral was appalled.

Roberta's eyes flashed. "Well, what could I *do*, Drake? We had to settle on *some* weapon or other. They'll all kill you very messily one way or another, but at least Joseph Bob hasn't ever had time to practice with one of these, so you'll have an even chance."

Maijstral took a deep breath. All was not lost. He could still try to fix this somehow, just as he fixed his last fight when he was at the Nnoivarl Academy.

"I'm sorry if I sounded upset," Maijstral said. "I *am* upset, of course, but not by you."

Her look softened. "I will have a staff sent to you tomorrow so that you can get the feel of the thing. We're borrowing some from a collector on Mars. He made it a condition that he witness the fight—he's always wanted to see the things used." She frowned. "The rules call for an objective witness anyway, so that seems all right."

Maijstral's mind raced. So, he thought, Joseph Bob would be practicing with his own dire staff as soon as it came down from Mars. Which meant that Maijstral could get to it and sabotage it somehow.

"Who did you say used these things?" he asked. "I didn't catch the name."

"The Hennese."

"And what are they? A religious sect of some sort?"

"No. A minor race. The Empire conquered them a few millennia ago, but they've subsequently become extinct."

Cold foreboding squatted heavily on Maijstral's breast. "And why did they all die off?" he asked.

"Well." Roberta reddened. "They kept fighting each other with dire staffs, for one thing."

"I thought as much. Thank you."

Cowards die many times before their deaths, as Shaxpur remarks in his newly translated play, *Tsar Iulius, "the valiant never taste of death but once."* After the conversation ended, Maijstral sat in silence for a long, endless moment, dying many times.

He could fix the stunner, he thought, but how could he fix a nest of glittering, sharp blades on the end of a *stick*?

This was going to take a lot of thought.

He rose and went to the service plate. "Roman," he said, "come and unlace me. I won't be going to dinner after all."

He seemed to have lost his appetite.

EIGHT

✿ ✿ ✿

The glories of Palancar towered toward the distant sun, layer after layer of coral and sponge, anemone and fans and gorgonia, every form and color in the world piled atop one another and reaching toward the sky. Among all this richness swarmed the fish, as brightly colored as the corals: grouper and barracuda, squirrelfish and angels, trunkfish and parrot fish and triggerfish.

Nothing was visible that was not alive.

Turn 180 degrees and there was only one ocean, a clear and perfect Cherenkov blue, reaching straight down a thousand meters and going on all the way to the mainland. The color was so blue that, looking at it, you could feel *blueness* prickling all the way along your skin.

Nothing alive was visible in that blue, nothing at all.

Nichole and Maijstral floated along the wall, hovering in the interface between the lonely blue and the bright, bustling swarm that was the coral wall. They communicated with one another along a cyphered link.

It was the only way, given the circumstances, they could achieve any degree of privacy.

"I wonder if we will find a splendid toadfish," Nichole said. "It's supposed to be the best. Quite rare."

"You heard that in your briefing, yes?"

"Yes. Of course."

Members of the Human Diadem were briefed before every appearance in order to give them something to view and talk about. They learned about the best people, the best art, the best food, the best architecture, the best sights, and—apparently—the best toadfish.

At least they were the best in the opinion of the Diadem's research staff, who were, of course, the best researchers money could buy.

Maijstral had lived without these briefings for several years now, and found himself perfectly content to exist without his every opinion being scripted ahead of time.

"I am surprised that the Diadem's researchers didn't offer to find a toadfish and tag it so that you could locate it and appreciate it properly," Maijstral said.

"They did. But I thought we'd prefer privacy."

"Thank you."

The two floated along a narrow passageway between two giant coral ramparts. Bright swaying tendrils trailed above them in the strong current like old friends waving good-bye.

"I have narrowed somewhat your range of suspects," Nichole said. "Alice Manderley arrived on Earth only yesterday on a liner from Qwarism, where she was released from prison last month."

"I see."

"Her bank account *has* registered a substantial increase which our researchers weren't able to account for—five hundred novae—but she may have signed some endorsement deal, or been paid for a commission that hasn't become public. The researchers will continue their efforts."

"They may as well not, since Alice is no longer a suspect."

"Drake," severely, "that's what they're *for.*"

"Well then. If you like."

Nichole continued. "Vanessa Runciter is in the Empire with her new consort, Lord Pasco."

"The foundation garment fellow?"

"Yes."

"I wouldn't have thought Vanessa would *need* that as yet."

"She has expensive tastes. I doubt it's the underwear she needs."

"True."

"Being in the Empire, of course, doesn't rule out the possibility of Vanessa's hiring it done, but it puts her so far out of communication with any hireling that it would make it impossible to coordinate anything."

"True."

"And your mother is also in the Empire, a guest at Lord Moth's hunting lodge."

Maijstral's relations with his mother were such that he had no objection to her inclusion among the list of suspects.

His mother held many grudges. That she would hold a lethal grudge against her only son was not absolutely out of the question.

A flash of deep paranoia lit Maijstral's brain. "She's nowhere near Vanessa, is she?"

"No. Pasco and Vanessa were clean on the other side of the Empire from Mothholm, on Krpntsz."

"Krpntsz? I heard the fishing is good."

"According to our researchers," airily, "the place is passé."

The water brightened as they passed from the shadowed valley to a plateau of white coral sand. Nichole looked about, frowned, and commanded her repellers to move toward the nearest coral castle.

A grouper, long as Maijstral's arm, floated nearby and wondered whether or not to ask for a handout.

"Have you considered Joseph Bob's brother?" Nichole asked.

"The Bubber?" Maijstral blinked. "No, I haven't."

"I presume he is his brother's heir, since Joseph Bob has only recently married and hasn't yet fathered a child. If you kill the Prince, the Bubber gets the title and everything else. He'd be one of the richest people on Earth."

"And he might be under the impression that I'm quite the dashing blade," Maijstral said. "Joseph Bob spent the evening talking about that stupid encounter I had in school—he made me sound perfectly heroic. Will might think I could kill his brother with a snap of my fingers."

"Think about it, Drake. He's the only person I can think of who would actually benefit from this situation."

Maijstral did just that, coldly considering the Bubber in the role of blackhearted conspirator. He didn't quite think that the Will he'd met was entirely up to the role, but then . . . a true blackhearted conspirator would seem perfectly innocent, wouldn't he?

Perhaps it had been the Bubber who'd suggested the dire staff, the ghastly weapon that would give Maijstral a good crack at killing Joseph Bob. And probably the Bubber could have opened the display case and removed the revolver simply by giving the proper codes. The only question was whether he had the ability to silently place the revolver in the ventilation shaft, and Maijstral rather suspected the answer was yes.

And if Will was really behind the whole thing, how could Maijstral prove it?

Tempting though it was to hang the Bubber upside down over the Grand Canyon, he suspected that if Will were really

blackhearted as all that, not only would the Bubber not confess, but he'd probably end up challenging Maijstral to a second duel following the first.

Of course, Maijstral thought, a bit cheered by the idea, he
could always let him *fall*. . . .

Thinking these thoughts, Maijstral followed Nichole
into a downward-slanting cave. A wall of bright silver fish
flashed on and off ahead, turning to and fro in unison, as if
they were a form of living heliograph sending a message.

"I also wonder about the Duchess of Benn, Drake," Nichole said. "You stole the Shard from her, after all. I wonder if
there's any ill feeling."

Thoughts of the Bubber fled Maijstral's mind as paranoia
closed in once again. Roberta—a force for evil! The *Black
Widow*—luring a man into her embrace, then *destroying him!*

The *dire staff!* his brain yelped. It was all part of her plot!

But after a brief, giddy moment in which the ocean did
backflips, rationality managed a cautious, delicate return.

"I think not," he said. "The circumstances of the theft of
the Shard were not such as to create a grudge. And besides, her
grace has favored me with an offer of marriage."

Nichole's perfect blue eyes, the exact shade of the great
deep, widened in surprise.

"Congratulations," she said softly.

"Thank you."

"It's a brilliant match."

"I wish I knew whether my brilliance was sufficient to
the occasion."

Her brows lifted in surprise. "You told her no?"

"I haven't given her an answer at all." When Nichole
continued looking at him, he added, "The matter of the duel
came up immediately afterward."

"I see." She looked away. "Perhaps someone in her family is opposed to the match."

Maijstral could hardly see Aunt Batty climbing about in ventilators, but then there was also Paavo Kuusinen, a fellow who seemed to have hidden resources.

"Paavo Kuusinen is here," he said. "You remember him from Peleng. He's the Duchess's attorney. And spy."

"He helped us on Peleng."

"He may have changed his mind."

"And the Duchess has a large family. There might be some thwarted suitor hanging about." She looked thoughtful. "I'll have the researchers get to work on them."

"Any other suspects?"

"The researchers have only had a few hours, Drake."

"*I* may have only a few hours."

"I will tell them to make haste."

The profound blue of the great deep beckoned ahead, surrounded by rust-colored coral fronds. Nichole and Maijstral floated from the dark cavern out onto the coral wall, into the light, the blaze of color.

"Perhaps," Nichole decided, "I shall tell them now. Shall we return to the palace?"

"As you like."

They floated back along the wall, each wrapped in thought. The ever-hopeful grouper followed, its own thoughts perfectly visible on its face. The magnificence of the reef, the clarity of the water, the warmth of the sun, made even Maijstral's predicament seem remote.

Strangely, Maijstral found himself wanting to get wet. Both he and Nichole were cloaked in their own private force fields, which kept air in while screening out both water and pressure. Air was provided through a little bottle and freshened through a rebreathing unit that clipped to the belt. Propulsion was provided by the same repeller units that powered personal fliers and Maijstral's darksuit.

This arrangement was convenient, and prevented both

the bends and nitrogen narcosis, but it lacked intimacy. The coral castles and darting fish that surrounded them were inspiring Maijstral to attempt a closer acquaintance.

If he lived, he reminded himself. If he lived.

The lights of the Underwater Palace were in sight when two other divers floated toward them.

"Why, hello!" said Laurence.

"What a coincidence!" said Deco.

Maijstral, certain that no coincidence obtained, nevertheless put on a civil face and introduced the two to Nichole.

"We're just going out to view the reef," Laurence said. "Shall we join you?"

"Alas," Maijstral said, "we were just going in. Don't let us keep you."

The two could not keep their dismay from reflecting on their faces. Maijstral and Nichole smilingly said their adieux and made their way to the airlock.

"I say," Laurence called after. "Were you lucky enough to see a toadfish?"

After entering through the airlock and turning in their diving gear, Maijstral and Nichole strolled to her suite, and the invincible Diadem security closed softly, silently, and inscrutably behind them.

Maijstral felt a knot of tension ease within himself. It felt so wonderfully safe here.

"Wine?" Nichole asked. "Coffee? Rink?"

"Rink."

"Rink for two, Daphne," Nichole said, speaking to a servant so professionally unobtrusive that Maijstral hadn't even realized she was present. Daphne poured drinks, served them, and at Nichole's command vanished into the aether from which Diadem servants came.

The only problem with the discreet, efficient servants

that came with the Diadem, Maijstral reflected, was that they were working for the Diadem, not for oneself. One couldn't have a private little fit of anger, a minor nervous breakdown, or a silent moment of drunken obliteration in the privacy of one's own salon without everything being reported to the media titans who controlled the Diadem, and whose job it was to exploit any of these perfectly understandable human vagaries for the entertainment of billions.

Maijstral and Nichole sipped and sat beside one another on a small sofa. Nichole kicked off her shoes and held out her feet.

"Do you like my feet, Drake?" she said. "I had them done on Cornish."

"They are fine feet, Nichole."

She frowned at them critically. "I loved them at first, but now . . . well, perhaps the nail area could be slightly reduced, don't you think?"

"They're *your* feet. I don't think it proper to express an opinion other than to say that in their present state they seem perfectly desirable feet to me."

She laughed. "You see what trivialities I concern myself with."

"Not entirely trivial, I suspect," Maijstral said. "Have I been selfish, talking only of my problems?"

Nichole sighed. "My problems are rather less urgent than yours."

"Nevertheless," Maijstral said, "you sent me a message when I was on Silverside."

"I was not happy then."

"Are you happy now?"

She bit her lip. "Navarre is going to accept Diadem membership. His designs are reaching a huge audience."

"Please give him my congratulations."

"And I have decided—I think—to leave the Diadem."

How many goddesses, Maijstral wondered, have chosen to abdicate?

"Are you certain?" he asked.

"I think so. It was that last play that did it, I think—I have discovered that I would rather be an actress than a celebrity."

"It has always been my impression that you were nothing less than superb at being both at once."

She smiled, touched his hand. "Thank you, Drake. But if one is a member of the Three Hundred, one is encouraged to take only those parts that enhance one's celebrity, that contribute to one's mystique and glamor. Any touch of the *real* is discouraged. And I find myself increasingly interested in the real." She looked thoughtful. "One is always attracted by what one does not possess, and whatever the many attractions of my current existence, reality isn't numbered among them."

"You were very fine in that play."

"The Diadem didn't like it. Neither did a lot of my fans."

"They will grow to adore it, given time. They just need to grow accustomed to your range."

Nichole sipped at her rink, tilted her head, looked at Maijstral. "You were offered Diadem membership," she said, "and turned it down. I'm afraid I was offended—at the time I interpreted it as a rejection of me . . . and so I rejected you."

"Things end," Maijstral said, "and it doesn't have to be anyone's fault."

"That's generous of you, Drake," Nichole said, "but it remains that the Diadem came between us. That barrier may soon be removed. And the Diadem may soon become a barrier between me and Navarre." She sighed. "The fact is, I'm a few days too late. Because if your unforgivably young and attractive Duchess hadn't beaten me to it, I would have proposed marriage myself."

Maijstral's lazy-lidded eyes opened to their widest possible extent. Only through force of will did he manage to keep his jaw from dropping.

Nichole's divinely blue eyes moistened. "And damn it," she said, "now that girl could get you *killed.*"

Maijstral's social antennae might not have been functioning at their best in the last few days, but at least he knew when to take a woman into his arms and kiss her.

He was, he thought to his amazement, perfectly safe here. Not even Colonel-General Vandergilt would be likely to get through the perfect wall of Diadem security.

Only one thought clouded his mind. "Where," he asked through a haze of kisses, "is Navarre?"

"One of the moons of Jupiter. Designing someone's yacht."

At least this spared Maijstral from the possibility of another challenge.

Safe, he thought. *Safe, safe, safe.*

It made Nichole all the more desirable.

NINE

❋   ❋   ❋

Some hours later Maijstral left Nichole's suite in order to dress for supper. There was to be some manner of spectacle beforehand, in the Shrine Room, with Prince Hunac and his assistants carrying out one of the rites he was permitted to perform in public.

Maijstral stepped into the central reception area and felt a cold hand touch his neck, the uneasy sensation that he was out of Diadem security and anything could happen to him now.

"Sir."

It was Paavo Kuusinen, wearing a green suit of the latest Constellation cut and looking, as usual, perfectly inscrutable.

"Mr. Kuusinen," sniffing his ears, "is her grace here?"

"No. She and the Bubber are still making preparations for the encounter tomorrow. It is a surprisingly complex business."

Maijstral's blood curdled at this reminder of the following dawn. He continued moving across the reception area toward his own apartments, and Kuusinen followed.

"I am charged," Kuusinen said, "along with the other reason for being here, with sending you her loving regards."

"And your other reason?"

"I have brought your dire staff, sir, along with a mock-up weapon should you desire to practice. I would be honored to be your partner in that practice if you should so desire."

Maijstral could feel sweat popping out on his brow at the thought. "I suppose a little practice would not be amiss," he said. At least it might give him some idea how to sabotage Joseph Bob's weapon.

"Perhaps after supper," Kuusinen suggested.

"Perhaps."

"I had the weapons delivered to your rooms."

Where, no doubt, they would stand propped up in the corner like sentinels at the gate of the Beyond, grim reminders of the fate to come.

"Thank you," Maijstral managed. "I wonder, Mr. Kuusinen, if—"

"Maijstral! Oh, Maijstral!" Laurence approached, smiling, his diamond winking. "I was wondering if—"

"I beg your pardon," Maijstral said without breaking stride, "but I have no time at present. Perhaps later—?"

"Ah. Oh." Laurence blinked, left behind in the dust. "Very well."

"Mr. Kuusinen," Maijstral continued, "I wonder if you would apply your splendid mind to the matter of the Bubber."

"Yes?" Kuusinen was all attention.

As they walked down the corridor toward Maijstral's rooms, Maijstral outlined Nichole's notion that the whole business of the duel might be the result of a plot by the Bubber to inherit the Princedom of Tejas.

"A provoking theory, sir," Kuusinen said. "But if it is true, how may it be proved? And proved by tomorrow morning?"

"*Proving* is precisely the matter to which I hope you might turn your mind."

Kuusinen gave it a few seconds' thought. "Amateur thieves often make mistakes, I should imagine," he ventured. "Leaving fingerprints, say. But there would be no surprise should the Bubber's fingerprints appear on the stolen revolver. He may have handled it frequently."

A thought—a wonderful, glorious thought!—occurred to Maijstral. "There are other places to leave fingerprints," he said. "Inside the duct, for example."

"Ah." Kuusinen nodded. "But did the police examine the duct for fingerprints? Or gather any other kind of forensic evidence?"

"No. His Highness declined to sign a complaint against me, and they terminated their investigation. But—" Maijstral found himself growing cheerful. "But I could go into the duct, tonight, with methods of detecting fingerprints, to see if I could find any latent evidence."

Kuusinen gave this further thought as well. "I'm afraid that you're hardly an unbiased witness," he said. "One might do better at asking the Prince if he would be willing to hire a private firm to examine the duct."

"I'm scarcely in a position to do that."

"Perhaps her grace, however, is. In her capacity as your second."

Hope blossomed in Maijstral, and he found himself walking for a moment with buoyant tread, but further thought cast him down again.

"But, acting as my second, she'd have to ask through the Bubber," he pointed out. "And if he's guilty, he won't let it happen."

"Ah." Kuusinen frowned. "Well, perhaps it will work and perhaps it will not. I will communicate with her grace on the matter nonetheless."

"I would be very appreciative."

Maijstral went through the complex procedure necessary to enter his booby-trapped room without tripping every alarm within a hundred leagues, and then he and Kuusinen entered.

"I see the dire staff is here," Kuusinen said. "Would you like me to demonstrate?"

Panic throbbed in Maijstral's heart at the very thought.

"Oh," he said, "there's plenty of time for that."

Kuusinen seemed a bit surprised. "Very well," he said smoothly. "Perhaps I should take my leave and give you a chance to dress for supper."

"I thank you for your efforts. And when you speak to her grace, please give her my love."

"I will."

Did he love the Duchess? he wondered as he saw Kuusinen to the door. Did he love Nichole? The answer to the first question, he suspected, ranged from *quite possibly* to *very likely,* and to the second *yes, probably,* but that provided no solution to the question of whether he wanted to marry either of them.

It was legally possible to marry *both,* of course, but he suspected the women in question would not be open to the suggestion, and in any case the solution was more likely to double, rather than answer, his dilemma.

He glanced over his shoulder at the dire staffs and shuddered.

The staffs, he realized, *did* offer a solution to the question of marriage, but one he would rather not consider.

In a mood to break bones and bang heads, Roman entered Maijstral's room. His naked skin was a shedding, flaking, burning torment, and he felt as if molten metal were coursing along his nerves. His muzzle, where the new age-ring was growing, was on fire.

Annihilation seemed a worthwhile alternative. Lacking that, he would have happily settled for the cheerful oblivion of psychopathic violence.

Unfortunately neither seemed likely. Instead Roman found Maijstral in a contemplative mood, studying the genealogy that Roman had prepared.

"You called, sir?" Roman said.

Normal words for a servant to address to his employer, but there must have been something odd in the inflection, because Maijstral gave a start and looked wildly at Roman for a moment, as if a threatening stranger had just entered and growled out a threat. But Maijstral's heavy-lidded eyes shuttered again, and he looked again at the long scroll.

"I observe you have left room for my descendants," he said.

"Yes," Roman said. Normally he would have said something more polished, along the lines of, *Indeed, I hope to be able to inscribe each happy event, and soon,* appropriate sentiment mixed with a decided hint that it was high time Maijstral got betrothed to his duchess. But in his current crazed condition, complex sentences were rather beyond him, and simple declaratives were more the thing.

Maijstral continued gazing at the scroll.

"I have spent the day with Miss Nichole," Maijstral said.

I trust the sojourn was pleasant would have been something along Roman's normal lines at this point, but the thought of Nichole—he had always been passionately fond of Nichole—sent his thought-impulses veering off into any number of unexpected byways, and he managed no reply at all.

Maijstral, who had raised one eyebrow in anticipation of a reply, waited for a moment and then lowered it. He pursed his lips and gazed at the scroll again.

"She tells me that she is considering leaving the Diadem," he said. "And she has also favored me with a proposal of marriage."

Roman's ears flattened in amazement and his tongue flopped from his muzzle. His thought-impulses scattered, reformed, scattered again. *Nichole!* Always his favorite—the only human to cause him to forget his usual prejudice against actresses and celebrities. But . . . but . . . *duty!* It was Maijstral's *duty* to marry the Duchess.

Nichole!

Duty!

Nichole!

Duty!

The conflicting notions volleyed away in his head for a few seconds, and then he managed to pull himself together and croak out a question.

"Did you give her an answer?"

Which was pretty good, under the circumstances, though his normal line would have been, *Did you favor her with a reply, sir?*

"The matter," Maijstral said, "is still under discussion."

"Hrrrr," said Roman, a sound of frustration much like a growl.

Couldn't his employer make up his mind about *anything?* The Duchess was clearly a perfect, brilliant match, but if Maijstral was *determined* to be feckless and irresponsible, then running off with an actress was the perfect way to do that, and Nichole, to Roman's way of thinking, was the perfect actress.

Pick one or the other! he wanted to roar. *Either one will do!*

He stifled these thoughts, though the effort cost him. Hence, "Hrrrr."

He would have apologized, but Maijstral seemed not to hear. Maijstral rose from his chair and held out his arms.

"The supper costume, please," he said. "The white suit tonight, with the gold braid. If I must spend the evening mirroring Nichole's glory, I may as well wear the most reflective thing I've got."

The Shrine Room featured stone tablets of intricate workmanship that prescribed the rite now being performed by Prince Hunac. There were chants, the drinking of ritual intoxicants, offerings of quetzal feathers, flowers, and fruit, and blood drawn via a silver needle in the shape of a stingray spine—the genuine article would have been used by Hunac's ancestors, but fortunately the concept of hygiene had entered the life of humanity since then.

It was difficult to see Hunac, partly because of his short stature, partly because he was enveloped by a feathery ritual costume. Fortunately, media globes floated overhead at all the best angles, and the results were transmitted to screens set in the back of the room.

The crowd watched respectfully from the sidelines, facing either toward the ceremony itself or the handy video screens. Nichole stood in the very front of the crowd—it was her due as a member of the Three Hundred—and Maijstral stood at her side and paid as much attention to the crowd as to the ceremony itself.

He was beginning to develop a morbid interest in ritual bloodletting.

Alice Manderley hovered in the back of the room, watching neither the monitors nor the ceremony itself. Perhaps, Maijstral thought, the sight of blood was unappetizing to her. He felt a certain sympathy for a kindred soul.

Or perhaps she was looking for her husband Kenny, who was not present. Doubtless he was advancing his career somewhere else in the palace.

Aunt Batty stood opposite Maijstral in the front row and

watched with an expression of polite attention. Maijstral could only guess what a Khosali gentlewoman would make of this sort of ritual. Probably, he concluded, nothing very positive.

Standing next to her in his green suit, Paavo Kuusinen watched everything very carefully and, as was his wont, let no detail escape his eye.

Midway back in the crowd, Maijstral could see Major Ruth Song, who still looked very like Elvis Presley. Next to her was a red-faced man in a uniform that Maijstral didn't recognize. As he glanced over the crowd, Maijstral accidentally locked eyes with the man and received a glare of hatred and defiance, a stare of sufficient emotional violence to cause a chill of alarm to travel through Maijstral's nerves.

Maijstral looked away. He didn't even know the man. Perhaps, Maijstral thought, he had intercepted a glare meant for someone else.

Laurence and Deco, Maijstral observed, were purposefully making their way through the crowd toward him, or rather toward Nichole. Maijstral sighed. Introductions, at this stage, were inevitable.

The intoxicants, whatever they were, had Hunac fairly loopy by the end—he was swaying on his feet and there was a broad, white, lopsided grin on his face. As the ceremony concluded the crowd tapped their feet in the pattern for reverence, though a few of the humans in the group banged their hands together in applause, a startling sound that the Constellation Practices Authority recommended as a more human custom than the Khosali practice of foot-tapping. The uniformed man with Major Song, Maijstral observed, was one of the more insistent hand-bangers.

Nichole turned toward Maijstral. "That was most enlightening," she said. "Did Hunac get up to all that at school?"

"Legend says he did. I never knew anyone who saw anything, though."

"Maijstral," said Laurence, who, now the crowd was dispersing, had finally reached his goal. "That was enthralling, don't you think? A link to our barbaric past."

"Odd to think of the universe being maintained in such a manner," Maijstral commented, and then turned toward Nichole to do his social duty. "Nichole, may I present—"

At this point a large fist filled Maijstral's eye and he went down. He blinked up from the floor in amazement and saw the large red-faced man standing over him and glaring at him. Major Song tugged at the man's uniform sleeve.

"You're a dirty rat-lover!" the man proclaimed. "That apology—hah! I've never seen anything so insincere."

"Milo," Major Song said, tugging, "don't do this!"

Maijstral could think of nothing better to say than, "Who *are* you?"

"What you said was an insult to everyone who died in the Rebellion!" the man went on. "I challenge you, you rat-loving thief!"

Major Song gave up her tugging. "He's drunk," she said apologetically to the crowd at large, accompanying her comment with a hands-up boys-will-be-boys gesture.

"Who *are* you?" Maijstral asked again.

"Robert the Butcher was a disgrace to humanity, and so are you," the man opined.

At this point the crowd, which had been agitated, suddenly fell silent. Prince Hunac had arrived, surrounded by his assistants. Maijstral observed that the assistants were dressed in full-feathered regalia and carried wooden swords edged with obsidian as well as large clubs consisting of a suggestively shaped stone lashed into the crotch of a stout stick.

The assistants were rather short, but their demeanor was of an intense, ominous, and unfriendly nature.

"Who profaneth the rites?" Hunac demanded, speaking—oddly enough—with the full majesty of High Khosali.

Maijstral knew a cue when he heard one. He pointed at Milo.

"*He* profaneth them!" he said.

Prince Hunac snapped his fingers, and Milo, whoever he was, was promptly engulfed by Hunac's feathered entourage. Thumps, thuds, and yelps of pain accompanied his exit from the Shrine Room. Major Song followed, waving her arms and asking them, please, to stop. Which, it should be pointed out, they did not.

Kuusinen and Aunt Batty broke through the crowd. Maijstral looked at Prince Hunac.

"Who *was* he?" he asked.

Prince Hunac grinned broadly and giggled as the intoxicants caught up with him. His pupils were wide as saucers. Considering what he'd been drinking, it was a significant accomplishment to have managed High Khosali at the height of the crisis. He dropped into the simpler forms of Khosali Standard. "Never saw that man before," he said. He offered a hand. "Would you care to stand?"

"Thank you."

Maijstral accepted Hunac's hand, but Hunac was unsteadier than Maijstral, and there was a certain amount of tugging back and forth before Kuusinen intervened to help Maijstral rise. Nichole's welcome arms steadied him as he found his feet.

"Are you all right, sir?"

"A *complete stranger!*" Maijstral complained to the world at large, and then, "I'm getting tired of being punched."

"So is your attacker, I imagine," Hunac said cheerfully. "You'd best get some patches on that shiner."

"Yes, I suppose." Media globes were swooping in, and it was clearly time to leave.

"Let me go with you, Drake," Nichole said.

"Gladly."

"I say. Maijstral," Laurence began, submerged in the crowd, "I believe you were about to introduce me—"

Maijstral and Nichole were already gone.

"I wonder if you underestimated the strength of public feeling," said Mangula Arish, "in regard to your controversial statements yesterday."

"*What* controversial statements?" Maijstral snarled.

Now that he was physically safe, Maijstral found himself with the luxury to grow angry. How *dare* these people? Who did they think they *were*?

He and Nichole were hastening down a palace corridor to his rooms. Only a reporter, it seemed, would have the nerve to interrupt them. She had to hop alongside in order to keep up with their rapid pace, a form of locomotion that made the bell-shaped skirt look as if it were being rung repeatedly.

"Your alleged apology for the acts of your grandfather. There are those who have found it wavering and insincere, even mocking."

In truth, Mangula's editor had done an outstanding job with the unpromising material—it had been a slow news day, otherwise he wouldn't have bothered. He'd edited Maijstral's words to maximize their potential, then sent the edited versions to the usual political hotheads, who were always eager to get their faces on video.

He had succeeded beyond his own cynical expectations, though he didn't think the controversy was good for more than a day's play. If Maijstral actually ended up in a duel and got killed, however, he could count on running the story for at least two or three days.

By then there might be some *real* news to broadcast.

"There are those who claim that you should be forced to

apologize again for the nature of your remarks," Mangula went on.

"Apologize for my *apology?*" Maijstral said.

Everyone, he realized, simply *everyone,* was trying to kill him. He was going to get a few necessities from his room, he decided, and move into Nichole's suite and never come out. He would be surrounded by Diadem security until he left the planet. And then he'd recruit his own guards, a solid wall of muscle to stand between him and an inexplicably hostile universe. . . .

"Perhaps in view of the fact that you've been set upon by an outraged citizen," Mangula led on, "you might consider an apology of greater depth and sincerity."

"He was set on by *one drunken man,*" Nichole pointed out. "That's hardly a lynch mob."

Maijstral turned the corner just before his room, intent only on escape from this inquisitorial nightmare, and then saw, silhouetted against the distinctive, intricate design of the hallway's Bludarsian Seawood panelling, a peculiar shift of light, of color, of pattern. A perfectly familiar shift, though usually he only saw it when he was stealing something and caught a glimpse of himself in a mirror, cloaked by his darksuit. . . .

Triumph sang in his nerves. *Got you!* he thought.

Anger and exultation mingled in Maijstral's nerves, a perfectly dangerous combination. The spitfire slid from his armpit into his hand with practiced ease. He flung himself prone on the carpet, and—as Nichole and Mangula yelped in alarm—Maijstral opened fire.

Got you got you got you!

Stylish energies flamed off invisible shields and scorched the walls. Alarms clanged. Bright purple fire-retardant foam poured from the ceiling fixtures. Whoever was in the darksuit fled as Maijstral poured fire after.

"*What* . . ." Mangula got out, and then there was the

hum of a stunner—the burglar returning fire—and Mangula flopped to the carpet, suddenly unstrung. Her sculptured hairstyle was melting rapidly. Her silver media globes thudded to the ground like overripe metallic fruit. The mystery figure disappeared around the L-intersection at the end of the corridor.

Mangula spoke with great effort and severity as Maijstral rose to his feet.

"Gleep," she said.

"Call security!" Maijstral told Nichole—perfectly pointless after all this, but it would give her something to do and keep her out of the line of fire—and then he sprinted after the intruder, for all the world like the character that Laurence played in the vids.

His feet, slicked by the foam that was pouring from the ceiling fixtures, promptly slid out from under him and he crashed face-first onto the purple billows.

Laurence's character never had these problems. Especially not when he was wearing a white suit.

"Fnerg," Mangula said with satisfaction.

Maijstral rose and slid, slipped, and skated down the hallway. Presumably whoever was in the darksuit could fly, and would have got a good lead on him by now.

"Snerk," Mangula commented.

As he approached the L-intersection he wondered whether to charge ahead or slow down and proceed cautiously in case the stranger was waiting there with a weapon. He opted for the better part of valor, but then to his alarm found that the slick foam under his feet wasn't about to let him put on the brakes. His momentum carried him inexorably out into the intersection, and so he raised the spitfire and squeezed off a few more shots—suppressive fire, he hoped desperately— and then he slammed into the wall hard enough to make his teeth rattle.

"*Yibble!*" Mangula shouted triumphantly.

The intruder had long since fled. Maijstral's shots had only caused more foam to rain down. He charged down the corridor, banged through a series of doors that looked suspiciously ajar, and then found himself in the submarine pen, a cavernous dome built on a plateau of white sand, with a tunnel leading downward and opening onto Palancar Wall.

There was a small private submarine diving into the tunnel amid a gush of bubbles.

Maijstral fired, causing a cascade of steam but no visible effect on the submarine other than to vaporize one of its running lights. The villain was getting away! Desperately he looked about for a submarine he could call his own.

"Submarine!" he shouted. "Open!"

Three unlocked canopies obligingly popped open, all small subs that Prince Hunac kept for the convenience of his guests. Maijstral hopped into the nearest, a colorful green two-seater with a transparent canopy.

"Power up!" he said. "Close hatches!"

"Very good, sir," said the submarine. The instrument panel flickered to life. The controls seemed similar to an aerial flier—not surprising, considering that a submarine was just an aircraft adapted to another medium.

"Follow the submarine that just left," Maijstral said. "Top speed."

"Flank speed is not possible in the docking area."

Maijstral clenched his teeth. Hard-wired safety mechanisms, in his experience, always led to frustration.

"As fast as possible, then."

"Very good, sir." The submarine cast off and thrashed toward the tunnel entrance. Air bubbled out of ballast tanks as it began to submerge.

"Do you carry any weapons aboard?" Maijstral asked hopefully.

Artificial intelligences are incapable of surprise.

"No, sir," it said.

So much for the cheerful fantasy of a volley of torpedos to precede the submarine out of the tunnel.

The surface closed over Maijstral's head. The submarine angled down toward the brightly lit tunnel.

"Hurry," Maijstral urged.

"I am proceeding with all possible speed in view of necessary safety precautions."

Maijstral could only hope that the intruder's submarine was as obstinately safety-minded as his own.

The submarine entered the tunnel. The engine noise, magnified by the close quarters, throbbed in Maijstral's head. He wiped purple foam from his white dinner jacket.

"Is there any possibility of establishing communication with the palace?" he asked.

"I could surface to extend a radio aerial," the submarine offered.

"Never mind. Is there any way I could keep the palace informed of my location?"

"I could use active sonar."

"Please do so."

"It would be unsafe to use sonar in the tunnel. I will commence pinging as soon as we reach open water."

"Where is the other sub?"

"I have no readings on my sensors."

The submarine floated effortlessly from the tunnel and into the astonishing blue of the open water. A horrid groaning noise ensued, causing metallic objects in the submarine to rattle alarmingly. Maijstral's nerves leaped.

"What was *that?*"

"A sonar ping, sir. Shall I discontinue active sonar?"

"No. Follow the other sub and keep on pinging."

"Very good, sir."

Another groaning noise rumbled through the sub's

frame. Why, Maijstral wondered, was it called a ping when it sounded more like a cetacean in the depths of some unmentionable gastric agony?

Running lights appeared ahead. "I see a submarine!" Maijstral said. It was getting closer.

"That is the craft you have asked me to follow. It has suffered damage to one of its running lights, violating safety regulations, and its autopilot is returning it to the docking bay."

Delight filled Maijstral. He had never felt like cheering a hard-wired safety mechanism before.

"Follow the sub into the dock, please," he said cheerfully.

"Very good, sir."

The two submarines passed each other, Maijstral's sub groaning in welcome, and Maijstral peered from his cockpit for a glimpse of the intruder. He was disappointed: the stranger was still wearing a darksuit, and all Maijstral could see in the other cockpit was a camouflage hologram the color of the blue ocean, marred here and there by clumps of purple fire retardant.

The submarine itself was the same two-seater sport model as Maijstral's, bright blue. Apparently the intruder hadn't planned to make an escape by submarine and had been forced to grab the first sub available.

Then the intruder's submarine gave a lurch, banked in an abrupt change of course, and sped off in a northward direction, increasing its speed.

"What happened?" Maijstral demanded. "I thought the other sub was returning to dock."

"Someone must have overridden the submarine's safety mechanisms. I will report this violation as soon as we reach our destination."

"Follow that sub!"

"Very good."

The stranger presumably had a full complement of burglar tools and the ability to override the programming of artificial intelligences. All Maijstral had were his pistol and a couple of knives he hadn't as yet removed from their sheaths. Still, if he could keep the enemy in sight, marking his location with active sonar, he should be able to attract rescuers who would help him overcome the intruder.

Maijstral's submarine appeared to be gaining on the intruder. Perhaps the intruder was not as good a pilot as Maijstral's autopilot. Maijstral's heart cheered.

Then the intruder sub peeled away from the reef, diving and circling simultaneously. "Follow!" Maijstral commanded. Diving planes made adjustments and the submarine heeled over like a falcon stooping, in slow motion, on its prey.

The submarines spiralled down into the deep, one after the other. Blackness surrounded them. Maijstral had to crane his neck left or right to keep his target in sight.

He peered out to starboard and saw the other sub slip under them, still heading for the bottom, and then leaned out to port and, after a few seconds, saw the intruder reappear. But its orientation seemed different somehow, and Maijstral's brow furrowed as he tried to work out what had changed.

"It's coming up!" he said.

Maijstral's own submarine lurched as diving planes moved to a new attitude. "The other submarine is not following safe proximity procedures," the sub said. "I will report it at the first opportunity."

Maijstral's heart gave a lurch. "What do you mean by safe *proximity*—" he began, desiring clarification.

"We are in danger of collision," the submarine announced.

The other submarine's silhouette narrowed as it presented its bow toward Maijstral. "It's trying to *ram* us?" Maijstral yelped.

"Yes, sir," the sub remarked conversationally. "I am commencing evasive—" Its tone changed radically as a clanging alarm began to sound. "Collision alert!" it shouted. "Prepare for impact!"

"Prepare *how?*" Maijstral demanded, his heart flailing as he saw the other submarine's bow growing larger. "What am I supposed to—"

Bright yellow foam exploded suddenly into the cabin from a dozen inlets, covering everything and hardening almost instantly. Maijstral was frozen in mid-complaint, mouth half-open. Frantically, he tried to gulp air. There was a hideous crash and jarring that ran up Maijstral's spine, and he felt the submarine roll alarmingly.

Maijstral tried to move, but he couldn't. The foam had frozen him in place. He couldn't see anything, but his sense of balance suggested that he and his submarine were inverted and heading for the bottom.

"Collision foam has been deployed," the submarine said, voice muffled by foam. "It should be possible to breathe through it with effort, but it will dissolve in a few seconds."

"*Hwa hoing hon?*" Maijstral demanded, mouth frozen with foam. The submarine nevertheless seemed to understand his demand.

"We have suffered damage to the diving planes," the submarine said. "We are compelled to continue at a downward angle until we reach the bottom."

Terror clawed at Maijstral's heart. "*He're hinking?*"

"Hull integrity is at one hundred percent," the computer reported. "We will wait at the bottom until rescue can reach us. Please try to remain calm."

"*Halm?*" Maijstral demanded. They'd been rammed by the enemy and were sinking, and Maijstral had been frozen into a block of quick-hardening foam, and he was supposed to remain *calm?*

"*Halm?*" he demanded again.

The foam was beginning to loosen its grip. Maijstral fought to free one arm, then tore away bits of foam until he could remove the pieces around his mouth.

"What about the other sub?"

"It has also sustained damage. It has undergone an emergency blowing of its ballast tanks, and has made an uncontrolled ascent to the surface." The computer adopted a bitter tone. "Its pilot will be severely disciplined when word of this reaches the authorities."

Maijstral could only hope so.

For himself, he suspected that the first person he was going to see would be Colonel-General Vandergilt.

TEN

❖ ❖ ❖

The first person Maijstral saw, as his submarine was towed back into dock, *was* in fact Colonel-General Vandergilt. The second was Prince Hunac, still in his feathered costume, and the third was Mangula Arish, who seemed pale and unsteady but whose media globes gleamed bright and ferocious.

Nichole was not to be seen. Probably Diadem security had her under lock and key.

The sub nudged up to the dock, and the canopy hissed open. Maijstral stepped onto the dock, and Prince Hunac ran up and hit him on the chest. The clenched hand bounced off without making much of an impression.

"Yes?" Maijstral said, puzzled.

Hunac thumped him again. He kept bounding up and down on the balls of his feet, and his bright pupils looked bigger than his fists. "You abused my hospitality, you thief!" he screamed. "I challenge you!" He had lost his grip on High Khosali and spoke in Human Standard.

Maijstral realized that Hunac was only hitting him in the chest because he couldn't reach his face. "Thief?" Maijstral said. He turned vaguely and pointed at the submarine. "But you got your sub *back,*" he pointed out.

Hunac kept bouncing up and down. Somewhere in his mind Maijstral registered the fact that he had never before seen anyone who was literally hopping mad.

"I'll cut you to pieces!" Hunac said, and punched Maijstral's chest again.

Everyone, Maijstral was reminded, was trying to kill him. Or marry him. Or maybe both. There didn't need to be a reason, it was just this *thing* everyone had agreed to do at some secret meeting to which Maijstral had not been invited.

"You'll have to stand in line," Maijstral said. He picked Prince Hunac up bodily and moved him out of the way, and then began his weary trek to Nichole's quarters.

It was safer than anywhere else he could think of.

Nichole's household, of which Maijstral's soon became a subset, moved within the hour to an exclusive resort hotel outside Havana. Diadem security, appalled at their precious human commodity becoming involved in a firefight in a presumably secure place like the Underwater Palace, had called in the reserves, and soon squads of large, grim humans and even larger, grimmer Khosali were patrolling the corridors, the roof, and the public areas doing the things that security people normally do—talking into their sleeves, patting the hidden pockets that concealed their weaponry, and scrutinizing hapless tourists who were left to conclude, from their somber and ominous appearance, that there was some kind of international crime convention in town.

Maijstral, once he'd showered off the foam and changed into a dressing gown, merely lay on the bed in the darkness of his room and stared at the ceiling. He'd slammed down three brandies, but never felt less drunk in his life. Adrenaline had burned off the alcohol the second it reached his system.

He was, he realized, doomed. Three challenges in three days, and all for things he hadn't done, and there was no earthly reason why the challenges should stop now.

The stranger, of course, had got clean away. Summoned a waiting flier once the submarine surfaced, and was last tracked over the mainland, flying low to avoid detection.

Maijstral had, eventually, found out why Prince Hunac was mad at him. One of Prince Hunac's priceless prehistoric steles had been found under Maijstral's bed. The intruder had planted it there, clearly, just before Maijstral arrived and began shooting. Maijstral had encountered the perpetrator making an exit, not as he'd assumed during the break-in itself.

Prince Hunac, whose reasoning faculties had not been at their best following his consumption of whatever was in his ritual beverage, had assumed that Maijstral and the stranger were partners, that something had gone wrong with their plan, and that Maijstral and the stranger had been attempting their getaways when their submarines collided.

There were any number of problems with Prince Hunac's theory, but he wasn't in any condition to make a more logical construction, and Colonel-General Vandergilt, happy with seeing Maijstral again in trouble with one of his hosts, had not been inclined to change the Prince's mind.

Three challenges, Maijstral thought despairingly, in three days.

He was the Hereditary Prince-Bishop of Nana! he protested. How *dare* these people challenge a man of the cloth!

He tried vainly to visualize a strategy that could get him out of at least some of the fights. But every thought was interrupted by the chilling image of Joseph Bob raising the bladed end of a dire staff for the coup de grace.

The dire staff. He was going to have to do something about that.

He sprang from the bed, ready to don his darksuit and head for his burglar equipment, but at that moment the phone chimed. He went to the service plate and touched the ideogram for "phone," then another for "image."

"Hello, Drake." The Duchess looked at him with level violet eyes. "I hope I'm not interrupting your rest."

"I wasn't sleeping."

She didn't seem surprised. "I had a hard time finding where you were. And then I encountered some functionary who didn't want to forward the call."

"I'm hiding out. Nichole has much better security than I do, and—well—it seemed the best thing to make use of it." He stepped toward the bed and sat on it so as to make it clear to Roberta that if he was not-sleeping tonight, he was not-sleeping alone.

It wasn't that he was immune to the thought of Nichole's comfort, but he had never felt less erotic than he did right now. Plus, he needed to be alone in order to skulk.

"I'm sorry if I neglected to communicate with you," he said. "My life has been . . . overwhelming . . . of late."

"So Kuusinen told me. It's obvious that you are the victim of a conspiracy."

He forced a haunted smile. "I would like to think so. If these are all random occurrences, then the universe is far more erratic than I'd ever suspected."

Roberta showed no sign of amusement. "Kuusinen said that you suspected the Bubber."

"Yes."

She gave a little shake of her head. "I don't think your theory holds water. He can't be responsible for what happened at the Underwater Palace."

He can if I *say* he is, Maijstral thought, but there was too much sense in what Roberta had just said.

Roberta's look softened. "Besides," she said, "he's been working constantly to prevent the duel. I've seen him try, but

Joseph Bob won't see reason. Will's terrified that his brother will be hurt."

"A good sociopath would be able to imitate those emotions quite well," Maijstral pointed out.

The Duchess looked doubtful. "If you say so," she said.

"I'm open to any other theories," Maijstral said.

She bit her lip. "I don't have one. And we've only got a few hours."

"Yes."

Doomed, Maijstral thought. The word, rolling about in his brain, had a certain orotund majesty, like a tolling bell.

Doomed, doomed, doomed.

Roberta cleared her throat. Her eyes were shiny and she was blinking hard. She tried to make her tone businesslike. "I've arranged for a medical team to be present. There will be media globes recording the event to show that it will be fair. Kuusinen said that you accepted his offer to practice with the staffs, but that there wasn't an opportunity."

Roberta's tears were beginning to have their effect upon Maijstral. His own eyes stung. He wanted to sit in the dark and have a good long cry.

"I'll pick you up half an hour before sunrise," Roberta said.

"I will look forward to seeing you," he said.

For the last time, his inner voice added.

They both rang off before the call got too soppy. Maijstral dried his eyes and got his darksuit from the closet. He put it on and felt better at once.

He'd fixed one duel, he thought, and by the Active Virtues he'd fix a hundred if he had to.

The Bubber frowned into the phone pickups that were transmitting his image to Joseph Bob. "I think Maijstral has a good case," he said.

"For stealing from me?" Joseph Bob asked. The Prince was in the act of practicing with his weapon. Light glinted off the wicked blades of the dire staff as he advanced, whirling the staff before him.

"Maijstral's got two more challenges in the last two days."

Joseph Bob halted, frowned, grounded his weapon. "They're not going to fight him first, are they?"

"No. Of course not."

"So what's the problem?"

"It bolsters Maijstral's case that there's some murderous conspiracy involved."

Joseph Bob hoisted his weapon again. "Well, *I'm* not a conspirator," he said.

"Of course not. But if it were to turn out that you were the *dupe* of a conspirator, it wouldn't look good for us."

Joseph Bob thought about this for a moment, twirling the staff idly.

"I'm just looking out for our interests, J.B.," the Bubber added.

Joseph Bob nodded. "You've a point there," he conceded. "But it also doesn't look good if I let people steal from me." He gave another brisk nod as he came to a decision. "Tell you what—if it turns out there's a conspiracy involved, I'll challenge the conspirators, too, for daring to use me in their plans." He gave a boyish grin. "*That'll* take care of it."

Still grinning, he lunged with the weapon, meanwhile giving out the paralyzing Yell of Hate recommended by the best combat instructors.

The Bubber sighed. "Well," he said. "If you're *sure.*"

"Of *course* I'm sure," Joseph Bob said, falling briefly on guard, and then he attacked again. "*Yaaaaaah!*" he shouted.

The Bubber terminated the call and walked into the other room where Her Grace of Benn waited. In order to have neutral territory in which to conduct negotiations, they had rented a room in Key West, and the place suffered from an overindulgence in the rustic and picturesque: woven palm frond lampshades, fishnets drooping from the ceiling, an ashtray made to resemble a starfish.

"Didn't work, I'm afraid," the Bubber said.

Roberta made a face. "It was worth a try."

"It was a good argument. *I* would have been convinced. But J.B. is having too good a time to really pay attention to quibbles." He sat next to Roberta and patted pockets for his cigaret case. "He's enjoying this belated discovery of martial ardor far too much," he said glumly. "It's being brought up in a house full of weapons, I suppose, and early exposure to all the stories about our ancestors' prowess . . . the warrior spirit was bound to break out sooner or later. I'm just sorry it's wrecking your engagement."

"If it *is* an engagement," Roberta said, equally morose. The Bubber produced his cigaret case and then looked at it for a moment as if he couldn't remember why he'd been searching for it.

"Could I have one of those?" Roberta asked. "It's bad for training, but occasionally one has cravings."

He handed her a cigaret and began a search through pockets for his lighter, but Roberta found hers first. They puffed in somber silence for a moment.

"He's run off to Nichole," she remarked. "I suppose there's nothing in it—she's an old friend and everything—but I'd much rather he'd run off to *me.*"

The Bubber did his best to be helpful. "Well, he couldn't, could he? I've been taking up all your time."

Roberta rose from her cane chair. "There's nothing left to arrange, is there?" she said, and walked toward the door. "I might as well try to get a few hours' sleep."

"You think you can sleep?" the Bubber asked in surprise. "I know I won't catch so much as a wink."

She hesitated by the door. "Well," she said. "I suppose you're right."

"There's an all-night bistro down the street," the Bubber said. "Perhaps we could have some coffee and a pastry."

"Oh." Roberta tilted her head and considered. "I suppose I might as well join you," she said. "The coffee will be welcome, but I don't think I could eat anything."

The Bubber flicked ashes into the starfish ashtray and rose, then hesitated on his way to the door. "I say," he said. "Would you mind if I asked you a question?"

"Go ahead."

"I haven't—er—bungled this horribly, have I? I haven't got my brother killed without realizing it?"

Roberta smiled and patted his arm. "You've done very well," she said.

"Oh." A surprised look crossed the Bubber's face. "Well. That's all right, then."

Maijstral left the hotel after telling the security people he needed some time alone, and flew off with the impression they were happy to see the back of him. Once in Tejas, he scouted the perimeter of Joseph Bob's estate, then left the car, activated his darksuit, and flew on silent repellers to the Prince's huge manor house.

His plan was simple. He'd sabotage the stunner on the one end of Joseph Bob's dire staff so that it wouldn't work at all, and then take care of the bladed end through the use of a resonance ring, a clever bit of burglar's paraphernalia intended for use on barred windows. The ring would snap around the bar in question, then find the frequency of the metal. A resonance effect would be set up that would shatter the crystalline bonds holding together the metal's molecules. The metal would weaken, then come apart.

Maijstral planned merely to weaken Joseph Bob's staff near its bladed head. Then, first thing in the fight, he'd take a swipe at the blades, and the thing would come off.

Everyone, he hopefully presumed, would believe that the old weapon suffered from metal fatigue, or perhaps just conclude that Maijstral was a far stronger warrior than he looked.

After disabling Joseph Bob's weapon, Maijstral would keep hitting away until he'd either won or the seconds put an end to it. Either way, honor was satisfied, and he would decline any challenge to a second encounter.

Maijstral broke into Joseph Bob's house easily enough, then headed for the exercise room, where Joseph Bob might have been practicing with his weapon. No dire staffs were to be found. He went to the study, in case the dire staff was hung on the wall with Joseph Bob's other weapons, but it wasn't there, either.

Good grief, Maijstral thought, is he *sleeping* with the damned thing?

He floated up to the regal apartments and glided to the door of the Prince's room. He deployed his scanners, but the audio scanner failed to report the sound of breathing, and the infrared scanner detected no body temperature.

Maijstral peeled the lock and entered. No one sleeping here: the bed had not even been turned down. No dire staff.

An uneasy feeling began to creep up Maijstral's spine. No, Maijstral thought, the Prince was just spending his last night with his Princess. Where was Arlette's room?

Arlette's room proved empty as well. Maijstral felt his mouth go dry. He flew along the corridor, peeling locks and entering rooms. The whole family had left, and Maijstral didn't know where.

Terror beat a tattoo in his heart. He wiped his forehead and tried frantically to guess where the family might have gone. Somewhere closer to the site of the duel, perhaps, Key

West or Miami or even Havana. They might be in the same resort as Maijstral and Nichole!

The point was, he didn't know. He had no knowledge of what holdings the Prince or the Bubber might have in the Caribbean, and he had no idea, on such short notice, how to find out.

What, he considered, would happen if he just got back in his flier and zoomed off to continue his life as if nothing had happened? Live off his loot, or perhaps check into a New Puritan monastery and announce that he'd found God.

He would be disgraced, of course. Most if not all of his friends would drop him. There would be no question of marriage to the likes of Roberta or Nichole—they'd flee in disgust at the very mention of his name. He would no longer be able to float about at the top of society, picking his scores and earning a good living from commissions. The Imperial Sporting Commission might well revoke his license, which would mean that he could be arrested much more easily. If he ever needed money, he'd have to sneak about, travel incognito, and take down vaults and storehouses just for the money, and he'd be very, very vulnerable to the police.

And all because he didn't want to get killed. How fair was *that?* he wanted to know.

But the thing that really chilled his blood was the realization that Roman might leave his employ. Roman had standards. Roman was devoted to all the ideals implied by that scroll he'd created: family and honor and nobility. Maijstral didn't believe in any of these things, but Roman did, and if Maijstral betrayed them all in one fell swoop, then Roman, he was sure, would be compelled to leave him.

How could he survive without Roman? Roman was his prop, his anchor, the one certain, unequivocal thing in his difficult and equivocal life. Roman was *home.*

Roman had saved Maijstral's life a dozen times. If

Roman left, Maijstral might as well be dead anyhow.

And if he was going to die, the duel was as good a place as any.

But still, there had to be an escape. He gave desperate thought to the matter.

Well, he thought, he was here in Joseph Bob's house; he had sufficient gadgets to get him access to Joseph Bob's computers; and they could very likely get him a list of the family holdings. It might be possible to find that dire staff yet.

He might as well get busy. He had nothing else to do than die.

"Roberta?"

"Yes?"

"It's time to get in our aerocars and pick up our duellists."

"How far do you have to go?"

"Only as far as Key Largo. My brother's staying at the estate of Lord Pony. J.B. wanted to be able to practice with the staff and not have to deal with any interruptions. He hasn't told anyone he's there except family."

"Well, I don't have much farther to fly myself."

"Havana, yes?"

"Yes."

"A lovely place. You might stop there on your honeymoon, if things work out."

Beat.

"Was that a really tactless thing to say?"

A sigh. "I don't think so. But I'll give it further thought, if you like."

Doomed, doomed, doomed.

The word rang through Maijstral's head as he stood wrapped in a cloak on the verge of the sea.

Doomed, doomed, doomed.

He had found a list of all of Joseph Bob's possessions in the Caribbean. He had flown to every single one of them, his desperation increasing with the cumulative realization that neither Joseph Bob nor his dire staff was in any one of them.

Doomed, doomed, doomed.

Finally he'd run out of options. He had nothing to do but return to Havana, pick up his staff, head out to the Dry Tortugas, and die like a gentleman.

Doomed, doomed, doomed.

He shifted his weight on the sand and gazed out to the dark, predawn sea, hoping that someone would sail over the horizon to his rescue—smugglers, pirates, Colonel-General Vandergilt, anyone.

Doomed, doomed, doomed.

After his return to Havana he'd figured he might as well give fighting a chance, and he'd had Roman give him a lesson with the dire staff. It had been a disaster. The staff was solid steel and immeasurably heavy—every movement seemed to take forever and left him panting for breath. The wicked nest of interlaced blades on the end of the staff were appallingly sharp. He'd fired off the stunner once by accident and put his own foot to sleep.

He could not rely on martial prowess. And his only chance to rig the outcome had failed.

Doomed, doomed, doomed.

"Drake? It's time."

Roberta touched him lightly on the shoulder.

"I need to do your hair."

He gazed at the sea while Roberta tied his hair back with a ribbon. Then he turned and followed her to the designated spot. He took off the cloak, and Roman approached and handed him his staff.

"Remember," Roman said. "Get inside him. Hit left and right."

Maijstral didn't understand a word of it. It all sounded

like the most inane babble in the world. "Yes," he said. "Thank you."

"Don't forget the Yell of Hate."

Maijstral nodded.

Roberta squeezed his arm. He felt the moist touch of her lips on his cheek. "Come back to me," she said.

Doomed, doomed, doomed.

Joseph Bob marched toward him confidently, the rising sun gleaming on his perfect blond hair. He looked utterly at home in this circumstance, and he carried his dire staff with confident ease. His lips were turned up in a slight smile. He looked as if he were on his way to a game of cards.

The only imperfection was the slight swelling around the broken nose—he'd removed his semilife patches so that they wouldn't interfere with his vision during the fight.

Doomed, doomed, doomed.

It was at this point, viewing his opponent, that resentment rose in Maijstral. How *dare* the man smile! How *dare* he look so perfectly at ease, so *sans-peur-et-sans-reproche,* so damned *happy to be here!* The man was a *fool.* A dupe. He was being used as a puppet by a legion of conspirators, and he neither knew nor cared.

"Ready!" The Bubber's voice broke and squeaked on the second syllable.

Combats with the dire staff begin *corps-à-corps,* with each staff held crosswise in both hands and touching, so that neither side could get off an easy shot with the stunner right at the start. Maijstral braced himself and pushed his weapon forward, felt Joseph Bob's weight as the two staffs came into contact.

Joseph Bob gave a little grunt of satisfaction as he leaned his mass into Maijstral. He was bigger and stronger and had longer arms, and the advantage was all his. Maijstral felt Joseph Bob's weight driving him into the ground like a tent peg, and dug his heels into the sand to arrest his backward movement. His arms were already tired.

"Begin on the count of three!" the Bubber shouted. *"One . . ."*

In the corner of his eye Maijstral could see media globes winking in the sun. This whole fiasco was being recorded in order to demonstrate to the authorities that it was fair.

Fair. The whole notion made Maijstral's blood boil. What was fair about a big, strong idiot being permitted to butcher a smaller, far more intelligent man?

"Two!"

Joseph Bob was a *moron!* A *simpleton!* How *dare* he be so casual about this?

"Three!"

Maijstral's resentment and indignation burst from his throat in a shattering scream.

"Yaaaaaaah!" he yelled.

ELEVEN

❀   ❀   ❀

Maijstral opened his eyes and blinked lazily at the ceiling. He yawned. He stretched. He rose from his bed and planted his bare feet on the floor and clenched his toes in the thick nap of the carpet.

He looked down at his knuckles. They were reddened and swollen and a bit sore. He flexed them in time with the clenching of his toes.

Voices were heard from the drawing room adjacent. Maijstral padded to the door, opened it, and entered the room.

Roberta, Nichole, and Kuusinen were watching a video and chatting. Glasses, bottles, and dirty dishes were strewn on tables. It was perhaps the twentieth time they'd seen the video, and they hadn't tired of it yet.

"Do you know," Roberta said, "I believe this is the first time I've ever seen one human being climb another."

In the video, Maijstral and Joseph Bob were facing each other, each with dire staff braced. The Bubber called out commands. And then, before Joseph Bob could move, Maijstral

screamed, batted the Prince's dire staff out of the way, then
threw down his own weapon and launched himself at his foe.

"Clever," Kuusinen commented. "Butting His Highness
on his broken nose that way."

Maijstral couldn't remember any of it. He could view the
video almost as if he were watching Laurence play some Maij-
stral-analogue in a fictional adventure. He was fairly certain
that his head butt to Joseph Bob's nose was an accident, but he
couldn't swear to it.

On the video, the Prince lurched as Maijstral climbed his
front like a squirrel climbing a tree. Maijstral bit, punched,
butted, and gouged. He screamed aloud the entire time. The
Prince staggered, dropped his staff, and fell backward to the
sand with Maijstral on top. Maijstral, still screaming, sat on his
chest and hammered his head into the sand with his fists until
Roberta and the Bubber dashed in to seize him and drag him
off his prey.

"That's quite a Yell of Hate," Roberta observed.

"Drake looks like an *animal*," Nichole said, a bit wide-
eyed. Despite their long acquaintance, this was clearly an aspect of Maijstral that was new to her.

"Is it feeding time at the zoo?" Maijstral asked. They all
turned to him in surprise. Nichole flushed with embarassment
at being overheard.

Silent entrances were a signal feature of Maijstral's profession.

"Slept well?" Roberta asked.

"I think I can safely say it was the sleep of the just."

He sat beside Roberta on a settee and she took his hand.
"We've been discussing you," she said. "And we've come to
some conclusions."

"Other than the observation that I'm an animal?"

"That, too."

Maijstral flexed a hand and wondered a bit at the video

he'd just seen. His astonishment at himself was still in a very tender state. He had some years before concluded that he no longer possessed the ability to surprise himself, and over time he'd managed to reconcile himself to the idea that he was incapable of facing physical danger; but the video was clear evidence that his notions of himself needed an overhaul.

If only he could *remember*. He couldn't recall a thing from the moment the Bubber counted three till Roberta and the Bubber hauled him off the Prince's splayed and hapless form.

Nichole turned to Kuusinen. "Mr. Kuusinen, I think, can outline the substance of our conversation."

"Could you call for dinner first?" Maijstral asked. "I'm starving."

He hadn't, he realized, eaten in days. His meals kept getting interrupted.

Maijstral's dinner was ordered from room service, then he poured himself champagne from a half-empty bottle that was sitting convenient to hand in a silver bucket. Kuusinen frowned, settled himself in his chair, and began his summary.

"It's obvious enough that you are the victim of a conspiracy," he said. "Our difficulty is that, while we can eliminate any number of suspects, we still have no firm idea who is behind it all, or what that person's motive might be.

"The conspiracy would seem to be aimed at getting you challenged by those people who have consented to be your hosts while you've been staying on Earth. The first attempt, at the home of the Prince of Tejas, was successful—"

A memory bubbled, like champagne, to the surface of Maijstral's mind. "It wasn't the first," he said suddenly. "When I was staying with Lord Huyghe, Conchita Sparrow saw someone in a darksuit hovering outside my window. The intruder fled, and I've assumed all along it was a police spy of some sort, but now it seems likely the stranger was a member of the conspiracy."

Kuusinen nodded. "That datum somewhat alters the time scheme," he said. "Your enemies are very well organized. Perhaps we should begin by itemizing their knowledge and capabilities."

He held up a finger. "First, they're aware of your travel schedule, and have laid plans in advance." Another finger. "Second, they include in their number a burglar of considerable prowess—Roman informed us that he had booby-trapped your room in the Underwater Palace such that it would have taken a burglar of no small competence to break in undetected, and of course it would have taken an extremely capable burglar to have stolen Prince Hunac's stele in the first place."

"That leaves out the Bubber," Roberta said. "Will probably could have stolen and planted the pistol, but he wasn't anywhere near the Underwater Palace, and nothing in his background suggests he could at any point in his life have acquired any competence as a thief."

Maijstral frowned into his champagne. "I have given some consideration to the notion that Drexler might be responsible," he said.

"Roman informs us," Kuusinen said, "that he and Drexler were dining together in the servants' hall of the Underwater Palace when you came across the burglar."

"Oh."

At this point the door chime gave a soft, shimmery noise; and three individuals, uniformed as splendidly as fleet admirals and operating in efficient silence, delivered Maijstral's dinner and swept away the dirty plates. The conversation suspended itself while they were in the room. It was always possible that one of them had been corrupted by the media.

As the grand potentates of room service bowed their way out, Maijstral applied himself to his plate. Sea lion Provençal, one of his favorites, mixed vegetables in season, and little heads of khronkh, fried crispy.

Kuusinen frowned and looked at his hand, with the first two fingers extended, and quite visibly rewound his summary, mentally replayed his earlier remarks, and then, once he located himself, recommenced. He thrust out his third finger.

"Three," he said. "The conspirators seem possessed of an undying, obsessive, seemingly irrational hatred toward you yourself, Mr. Maijstral. Who do you know that hates you so much?"

Bewilderment settled about Maijstral. "I can't think of anyone I've offended that badly," he said. "Fine, I've *stolen* things from people, but *still...*"

"*I* still wonder," Nichole added, "if perhaps the two burglaries are unrelated. Perhaps the first was planned for some perfectly rational reason—by the Bubber, say, as a scheme to get his brother's property—and the second was planned by someone who had heard about your problem with Joseph Bob and wanted to exploit the situation somehow."

"Who?" Kuusinen asked.

"Alice Manderley, perhaps?" Nichole ventured. "She *is* a first-class burglar and is, I presume, capable of breaking into Drake's room...."

"But why would she do it?" Roberta interrupted. "What could her scheme have been?"

"Who knows? Drake interrupted it. Perhaps she wanted to steal a whole lot of steles, and planted one under Drake's bed so he'd be the one to bear the blame."

Kuusinen looked at Nichole levelly. "You pointed out, I believe, that she was in attendance at Prince Hunac's ceremony, and therefore unable to break into Mr. Maijstral's room."

Nichole's face fell. "Oh. I *did* say that, didn't I? I forgot."

Maijstral cast his mind back to the ceremony. "I wouldn't write her off entirely," he said. "I saw her at the ceremony, but she was wandering in the back of the room, away from everyone. And her husband was not with her."

"You believe her husband capable of taking the stele?" Kuusinen asked.

"I don't believe Kenny is capable of tying a bootlace without her help," Maijstral said. "But Alice might still have planted the stele while Kenny wandered about the ceremony wearing a hologram of Alice. It's misdirection, a basic element of magic. The fact that Alice wasn't a part of the crowd, and wasn't talking to anyone, might serve as evidence."

"It's a common tactic burglars use to mislead people," Nichole added. "Drake used to do it all the time."

"I still do."

"I'll keep my researchers busy regarding Alice Manderley," Nichole said. "And her husband."

"You might check again the list of high-rated burglars on Earth," Maijstral added. "There can't be many who are capable of leaving something the size of a Mayan stele in my room without setting off at least one of the traps I'd set."

"We're also checking everyone at Prince Hunac's party."

"And speaking of the party," Maijstral said, and felt his injured eye give a twitch. "Who was that Milo person?"

"Captain Milo Hay," Kuusinen said promptly. "He is the fiancé of Major Ruth Song, the Elvis impersonator."

"I didn't steal anything from *him*," Maijstral said. "Is he a participant in this conspiracy or not?"

The others looked at each other. "We don't know," Kuusinen admitted.

"He called me a 'rat-lover,' " Maijstral said, "and this was the second time I've heard about rats, the first being from Kenny Chang, of all people, and in connection with the Security and Sedition Act. What is a rat exactly, and why is loving one supposed to be so bad?"

The others looked at each other uneasily again. "A rat,"

Kuusinen said finally, "is a scavenging Earth animal widely regarded as a destructive pest. On account of a fancied resemblance, certain organizations in the Constellation have applied the term to the Khosali."

Distaste narrowed Maijstral's heavy-lidded eyes. "The 'prohuman' element, I presume," he said, deliberately inserting the quotation marks in his tone.

"Indeed," Kuusinen agreed. "Not coincidentally, the same people who are the most loud in support of the Security and Sedition Act, which will prevent nonhumans from advancing past a certain rank in the military and civil service, and subject the rest to random, intrusive investigation."

Roberta smiled grimly. "Investigation, one gathers, at the hands of our friend Colonel-General Vandergilt."

Kuusinen nodded. "Her among others."

Maijstral fingered his diamond ring. "Is Captain Hay another pillar of the Constellation's security establishment? I didn't recognize his uniform."

"Captain Hay did not in fact receive his rank from the Constellation military," Kuusinen said. "He is a member of something called the Human Guard, a paramilitary organization devoted to protecting the Constellation from alleged enemies foreign and domestic."

Maijstral nodded. "And Captain Hay—*Milo*—perceives me as an enemy of the domestic variety."

"As we can detect no connection between him and you or your family, we suspect his aggression toward you may have been motivated by ideology, yes."

"And drink," added Nichole.

Maijstral ground his teeth. He had encountered this sort of fanatic before—on Peleng they called themselves Humanity Prime—and he had found them a severe and constant trial.

Of course on Peleng he'd also got a lot of money out of them, so the encounter hadn't been all bad.

Maijstral looked down at his plate and realized that his meal was gone. He didn't remember eating it.

Perhaps he was beginning to suffer from random outbreaks of amnesia.

He was still hungry. He ordered another dinner identical to the first.

"Do I really have to fight this Milo person?" Maijstral asked. "I'd think ax handles in a dark alley would be more his style than a fair combat."

"He hasn't been heard from since his challenge," Roberta said. "Nor has any second. He may have sobered up and decided not to pursue the matter."

Nichole's face settled into a satisfied smile. "Or," she added, "Prince Hunac's guards are still pursuing *him.*"

"Major Song tried her best to excuse Milo's actions," Maijstral said. "I take it she is also a member of the Human Guard?"

"No," Kuusinen said. "She is in fact an officer in the Constellation Marines, though she is on extended leave to prepare for the Memphis Olympiad. Her grandfather, incidentally, was the late Fleet Admiral Song, hero of the Battle of Neerwinden."

As celebrated a military hero, Maijstral knew, as the Constellation's brief history offered. Neerwinden had been the first great victory for rebellious humanity.

"You'd think, with a grandfather as famous as all that, she'd know the difference between a genuine military and a false one," Maijstral said.

"She's a false Elvis," Nichole shrugged. "Her purchase on reality may not be of the highest order."

The discussion of Milo and Major Song had brought Maijstral's mind back to issues of personal survival. "Has Prince Hunac been heard from?" he asked.

"No," Nichole said, "though that's not surprising. Considering what he ingested yesterday, we suspect it will take him a lot longer to sober up than it will Captain Hay."

"I'd appreciate it if you'd appoint me as your second for both fights," Roberta said. "I'm experienced at it by now, and I have a tack I'd like to try with each of your foes."

"Yes?" Maijstral asked.

"My plans are different for each. With Hunac I'll try reason—all the arguments that *didn't* work with Joseph Bob, but might well work with someone less hungry for glory. I will simply offer him the evidence of a conspiracy and ask him to postpone things until we can find out who's responsible. He may prove amenable, though since his challenge was offered publicly, he may have a difficult time withdrawing entirely."

Maijstral's nerves gave a little wail at this conclusion. "Very well," he managed. "And how do you intend to handle Milo?"

Roberta looked at him levelly. "I plan to frighten the daylights out of him," she said, matter-of-fact. "And for that, I would like your permission to release to the media the video of your encounter with Joseph Bob. Milo may *really* want to reconsider when he sees it."

Maijstral showed his teeth. "When he sees my animal nature, you mean."

"Exactly."

"Besides," Nichole pointed out, "there's an army of media swarming just outside our hotel's perimeter. It's like an armed camp out there. We'll never be able to do anything unless we give them *something*, and I think the video and perhaps a press conference, with you, Drake, at your most outgoing and genial, if you please."

"I will try to summon such bonhomie as remains."

"It's only after we get rid of most of the press that we can enter into our plan."

Maijstral's eyebrows lifted. *"Our* plan?"

"Quite," Roberta said. "Since we don't know as yet who is responsible for your misfortunes, we've decided to go on a fishing expedition. Right now there's a wall of Diadem security around you, and it's unlikely anyone would try to penetrate it."

Maijstral felt a warm glow of inner gratification at this sentiment.

"But if you leave," Nichole added with a smile, "the conspirators may strike again. And that's exactly what we want."

A chill wafted up Maijstral's spine. "We want *what?*" he asked.

"We want to lure them into trying to frame you a third time," Roberta said. "And when they come, we'll be ready."

"We will?" Maijstral asked.

"Oh yes. We'll catch them, force them to confess, and get you off the hook. Nothing easier."

Maijstral had an intuition it was all going to be more complicated than that.

He looked from Roberta to Nichole and back again.

Taking dead aim, he thought. Magician's cant, and also what had been happening to him.

The conspirators, whoever they were, had taken dead aim at him in hopes of getting him killed or slammed away in prison.

Roberta had taken dead aim at him for her marriage scheme.

Nichole had done much the same.

Now the two of them together were about to put him in harm's way once more.

And Maijstral had the horrid, queasy feeling that he had no choice but to let them do it.

TWELVE

✿ ✿ ✿

The meeting with the press was going rather well,
Maijstral thought. Media globes winked in the sunlight over-
head. The courtyard of the hotel was filled with reporters.
Most of the questions concerned his encounter with Joseph
Bob—his "strategy" for victory, his "feelings" during the
fight.

Since he hadn't possessed the former, and couldn't recall
the latter, he was free to invent something that cast himself in a
suitably noble light.

Because their quarrel was based on a misunderstanding,
he said, he didn't want to kill Joseph Bob; and therefore he
resorted to fists.

His feelings, he reported, were such a mixture that it was
difficult to define any of them very well. He then let the reporters suggest emotions to him, and he picked the ones he
liked best.

Determination to win at all costs?

Yes.

Concern for Joseph Bob's welfare?

Naturally.

Fear?

"Well," he said, laughing, "of *course.*" And the reporters laughed with him.

One smiling young man waved a hand. "Have you heard of Laurence's offer to stand as your second for your other two fights?"

"Sorry?" Maijstral said. "Who?"

"Laurence. The video star who—"

"Oh yes! Laurence! Of course." Maijstral winced inwardly. "I'm sorry, I didn't hear—"

Somehow he knew he was going to pay for this.

Maijstral was mistaken in reckoning that the payment would not come immediately, however. At that moment an elderly man, white of hair and erect of bearing, strode from the crowd and brought his cane down on Maijstral's head.

"Dastard!" the old man cried in a passion. "I had the honor to serve under your grandfather, and I counted your father as a friend. How dare you disavow their cause? How dare you disavow your Emperor?"

Maijstral, from his position on the ground, rubbed his head and looked at the old man in amazement.

"Who *are* you?" he demanded.

"I am Baron Sancho Sandoval Cabeza de Vaca," the man said grandly, and pointed at Maijstral with his cane. "And *you,*" he added, "are a dastard! I challenge you to single combat."

Rage exploded in Maijstral. He jumped up, snatched the cane from the Baron's grip, and snapped it over his knee.

The Baron glared at him. He glared back.

"Perhaps," cried the voice of Mangula Arish from somewhere in the crowd, "you should again consider apologizing for your controversial remarks the other day. . . ."

Maijstral observed that Arish had her hair firmly lacquered back into place. On the whole, he preferred it limp and covered with purple goo.

"I think," Maijstral said, blood boiling, "this meeting is over."

He stalked back to the hotel and made his way to Nichole's suite. She looked up in surprise as he slammed the door behind him.

"Have we got *another* plan?" he asked.

Well, no, they didn't. So Maijstral and his suite flew on to Memphis, where they were to stay at the home of Tvar, a well-known art collector and an old acquaintance for whom Maijstral had performed several commissions. Tvar had been contacted by Nichole ahead of time and, no less immune to certain forms of glamor than the public at large, had been so dazzled by the call from one of the Three Hundred that the warning that she was likely to be burglarized by Maijstral's unknown enemies had only provoked in her a casual flick of her pointed ears.

"How *exciting*," she'd said, her tongue lolling in a Khosali smile. "Perhaps I will have a chance to *shoot these conspirators down like dogs*."

When this comment was relayed to Maijstral, the sentiment could not help but meet with his wholehearted approval.

On the horizon, Maijstral saw the minarets and domes of Graceland as he came in for a landing at Tvar's estate. He hadn't realized Tvar's place was so close. Before he'd stepped from his flier, Tvar emerged from the front door, arms outstretched in welcome.

She was a Khosalikh of medium build—a head taller than Maijstral, who was slightly above average height for a human—and was dressed extravagantly in a gown of rainbow texture that made her seem rather larger than she was. Her pointed ears peeked from a particolored turban ornamented with flashing gems. Chiming on her wrists were the bracelets that she'd commissioned Maijstral to acquire for her: they had once belonged to Lady Scarlett, the patroness of the poet who went by the name "Ptarmigan"—the bracelets were not very valuable, but Tvar coveted them for their associations.

She also had Lady Scarlett's liver in a cryonic reliquary on her mantel. She'd bought it at auction and hadn't had to use Maijstral as an agent for that one.

Tvar embraced Maijstral and sniffed his ears. "How pleasant to see you again!" she cried, and cocked her ears toward the boundaries of her estate. "I see you brought a flock of birds with you."

"Carrion crows, I'm afraid," Maijstral said, and glanced over his shoulder at the media fliers dropping to a landing outside Tvar's property.

"Hoping to follow you to your next duel, I imagine."

"And hoping you'll punch me while the cameras are looking," Maijstral added.

He turned as another, larger flier settled onto the lawn, and opened to reveal its passengers. "May I present Her Grace Roberta Altunin, the Duchess of Benn? And her aunt, the Honorable Bathsheba sar Altunin. Mr. Paavo Kuusinen."

There was a formal sniffing of ears. Tvar gestured toward the flier's roomy storage compartment. "Who's in the box?"

"My father, the late Duke."

"Shall we put him in the crypt, or give him a room?"

"A room, please," said Aunt Batty indulgently. "I'd like to have someone to talk to while the young people are going about their business."

"Anastasia?" the late Gustav queried. "Is that you, Anastasia?"

"No, Dad," Maijstral said. "Mother's not here."

"Anastasia isn't here?" The ex-Duke sounded disappointed. "I thought I heard her voice."

Maijstral maintained a grip on her patience. "You don't even like her, Dad. Remember?"

Ex-Dornier paused for thought. "Oh. Yes," he said. "That's right. I forgot."

"Isn't Nichole coming?" Tvar asked.

"Not at present," Maijstral said. "No." Tvar's ears drooped in disappointment.

The cold-coffin was shown to its room, and Roman and Drexler were set to work booby-trapping Maijstral's suite for the anticipated descent of Maijstral's unknown enemy. Maijstral, Roberta, and Aunt Batty were given a tour of Tvar's collection, which featured sensational artifacts mixed with sculptures and canvases that inclined in their subject matter toward the lurid. Probably the best was Mixton's *Baroness Kharniver Eating the Heart of Her Lover,* though Maijstral had a sentimental fondness for Actvor's *The Dying Ralph Adverse Gazes on the Shard,* which artfully balanced in its composition the glowing face of the dying burglar, the crystal glass of poison, and the fabulous, shining gem whose original, more luminous than any possible representation, Maijstral had first seen about Roberta's throat, and which he had in short order removed therefrom.

If Maijstral had an appropriate wall to hang the painting on, he might have acquired it for himself. But from his father he'd inherited practically no property at all, no wall, no mantelpiece, no alcove—nothing suitable for displaying anything fine, anyway. His entire domestic establishment consisted of Roman, Drexler, and a large assortment of luggage. If any great artworks came into his hands, they passed out as efficiently as they'd come.

Maijstral looked at Roberta and, with a start, realized that this situation might soon change. Roberta had walls and mantelpieces in abundance. If he married her, he could probably put anything he wanted on them.

What *would* he want on his walls? he wondered. And what steps would he have to take to make certain that none of his colleagues removed what he put there?

"And here," Tvar said, pointing to an instrument glittering in a case, "is the spoon that the Marquess of Tharkar used to remove his heir's eyes during an argument over dessert." Her tongue lolled in amusement.

"What was the argument about?" Batty asked.

"Dessert, as I said."

"I thought you said it was during dessert."

"The argument was *over* dessert, not *during* dessert. They fought over what flavor of sherbet to serve, I think." Tvar's eyes glittered with amusement. "You know, it is generally believed that the Khosali are a lot more steady, reliable, and law-abiding than humans . . . but I must say that when we go bad, we *really go bad.*" She cocked one ear toward Maijstral. "You know, Drake, you might consider spoons as weapons in your next combat."

Maijstral grinned with forced jocularity.

"I will if the other fellow will."

Roberta gave him a superior look. "Oh," she said. "And as to weapons, I have a much better idea than *that.* And by the way, if Captain Hay ever calls, may I borrow Roman for the meeting?"

"Hello?"

Roberta smiled as she saw who had telephoned her. "Will!" she said. "I hadn't expected to hear from you."

"I just called to let you know that J.B.'s been released from the hospital. He broke a cheekbone, and rebroke the nose and lost some teeth, and there are bruises and some nasty cuts—I think from that diamond of Maijstral's—but it's nothing that can't be repaired."

"I'm glad to hear it."

"Yes. He'll soon be good as new—better, once the teeth are replaced with implants." Pause. "You and I are still friends, aren't we? I mean, we can still speak to each other and everything?"

"Of course we can."

"Good. I'm relieved. Because I'd like to express my thanks for your part in forming Maijstral's strategy and keeping everything nonlethal."

"Well," a smile, "I'm afraid I can't claim credit for that. It was all Drake's doing."

"Oh. Well. I suppose I can't exactly call him and thank him, can I?"

"I don't see why not."

"Really?" Brightening. "Do you think it would be good form?"

"Certainly. It wasn't your fight, it wasn't your grudge. If we can all be friends again, so much the better."

"Wonderful. But I don't suppose . . ." A long pause.

"Yes?"

"I don't suppose I can resume my magic lessons."

"Well," laughing, "I think Drake is rather busy now."

"Yes. Of course. But still, it would be very nice to see you—to see you all again."

"I will look forward."

There was the sound of a chime.

"I've got to go, Will. I've got another call."

"Well. Talk to you later, then."

"I'll look forward to it."

Roberta switched to the other call and found herself gazing into the shaded eyes of someone who looked remarkably like Elvis Presley.

"Your grace?" the Elvis said. "I am Major Song. Captain Hay has asked me to act for him in the matter of his fight with Drake Maijstral."

"Ah," Roberta said. "I see."

She took a breath and steeled herself.

She knew exactly what she wanted to do.

Conchita Sparrow blinked in surprise when she saw who had phoned her.

"Miss Sparrow," Maijstral said, "are you busy?"

"I'd imagine that *you'd* be," she said. "What is it, three duels left?"

"I have no intention of keeping track," Maijstral said.

The score would be too depressing in any case.

"The media are full of the story," Conchita said. "Several of the broadcasters seem to have converted to twenty-four-hour Maijstral channels."

That, Maijstral reflected, was too depressing all by itself.

"I was wondering if I could hire you for a few days," he said.

Conchita looked puzzled. "You need me to build some gear?"

"No," Maijstral said. "Not really."

She grinned. "I can't imagine you want to hire me for my burglarizing skills."

"No. Not that, either. I want you to do a tail job."

"It's not really my line of work," she said, ears cocked forward with interest, "but I'm willing to give it a try. Who do you want me to follow?"

"Alice Manderley."

Conchita pursed her lips and whistled. "Well, now *that's* an interesting assignment."

"I thought another burglar would be more likely to understand any countermeasures she'd use. Are you willing?"

"Only too! Where do I find her?"

"The Underwater Palace for the moment, though I expect she'll be leaving in the next day or so. There's only one exit, not counting submarines, so I imagine she'll be easy enough to pick up."

"Sounds right as Robbler."

They spoke about fees and communication protocols for a while, then said their adieux. Maijstral turned away from his suite's phone pickups, a subdued green glow in his lazy eyes, and smiled.

Nichole had provided Diadem security's watch a list of all known burglars in the vicinity of Earth. Of those named, Maijstral judged that only Alice Manderley possessed the skills necessary to have neutralized all the alarms and traps in Maijstral's booby-trapped room at the Underwater Palace.

Which in itself wasn't conclusive, but it was something like a large pointing finger floating in the sky over Alice's head, inscribed with the ideogram for "inquire within."

If in the next few days, Alice took a little detour in the direction of Memphis, then Maijstral fancied he'd know what to do.

Captain Milo Hay looked as if he were battling a hangover in addition to his numerous contusions and bruises. His face was dotted with semilife patches and he moved uneasily, as if it hurt to exert himself.

Or perhaps he was made uneasy by Roman, whom Roberta had brought with her. Hay was apparently a professional xenophobe, and might therefore be expected to be wary of Khosali—but he might be indulged in this instance, as Roman was a sight guaranteed to produce unease in anyone with even the faintest grasp of sanity: skin wrinkled and gone from normal grey to bright pink, nose cracked and bleeding where the new age-ring was coming in, eyes starting from their sockets in a barely repressed psychotic glare.

He was the worst molter Roberta had ever *seen*. But apt, she concluded, to her purpose.

Captain Hay, despite his injuries and the effects of alcohol on his tender system, had nevertheless made an effort and donned the full dress uniform of the Human Guard, as splendid in its way as the white bejeweled outfit of Major Song, who—as ever—was dressed as Elvis.

"A *what?*" Major Song asked.

"Caestus," Roberta said, and fingered the studded leather straps she'd dropped on the table in front of Captain Hay. "It's an ancient Earth weapon, dating, I believe, from the time of the Romans. You strap one on each hand. I was surprised to find the caestus in the Khosali weapons lists, but there you go. They're a very inclusive sort of people."

Unlike others, her tone implied.

Hay picked up the straps and looked at the metal studs designed to crush bone, the hooks meant to tear flesh. He swallowed hard.

Immediately after Major Song's call, Roberta had flown to Alaska to meet with her in person. She wanted to handle this face-to-face.

Major Song hiked up her wide wrestler's belt. "Let me understand this," she said. "You *insist* on using this weapon."

Roberta straightened her spine and flashed a cold look at Captain Hay. "Your principal chose to strike mine with his fist. My principal insists he be allowed the chance to reciprocate."

"But this isn't according to form," Song protested. "You can't just dictate which weapons are to be used. It's up to both seconds to decide."

"Hitting someone without warning isn't according to form either," Roberta pointed out. She flicked her ears carelessly. "Of course, if your principal is afraid of facing the consequences of his behavior . . ."

Hay looked up sharply. "Hey. We never said that."

"We want to follow form," Major Song insisted.

"Let me point out that my principal has already fought one duel—just this morning, in fact. I assume you've seen it on video. He won a complete victory, of course, and with his bare hands." Roberta permitted herself to smile. "Of course, his antagonist was a friend whose continued existence my principal wished to preserve." She looked at Hay. "He doesn't know *you* at all."

A growling noise filled the room. Song and Hay looked in alarm here and there to find the source, and then seemed even more alarmed when they discovered the source was Roman.

Hay turned pale. "Say," he said. "Now, about these weapons . . ."

"That's why we insist on the caestus," Roberta went on. "It might be said that Captain Hay chose fists himself, when he struck my principal, and my principal chose the, ah, *intensity level* of the combat. If it's a formal duel, of course there has to be a chance of death. I'm informed that quite a few ancient Romans died in fights with the caestus, though of course there's a decent chance that, with those heavy studs and hooks, the loser will just be *mutilated* so severely they will be unable to continue . . ."

"*Wait a minute!*" Hay said.

"We *insist* on another weapon!" Major Song said, turning as red as her principal had turned pale.

Roberta looked at her. "Do you have another weapon in mind, or will just *any* other weapon do?"

Major Song opened her mouth, closed it, opened it again.

"I remind you," Roberta said, "that my principal has *nothing to prove* in the matter of his courage, while *your* principal, whose introduction to my principal was by way of a cowardly attack, has everything at stake—either he is a polite individual, fit to be seen in society, or he is not, and so far the evidence is not in his favor."

"Hold on here," Hay said. "All I did was *hit* the man. After what he said the other day, I couldn't help myself once I saw him. It was just . . ." He groped for words.

"A form of political protest," Major Song concluded.

"That's right," Hay said. "I don't see why it really *needs* to go any farther."

Roberta frowned, straightened herself, and looked at Hay. "Is it your contention that striking people is an acceptable form of political protest? And that there is no need for a fair combat as a consequence?"

"Well," Hay said, "yes, I suppose."

Roberta frowned, then shrugged. "If you insist." She turned to Roman and smiled. "I believe, Roman," she said, "that you have several political points to make with Captain Hay?"

Hay's eyes widened. He got out one word—*"Wait!"*—before Roman reached him.

Roberta closed her eyes during the worst of it. The meaty sounds of fists on flesh, the grinding of cartilage and the crack of bone, were quite graphic enough without her having actually to *watch* it.

Once a day for this sort of thing was enough.

Throughout the fight Major Song backed up against the wall and stared at the proceedings with horror. After Roman had finished, Roberta looked at her and nodded.

"I'm pleased we reached an understanding," she said, then took her caestus and left, fingering the media globe in her pocket through which she'd recorded everything.

The next visit would be to Prince Hunac. Unfortunately she anticipated that, with the Prince of Quintana Roo, she'd have to adopt a different strategy.

"Hello?"

Two perfect blue eyes gazed at Maijstral from the video. "Drake. I have some information."

"Oh yes?"

"Concerning the Baron Sancho Sandoval Cabeza de Vaca."

"Oh. Yes."

"He did in fact serve as a junior officer under your grandfather in police actions in Malaysia and on the Indian subcontinent. There is no indication that he and your grandfather ever met."

"I see."

"He and your father seem to have crossed paths on several occasions. They had an assortment of political groups in common."

Maijstral sighed. "No need to go into detail. I can imagine."

"I expect you can."

"The point being," Maijstral said, "*I* never met this man until he walked up to me and started hitting me with his cane. No glory is going to be won by thrashing an elderly nobleman in a fight."

And even less glory, Maijstral added to himself, if it was the elderly nobleman who happened to be the winner.

"I have been looking through the Imperial Sporting Commission's *Manual on Approved Formal Combat Systems,*" Maijstral went on, "hoping to discover if there is some way I can avoid fighting Sandoval, but all I've discovered is that if I object to Sandoval on account of age, the Baron is then allowed to find some strapping young brute as a substitute, and then I have to fight *him.*"

The blue eyes narrowed in concern. "How long is this manual?"

"Over two thousand pages, not counting all the statistics in the appendix. And, as I've discovered, it's not very well indexed."

There was nothing in the index, Maijstral had discovered,

along the lines of *Fights, weaseling out of.*

"Continue your researches, then. Perhaps I will assign several of the Diadem's people to it."

"The Diadem doesn't mind you using their resources this way?"

"Gracious, no. The research boffins love work that has a *real* application. They got all these degrees and things, and here the Diadem sets them to research fashion trends, dig out old video star gossip, and find out which exotic fish rates as a 'must-see' off Cozumel. They *love* having work out of the normal run."

Maijstral smiled. "Well. Thank you."

"And another thing. I've arranged things at Graceland. You will be granted use of the Jungle Meditation Room tomorrow afternoon and all night, beginning at sixteen o'clock."

"Thank you."

The blue eyes looked at him frankly. "I must confess that I was of two minds concerning this business of sending you on to Memphis instead of keeping you here. I may have thrown you into the arms of your young Duchess."

"I haven't forgotten our time together."

"Well," grudgingly, "see that you don't."

There was a gentle chime. "I have another call," Maijstral said.

"Au revoir, then. I'll talk to you tomorrow."

"It's been tomorrow for a couple hours."

"Later today, then."

The blue eyes winked out, were replaced by eyes of violet. The eyes looked very weary.

"Good news. I've settled with Captain Hay, and there won't be a fight. I recorded our entire conversation, so that if he tries to recant or make untrue claims, we can release our version and make him look ridiculous."

Maijstral's heart warmed. "Splendid!"

"I'm sending Roman back to you. And I've just spoken to Prince Hunac. He's still under the influence, a bit, of the stuff he took last night—and I think that's fortunate, because it made him quite suggestible. He has agreed to postpone any confrontation until the situation clarifies."

Maijstral's already-warm heart sparked to a furnace glow. "My dear, if the phone permitted it, I would kiss you full on the mouth."

"I'm too tired for kisses right now." With a yawn. "Prince Hunac has offered me a room here, and I'm going to take it."

"Sleep well."

"What you must do is speak to the media tomorrow and let them know that the Hay matter is settled, and that your quarrel with Prince Hunac is on the verge of being composed. That will force our opposition to make another move— they've *got* to try to frame you again, or give up their plan."

"Nichole just told me that Graceland has become available."

"Excellent. Then you must tell the media of your plans for a religious retreat."

"I will. I'm a hereditary prince-bishop after all—I'll tell the media I'm going to spend a whole night praying for peace."

Laughter lines formed about the violet eyes. "I keep forgetting you're a bishop. You're not very ecclesiastical."

Maijstral composed his face into an expression of piety. "I prefer to keep my devotions private, thank you."

"Well. I'm a hereditary abbess, so I suppose I should not criticize."

"Really? Which order?"

"The Reformed Traditional Hospice Order of the Blessed Spatula."

"Oh. The Spatulans. I've seen their abbeys scattered here and there."

"Yes. And since I'm an abbess, I've got to see the Spatula itself, in a vault in the City of Seven Bright Rings. It's supposed to be an emanation of Gulakh XII the Well-Versed, who is alleged to have ascended bodily to heaven after he retired from the throne."

"An emanation, is it? I wondered why they worshipped a bit of kitchen equipment."

"They take it out of the vault once a year and make a holy omelette with it, and then the celebrants all swallow a piece. The ceremony is quite moving."

"I'm sure."

"My piece was a bit leathery when I tasted it, though." Another lengthy yawn. "I really should turn in. It's been a long day."

"You've more than earned your rest."

"So have you. But you got a nap." Another yawn. "I'll think about Baron Sancho tomorrow."

"I have every confidence in you. Good night."

"Good night."

Maijstral sat for a long moment in his darkened room and contemplated the remarkable women, the galactic superstar and the nobly born Spatulan abbess, who seemed to have taken command of his life.

Not, considering the alternative, that he objected. Not exactly. But he found himself yearning for that blessed time when he had been convinced that he was captain of his fate. That time seemed very remote now, though it had only been a few days ago.

This conviction had been an illusion, as the past days had shown. What had happened? Had he ever really been in command of his life, or had he always been the victim of mysterious forces who had, just recently, turned malevolent and mysterious, whereas before they had been content to permit him to live in illusive ignorance?

He shook his head. He was too tired and beleaguered to work it all out now.

He yawned and picked up his copy of the Sporting Commission's *Manual*. It lay heavy in his lap as he flipped the pages: the sort of reading guaranteed to send him straight to sleep.

And then he encountered, purely by chance, a paragraph that brought him fully awake. Carefully he read it. And, even more carefully, read it again.

Very nice, he thought.

This might just do the trick.

THIRTEEN

❈   ❈   ❈

Media globes winked on high. Maijstral stood beneath the arched gate of Tvar's estate and smiled benignly at the assembled reporters.

"Furthermore," he continued, "I wish to announce that I accept the chastisement of my superior. I refer of course to the Baron Sancho Sandoval Cabeza de Vaca. I hope to reform my behavior, and I thank the Baron for calling my error to public attention."

Take that, Maijstral thought.

A sea of blank faces gazed at him. "What exactly does this mean?" someone asked.

"It means that I accept the Baron's assault as justified, and that I choose not to resent it."

"So you won't be fighting?"

Maijstral detected a tone of outrage in Mangula Arish's voice.

"No," Maijstral said.

There wouldn't be a fight unless Baron Sancho managed

another attack, and Roman and Drexler, standing at Maijstral's side with arms folded in the capacity of bodyguard, were there to prevent just that, as well as keep away any other senile delinquents with violence on their minds.

There was a *very* respectful distance between Roman and any of the crowd of reporters. Just *looking* at him caused any number of people to go pale.

And in the meantime, the Diadem's publicity people, at Nichole's behest, would whisper among the media that Maijstral had chosen this humiliating option out of respect for the Baron's age, and out of concern for his mental health, which—as was plain to observe—was not quite of the best.

But *Maijstral* would say nothing of the sort—nothing for the Baron to object to, nothing that could cause him to issue another challenge.

If Maijstral couldn't have it both ways, what was the point of being a celebrity?

Another reporter scowled up from the mass. "So with the Hay fight cancelled, and the Hunac fight postponed indefinitely, this means you won't be fighting any more duels in the near future?"

Maijstral managed a smile. "Once a week is enough, don't you think?"

The reporters' mood was surly. They'd come for blood—they *depended* on the spilling of blood, and plenty of it—and now it looked as if they were about to be deprived of their feeding frenzy.

"Do you think," Mangula Arish called, "that your opponents are having second thoughts after your victory over Prince Joseph Bob? Do you think their withdrawal might be a reflection on their courage?"

Maijstral resisted the temptation to bounce a rubber ball off Arish's hair, and on reflection judged the question an act of desperation. She was trying to reignite the duelling frenzy through name-calling.

"I have absolutely no reason whatever to question the courage of any of these gentlemen," Maijstral said, "and I hope that if any of my erstwhile opponents chooses to resent the insinuation, they will remember it was you, Mangula Arish, who made it, and not I."

The other reporters chuckled while Arish turned pale at the thought of three enraged, bloodthirsty duellists stalking her.

"I have only one other announcement," Maijstral said. "The nearness of death in the last few days has caused me to reevaluate the condition of my spiritual health. It has occurred to me that I have neglected the religious duties implied by my status as the Hereditary Prince-Bishop of Nana, and I have decided to go on a retreat for the purpose of meditation, fasting, and prayer. The administration of Graceland has very kindly made one of their meditation rooms available for the purpose. I will be going on retreat this afternoon, and will remain in seclusion for an indefinite period. Thank you."

Ignoring shouted questions, Maijstral made his way back to Tvar's manse. Roman and Drexler followed slowly behind, their purpose plain—to pound like a stake into the rich Tennessee soil anyone who might feel the urge to pursue Maijstral and hit him with a fist.

Maijstral entered the mansion and found Tvar waiting for him.

"How did it go, dear?" she asked.

He gave her a Khosali smile, tongue lolling.

"Very well, I think."

Later that day a tailor appeared for Maijstral's fitting. Maijstral didn't travel with his ecclesiastical garments any more than he carried the formal court dress to which he was equally entitled—both were designed for the Khosali physique anyway, and tended to make humans look stunted, aswim in a sea of fabric and ceremonial implements. The tailor managed the complicated ritual garments in jig time, and then Maijstral posed for a long time in his bishop suit, while Drexler thoroughly recorded his image with a holographic video camera.

Later that day one of Tvar's servants—a second footman—stepped out onto the lawn wearing a hologram of Maijstral's image, stepped into a flier piloted by Roman, and was carried off to the Jungle Meditation Room in Graceland. The media waiting before the gate duly followed, thereafter to wait like pilgrims outside the gate of Elvis's city.

The footman would be amply compensated for any fasting, meditation, and prayer he might, in the course of his impersonation, be compelled to undergo.

In the meantime Maijstral, wearing his darksuit and armed to the teeth, sat in ambush in the room next to his suite. Roman, Drexler, Tvar, Kuusinen, and Roberta were arrayed likewise. Tvar's estate now contained a remarkable number of passive detectors—nothing that would broadcast an alarm, for they didn't want any intruder to hear it and run away, they wanted the intruder to come right in and make herself at home.

Alice Manderley, or whoever else was responsible for Maijstral's dilemma, was going to have a nasty surprise in store.

The hours passed slowly. It was after twenty-six o'clock when Maijstral received a phone call on his shielded lines.

"Yes?"

"Mr. Maijstral, this is Conchita."

"Go ahead."

"For some reason I'm not receiving a picture—should I call again?"

"I'm not transmitting a picture. I don't want to activate any pickups."

"Are you on a *job?*"

"Something like that. What news?"

"I thought I'd let you know that Alice Manderley and her husband have left Quintana Roo, and they're flying north. I'm on her trail."

Triumph hummed in Maijstral's nerves. "Very good. Do nothing to alarm her."

"Everything's right as Robbler. She's not evading or anything."

"Excellent. Call again when you have an idea of her destination."

"Right."

Gleeful, Maijstral relayed this news to his confederates and told them to be ready.

Alice was going to have *such* a surprise.

The intruder was delayed only briefly by the screamers on the perimeter of Tvar's estate—they were neutralized by black boxes deployed by an assistant. The approach across the back lawn was made swiftly—a hint of recklessness there, Maijstral thought, there were potential detection problems flying across an open space wearing a darksuit, and the intruder was ignoring them.

Steal from my friends, will you? Maijstral thought fiercely.

The intruder flew to the second floor and began peering in windows. Maijstral restrained the impulse to huddle into the holographic camouflage of his darksuit. He was perfectly well screened from anything the intruder was likely to be carrying with him—energy detectors for the most part, intended to locate alarm systems.

Ram me with a submarine, will you? Maijstral snarled in silence.

The intruder located Maijstral's room without difficulty—some of Maijstral's gear had been left in plain sight to make it easy—and then the window alarms were neutralized swiftly with a black box. The window glass was sliced out and floated skyward on antigravity repellers. The intruder entered, darksuit automatically pulsing out minute compression waves that cancelled the minute compression waves caused by a body floating through the air.

Set me up to get killed, will you? Maijstral demanded.

The intruder floated into the center of the room and hovered, apparently making a survey. Then floated toward the wardrobe that stood in the corner.

Sending a mental command from the proximity wire in the collar of his darksuit, Maijstral triggered his ambush.

Hidden force-field generators slammed invisible walls across the windows, blocking the escape route. The intruder could neutralize them, but it would take time, more time than Maijstral planned to give him.

Roman lunged from the wardrobe, where expert devices had been concealing his body heat, respiration, and very existence. He had a stunner in one hand and a spitfire in the other. He used the stunner first. Energies splashed off the intruder's shields.

More doors crashed open. Micromedia globes deployed in formation, recording everything for scrutiny later. Roberta, Kuusinen, Tvar, and Drexler opened fire. Maijstral slid through his door somewhat less promptly, wary of stray bullets.

"*Surrender!*" Maijstral commanded, and opened fire with his Nana-Coulville spitfire rifle.

The intruder's form, outlined by blazing energies, bounced around the room as if buffeted hither and thither by the blasts of its attackers. Maijstral's detectors showed that its shields were clearly weakening.

"*Surrender!*" Maijstral shouted, firing as fast as he could.

The outside detectors showed that the intruder's assistant was soaring across the back lawn, zooming to the rescue of his employer, setting off a lot of alarms in the process.

The intruder seemed to gather itself as if to spring, then flew swift as an arrow straight for the open window. The arrow hit the shield headfirst with an awesome, meaty thud, then bounced back and drifted toward the floor as if stunned. Drexler, stray fire bouncing from his shields, leaped forward and slapped a palm-sized energy vampire onto the form.

The vampire began sucking energy from the intruder's darksuit and equipment. The holographic camouflage began to shimmer, vanish in places.

"We surrender! Don't shoot!"

The voice came from outside, from the intruder's assistant. Kuusinen sensibly turned his attention toward the newcomer, pointing his heavy chugger toward the window.

The last of the camouflage drained away, revealing the glassy-eyed, twitching form of Laurence, the actor.

"We wanted to teach you a lesson," Deco said, "after you were so mean to us."

"I *was?*" Maijstral said in surprise.

"You *ignored* us," Deco said. "You said you'd never even *seen* Laurence play you on video—and that *had* to have been a lie. A deliberate insult. What sort of person wouldn't watch himself on video?"

Maijstral tried to remember whether he was ever rude to Laurence and Deco, and came up blank. "I never saw the other fellow either," he said. "Anaya."

"It's as if we didn't *exist!*" Deco said. "And you wouldn't even introduce us to Nichole!"

"I wouldn't?"

Maijstral tried hard to remember. He couldn't recall anything about Laurence and Deco at all, other than the fact he'd spoken to them briefly once or twice in the Underwater Palace.

Actors! he thought. They were each a universe unto himself, invincible little egos oblivious to anything but their own boundless need.

"And then," Deco continued, "Laurence called a news conference, announced that he believed in you, and publicly offered to stand as your second for your duels—and what did you do? *You forgot his name!* You didn't even call us!"

Laurence, stripped of his gear and searched for weapons—he hadn't been carrying any—was lying miserably on the carpet in Maijstral's suite. Deco, his assistant, knelt next to him, vocal as his friend was silent. The others stood about them, weapons still in hand.

"It's just that kind of indifference that made us angry," Deco said. "So we decided to teach you a lesson!" He looked at Laurence. "It was my idea, actually. 'Why don't you just sneak into Maijstral's room and steal something?' I said. 'Show him that you exist! Show him that you're *important!*'" He nodded toward Laurence, then looked at Maijstral again. "That's what I said, and that's what we did." His expression turned resentful as he looked up at Maijstral. "You weren't even supposed to *be* here!" he said.

Kuusinen, sitting on the scorched divan with his chugger across his knees, frowned at them both. "Are you claiming," he clarified, "that you aren't responsible for the robberies in Tejas and Quintana Roo?"

At this suggestion, an angry growl emanated from Roman. Deco and Laurence were aghast at this sound, but Deco soldiered on.

"*Maijstral* is to blame for those!" he insisted. "They were *his* robberies, and they went wrong," he nodded primly, "just like ours."

"*Confess!*" Roman roared. "You were jealous! You tried to get Mr. Maijstral killed!" He seized Laurence by the collar and flung him into the air like a rag doll. He caught the actor before he hit the ground and shook him vigorously. Deco, protesting, jumped to his feet and tried to grab Roman's arm, but Roman only seized him with the other hand and shook him, too, then banged his two captives together.

Maijstral, observing, believed that he could watch this forever.

"Fine, fine!" Laurence shouted, speaking at last. "I confess! We did it!"

"But we *didn't!*" Deco protested.

"I confess!" Laurence affirmed. "Let us go!"

Roman dropped them both to the floor at once. "Details!" he demanded. "And make them convincing."

"Whatever you want," Laurence said, a huddled picture of misery and defeat.

At this moment there came the chime of a communications system, and a voice.

"Gleep," it said, somewhat muffled. "Fnerg."

Maijstral listened in puzzlement. He couldn't quite make out the identity of the caller, or the meaning or import of the words.

"Snerk. Yibble."

Roberta, eyes wide, leaped up from her seat. *"Batty!"* she cried, and ran for the door.

Maijstral, following at a run, felt his heart sink. Somehow, he knew, it had all gone wrong again.

He was right. When he ran to Batty's room, he discovered the old Khosalikh lying on the rug, floored by a stunner blast. The padded supports that had held the late Duke of Dornier's coffin were empty.

Maijstral's father, the late Duke of Dornier, had been kidnapped, and his coffin with him.

FOURTEEN

❀ ❀ ❀

Colonel-General Vandergilt was pleased, so pleased that a half-dozen loose strands of hair had escaped her helmet without attracting her notice. A victorious smile played about her lips as she watched a team of Memphis police collecting forensic evidence from Aunt Batty's room.

Aunt Batty herself had been taken to the hospital by Roberta. Stunner blasts could have unfortunate consequences for the elderly.

"It looks as if your gang is falling apart under the pressure," Vandergilt said.

"I don't have a gang," Maijstral pointed out.

"You're connected to all of these people that you're accusing. Laurence glorifies your crimes on video. Alice Manderley is a fellow professional." A superior look crossed her face. "Criminal gangs fall out—it happens all the time."

"Nevertheless," said Paavo Kuusinen as he frowned at Vandergilt, "a crime has been committed against Mr. Maijstral. Do you intend to investigate?"

"Of course," Vandergilt said. She noticed her dangling locks of hair and began methodically stuffing them back into her helmet as she spoke on, her voice cheerful and matter-of-fact.

"We'll do everything possible. Search the room for forensic evidence, put out an alert for the coffin and its, ah, contents. But of course, if we don't find the coffin by tomorrow midnight, it will legally become the property of the thief." Vandergilt looked at Maijstral and smiled. "An element of the current law which I believe you have often used to your advantage, Mr. Maijstral."

"But it isn't as if my father was a painting or a statue or a piece of jewelry," Maijstral said. "He's a *person*. There's no statute of limitations on kidnapping."

Vandergilt considered this. "Your father was declared dead, was he not?"

"Ye-es." Reluctantly. "Almost two years ago."

"Well then, he's not a person. He's inanimate—an *it.*"

"He may be in a box," Maijstral said, "but he still talks. Thinks, after a fashion. Isn't he a dependent, like a child?"

"I'm afraid not," said attorney Kuusinen. "The Constellation follows Empire law in this regard. After being declared dead, the elderly are considered keepsakes—like Lady Scarlett's liver, downstairs. Otherwise there could be no Imperial succession—no one could be crowned Emperor if his precedessors still retained their legal existence."

"Admirably put, Mr. Kuusinen," Vandergilt said with a thin smile. Her eyes glittered as they turned to Maijstral. "Another of those archaic Imperial laws causing trouble for you, Mr. Maijstral. What a pity that the Constellation Practices Authority hasn't got around to fixing that yet—but with the Burglars' Association putting up such resistance to the Authority's efforts to remove protections from Allowed Burglary, their other vital work has been delayed."

Another lock of hair was working its way from under the shiny brim of Vandergilt's helmet. Maijstral wanted to grab it and yank it out by the roots.

"Perhaps," Kuusinen said, perceiving perhaps the dangerous look in Maijstral's eye, "we should let the authorities do their work."

Maijstral withdrew, his blood simmering. Stealing his *father!*

It wasn't as if he'd exactly miss Gustav Maijstral if the late Duke dropped out of his life once and for all. But the theft itself was as vile an insult as he'd ever experienced. It wasn't as if Maijstral's father was in any way valuable property. The entire theft had been aimed at Maijstral himself. *Take this*, the theft said, *and suffer.*

The necessity for action coursed through Maijstral's veins. In another type of personality—the Prince of Tejas, say—the action might be to stand in fair combat on a distant beach, dire staff in hand.

Maijstral's character demanded another form of action.

He didn't want to fight. He wanted to *get even.*

"We need a council of war," Kuusinen said.

"Yes," Maijstral said.

"Perhaps at the hospital. Miss Batty may be able to give us some clues."

Maijstral could have said that she wouldn't—the most she would have seen would have been the vague outline of a darksuit against the window before the stunner blast rendered any perceptions unreliable—but he assented anyway.

He needed to get away from Colonel-General Vandergilt while he was still master of his passions.

It wasn't as if he would ever assault Vandergilt, but on the other hand the mental image of Vandergilt's home—a home stripped of all furniture, all clothing, all possessions— was floating insistently before his mental eye. But robbing

Denise Vandergilt would be a very, very dangerous thing to do.

And it wouldn't help a bit with recovering Maijstral's father.

Where am I?

A sinister laugh. *Welcome to . . . Hell!*

I don't recall being on a planet called Hell. I was—it was Earth, wasn't it? Yes, I'm almost certain it was. I was going to have cocoa.

There's no cocoa in Hell, Dornier!

Isn't there? We must be in the provinces. I will have some nice warm milk, then.

You can't have milk, Dornier. You're dead!

Oh . . . You're right. I forgot.

You won't forget it anymore, Dornier. You're in Hell— the afterlife designed for punishment.

Oh . . . ? Really . . . ? That sounds like a most unpleasant place.

It is. It's meant to be unpleasant.

Take me home at once. No—not home, take me to Earth.

You're in Hell, Dornier!

. . . There was some reason why I was on Earth. I forget.

Hell, *Dornier!* Hell!

I forget so much these days.

I said you're in Hell!

Yes, you keep repeating that. I wish you wouldn't. I heard you perfectly well the first time.

You're going to be here forever and ever! You're going to undergo eternal punishment!

Are you . . . Jacko?

Jacko! Of course I'm not Jacko!

Oh. I thought perhaps you might be. I thought I heard his voice.

I'm not Jacko, and this is Hell!

My dear fellow, I wish you wouldn't keep repeating that. You're becoming quite a tiresome person really.

You're going to be here forever and ever. Your punishment will never end.

Gracious, you do go on. Beat. I don't suppose you'd know if I could get a nice cup of cocoa, could you?

"Stealing Drake's father was a particularly malicious touch," Aunt Batty said. "I suspect we are looking for a person who is not entirely rational in his hatreds."

"Well," Maijstral wondered. "Who is?"

Batty was propped up on pillows and seemed reasonably comfortable in her hospital bed. Roberta's servants had brought her an embroidered nightdress and cap from her own wardrobe. The cap had two holes in it for her pointed ears.

If Batty was suffering any ill effects, they were well concealed. She lapped tea delicately from a saucer and seemed, on the whole, fully recovered.

Maijstral, Roberta, and Kuusinen sat in a respectful circle around her. Roman and Drexler were back at Tvar's place, making certain that the police neither stole anything nor planted any evidence. After the police finally left, Roman would fetch the false Maijstral back from Graceland and rescue the poor fellow from his regimen of fasting, meditation, and prayer.

Laurence and Deco were in police custody. Tvar, the householder, of a more practical and vengeful bent than the Princes of Tejas and Quintana Roo, had announced she intended to press charges.

Kuusinen dropped his teacup noiselessly into his saucer. "The thing that is beginning to signify," he said, "is the motif of the family that plays throughout Mr. Maijstral's recent experiences. The media demanding some sort of apology for the behavior of his grandfather, the late Duke Robert. Hay challenging him on account of his grandfather's behavior while Baron Sancho challenges him out of a misplaced loyalty to the same grandfather. And now Maijstral's father, who spent his life defending Duke Robert's behavior, has been kidnapped."

He looked levelly at Maijstral. "I think whoever is responsible for your predicament has a grudge against your entire family. Perhaps any hatred for you is incidental to hatred for your grandfather."

Roberta looked puzzled. "Who would hate your grandfather?"

"Thousands of people," Maijstral sighed. "*Tens* of thousands."

Roberta was startled. "Good grief. I know he was a famous Imperialist, but what exactly did he do to raise such ire?"

"Your question demonstrates that your education was on the Imperial side of the border—the Empire was so embarrassed by my grandfather that they don't talk about him much. He's barely mentioned in the official histories. But here in the Constellation, he's the bogeyman—the ultimate oppressor, the ultimate traitor, the ultimate bad example."

Roberta's eyes widened. "But what did he *do?*"

"Killed," Maijstral said, "tortured, threw people in prison without a hearing—here in the Constellation he's known as Robert the Butcher. He was far more excessive than any Khosali in defense of the Khosali Emperor. The Khosali were so appalled by his excesses that, after he fled to the Empire, they never employed him again—just let him live on his pension. They disbanded the Green Legion so that he'd never get the chance to use it in another war. One reason that I don't use my title is that I don't want to be called *Dornier*—it's a term of loathing here."

"*Tens* of thousands," Roberta repeated. "That's a lot of suspects."

"Mr. Maijstral's problems didn't begin till he arrived on

Earth," Kuusinen observed, "so I think we can narrow our investigations to Earth residents."

Maijstral wanted to grind his teeth. "I *meant* tens of thousands of Earth residents," he said.

"I think I may be able to narrow your range," said the voice of Conchita Sparrow. Camouflage holograms shimmered off, and she appeared above them, hovering near the ceiling. She flashed a grin at her own ingenuity and then dropped to the floor. Her grin froze as she observed that Roberta was pointing a very businesslike pistol at her.

"Am I interrupting something important?" she asked.

"Roberta," Maijstral said, "may I introduce Conchita Sparrow, a colleague. I have hired her to perform certain investigations on my behalf."

"I would have dropped in earlier," Conchita said, "but there were cops all over Tvar's place, and I preferred not to call attention to myself."

"Very wise of you," Maijstral said.

Roberta put her pistol away, folded her arms, and looked severe. "I wish you had told me that you were employing an agent," she said.

Maijstral, having seen that stern expression before, decided to tread warily.

"My apologies for not telling you," he said. "But you were on your way to Cozumel at the time and since then, well, we've been busy." He looked at Conchita. "You have news?"

Conchita eyed Roberta warily. "Can I talk in front of these people?"

Roberta's eyes flashed.

"You may," Maijstral said hastily.

"Well," Conchita said, "I was following Alice Manderley, but I lost her."

"Is that *it?*" Roberta demanded. "That's all you have to report?"

Conchita flashed her an annoyed look. "As a matter of pickles, it ain't," she said, and then turned to Maijstral. "She was in this bright orange Iridescent flier, a real flash job, and got in the flier with her husband. She opaqued the glass as soon as she took off, so I only had the Iridescent to follow, but the flier is so distinctive that there really wasn't any problem. I followed her flier to a garage in Alburquerque. A medium-sized cargo carrier flew out a few minutes later, followed by Manderley's flier, and so I followed Manderley. But when the flier landed in Vancouver, only the husband got out. Manderley had given me the slip."

"Was the cargo flier large enough to carry, say, a coffin?" Maijstral asked.

"You bet," Conchita said. "And there's more. After I lost Manderley, I thought I'd fly to Memphis and see if you had any more instructions for me. And as I was coming in for a landing, I saw the cargo flier taking off from that patch of woods just north of here."

"The *same* cargo flier?" Kuusinen asked. "You're sure?"

"Photon Twelve, brown with white stripe, registration number HHD458772N," Conchita said.

Kuusinen nodded. "Very good, Miss Sparrow," he said.

"I figured something was up, so I followed the flier. But it didn't go very far—it just hopped over the trees to Grace-land and landed there."

"Graceland?" Roberta said in surprise.

"*Graceland?*" Maijstral wondered.

"Graceland?" said Kuusinen.

"Oh my," Batty said, her ears cocking forward with interest. "*Graceland.*"

"Graceland," Conchita smiled, and then continued. "She landed in one of the central landing stages, right in the middle of the whole complex. The airspace was restricted and I couldn't hover overhead indefinitely, and anyway the flier moved under cover almost at once. I tried to find some place to observe from, but I couldn't see anything, so I thought I'd better give you a report. But when I got to Tvar's, I saw the place swarming with cops, so I waited until you came out, and then I followed you here."

"My compliments, Miss Sparrow," Kuusinen said. "You have done very well indeed."

Roberta produced her pistol again, twirling it around her finger. "I think it is time to get our hands on this Alice Manderley," she said. "Perhaps we can lay an ambush near Graceland and wait for her to leave."

"She could be anywhere by now," Conchita pointed out.

"We should get ahold of Kenny Chang," Maijstral said. "Alice will do anything to keep us from damaging her husband. For some inexplicable freak of character she's devoted to him."

Get even, he thought, and a little triumphant hum smiled its sinister way along his nerves.

He rose from his chair and turned to Batty. "If you'll forgive me," he said, "I'd like to set Roman and Drexler to work." The thought of Kenny Chang in Roman's hands caused him to smile. "We have a long night's work ahead of us," he said.

"Have a lovely kidnapping, dear," Batty said. Maijstral and Batty sniffed ears, and Maijstral left, followed by Kuusinen. Roberta remained behind to comfort the invalid.

From the hospital lobby, Maijstral called Roman to ask whether he'd gone to Graceland to pick up the false bishop, and was told that the police were just leaving: Maijstral told him to wait. He then called Nichole. When her hologram appeared, her face showed concern.

"Well timed, Drake," she said. "I was on the verge of calling you. My researchers have come up with some alarming news concerning Alice Manderley."

"That she stole the stele, and took my father's coffin this afternoon?"

Nichole received the news without surprise. "Indeed yes—or so the information implies. Your . . . *losing* . . . your father in such a way distresses me."

"You've heard?"

"Of course."

"Have you heard that Alice took him to Graceland?"

She looked thoughtful. "No. I hadn't heard that. But it makes sense in light of what I'm about to tell you."

"Indeed?"

Nichole's admirable brow wrinkled. "Are you speaking privately?"

Maijstral glanced over his shoulder. "Mr. Kuusinen is here."

"Could you engage the screen, please?"

Maijstral hesitated for a moment, then nodded. "If you wish."

He turned to Kuusinen. "My apologies, sir."

Kuusinen acknowledged the apology with a graceful wave, and Maijstral activated the privacy field. He turned to face the phone pickups.

"Yes? Why the urgency?"

"I have some financial information, gathered quite illegally, and I would prefer not to have to admit how I got it before any third parties. Particularly an attorney who seems to be infamous for remembering odd facts and who may have some professional obligation to speak honestly in front of a judge."

"I recall your mentioning that Alice had received a sum of five hundred novae," Maijstral said.

"Yes, though all that information cost me was an inscribed recording of my last play. The *next* mass of data is going to cost me a private dinner with the Chief Auditor of the Constellation Bank."

"I am sure anticipation has him all aquiver." Maijstral laughed. "Nichole, have I mentioned lately my exceeding admiration for you? Your resources never cease to amaze."

"Oh, my news is amazing all right. Alice was paid five hundred novae just before she arrived here from Qwarism. She was paid another five hundred within hours after the stele turned up under your bed. And she was paid a third five hundred earlier this evening, after your father was stolen."

"Fifteen hundred," Maijstral said. "That's a pension generous enough to support Alice for life. Or Kenny for a month. But who can afford to pay them sums that large?"

Nichole looked at him levelly. "The money came from the account of Major Ruth Song."

Maijstral was staggered. "The *Elvis?*"

Nichole gave an incredulous laugh. "That explains Graceland, doesn't it?"

Maijstral tried to rein in the astonished thought-imps that seemed to be running amuck in his brain. "Here I thought she was merely a political crank. Now I discover she's fanatic enough to spend a fortune to kill and discredit me."

"Remember her grandfather, the Fleet Admiral? The Nelson of Neerwinden?"

"Yes."

"Well it turns out his *first* wife, no relation to Miss Song at all, died in police custody in a roundup of the relatives of rebel leaders."

"A roundup ordered by my grandfather."

"Exactly. Though it appears that her death was an accident, a mistake by the doctor called in to treat her for some long-standing condition."

Maijstral tried to work this out. "So Major Song has organized this complex and highly expensive conspiracy in order to avenge the death of some stepgrandmother she never met and isn't in any case related to?"

"So it appears."

Maijstral shook his head. "There's got to be more to it than that."

Nichole looked exasperated. "She's just *crazy*, Drake! You don't need any other explanation than that. She not only inherited her political convictions from her grandfather, but her religious ones as well. The late Fleet Admiral Song became a convert to Elvis late in life, and he endowed Graceland with one of its showiest pavilions. He's buried in the mausoleum and sleeps forever in the Arms of Elvis. Major Song is one of the most important lay sisters in the faith, and she has an apartment in Graceland itself."

Maijstral stiffened. "I have a feeling she's got something in that apartment that I want back."

"Very possibly."

"I'll go there directly. But in the meantime I need you to call Kenny Chang and arrange an appointment with him. Tell him you've got a part that's just right for him, and that you'd like to meet him as soon as possible. Tomorrow morning would be nice. Can you do that?"

"Of course. And I take it that it will be you and Roman who keep this appointment, not me?"

"Naturally."

She gave a sigh of relief. "Oh, good. Kenny's so utterly dreary I'd hate to have to really meet him. The phone call will be bad enough."

Maijstral bowed toward the pickups. "Thank you, my dear. I'll call you tomorrow."

He made as if to leave, but Nichole fixed him with an urgent look. "One more thing, Drake. This is important."

"Yes?"

"Major Song has made other payments."

A warning hum sounded in Maijstral's mind.

"To whom?"

"Drexler. Three payments of twenty novae each. The first a few days before you arrived on Earth, then just after the Tejas theft, and again just this afternoon."

Maijstral looked down at his hands and found they were miming the act of closing around Drexler's throat.

Taking dead aim. That's what Song and her conspirators had done to him.

And he was about to take dead aim himself.

"*Thank* you," he said. "I will deal with this at once."

"I know you will, Drake. Give my love to Roman, will you?"

"Oh absolutely." He smiled. "Once he's finished giving *my* love to Drexler."

Maijstral hastened into the servants' parlor, followed by Tvar.

"Roman," he said. "Drexler."

"Sir. Miss Tvar."

Roman and Drexler rose hastily. They had been monitoring Tvar's security gear on the unlikely but hopeful theory that the mystery burglar might return.

"Oh. Sorry." Maijstral, bustling into the room, had brushed against Drexler.

"My fault, boss."

Maijstral smiled at him thinly. "Yes. I'm afraid so."

Drexler's ears cocked forward. "Boss?"

Maijstral stepped back and regarded him. "I confess a certain surprise to discover just how cheaply you work."

Drexler's fingers twitched, advancing toward the opening of his jacket. His sturdy body seemed to inflate slightly. "Boss?" he said.

"Alice Manderley was paid more than you by a factor of more than twenty, and all for doing the same job. Stealing, I mean, and planting the goods in my room."

Drexler made his move, his hand diving into his armpit. His eyes widened and his ears cocked forward.

"Looking for this?" Maijstral said, and produced the pistol he had just snaked from Drexler's holster.

Maijstral's next line would have been, "Roman, secure this traitor!", but he never got it out.

Roman had anticipated him. Drexler barely had time for a yelp of dismay before Roman had seized him by his crotch and throat, upended him, and dashed him skull-first to the floor.

There was a horrible crunch as vertebrae compacted. Drexler collapsed, his limbs atwitch. Maijstral frowned down at him.

"Roman," he said, "I wanted him in a condition to answer questions."

"Sorry, sir."

"Well." He shrugged. "As long as he's unconscious, search him for further weapons and any communications or flight devices. Then—" He turned to Tvar. "If Miss Tvar will provide us with the room in the house most resembling a jail cell?"

Tvar's tongue cheerfully lolled from her muzzle. "Lightless?" she asked. "Airless, dark? With stone walls to prevent any escape by burrowing?"

"Something like that, yes."

"I believe I have a place suitable to the purpose. It's the room in which Savage Simon used to confine his victims—I bought it entire and had it shipped here from Kualu." Her expression brightened. "I also have a number of his original instruments. For atmosphere."

Maijstral turned back to Roman. "Secure Drexler and put him there. We'll talk to him when he's conscious."

"Very good, sir." Roman took a detector and began patting Drexler down. Finding nothing suspicious, he picked the other Khosalikh up by the collar and dangled him like a child's doll.

Maijstral turned to Tvar. "Miss, if you could show Roman to the dungeon?"

"Delighted."

"Roman, after you've secured the prisoner, I will require you to take me and Conchita Sparrow to Graceland."

Roman paused in the act of carrying Drexler from the room. "Miss Sparrow, sir?"

"We're going to need a tech," Maijstral said, "and she's available."

"Hrrrr," Roman growled meditatively. Then, "Very good, sir."

"Carry on."

Maijstral, busy though he was, paused for a moment to enjoy the sight of Roman carrying away the unconscious Drexler.

Though he could not realistically consider himself the captain of his fate once more, Maijstral thought, he'd at least managed a self-promotion. To warrant officer, perhaps, or maybe even lieutenant.

FIFTEEN

❀   ❀   ❀

*Y*ou were a spy for the Empire, Dornier!

A spy? Oh don't be silly. What do you take me for, a member of the Secret Dragoons?

You belonged to the Imperial Circuit. The High Custom Association. The Nostalgia Party. The Imperial Armed Forces Relief and Reunion Society. The Empire Party. The Old Nobles' Association. . . .

Oh yes, the Old Nobles. What a splendid bunch of fellows they all were.

You conspired with them! Conspired against the Constellation!

We had such splendid plans for when the Emperor returns . . .

You admit it!

Of course. None of it was secret. You can read our minutes in our publications. . . .

It's the secret parts I want you to confess. Who gathered the information? Who were the spies?

I don't know what you're blithering about. . . .

The Old Nobles' Association! Who were the spies?

The Old Nobles . . . so jolly. So jolly.

What were their names?

You aren't Bertie, are you?

Bertie? Who's Bertie?

Such chums we were. We went to school together, you know.

I'm not Bertie!

Such a fellow for pranks he was. This is just like one of Bertie's jolly games, you know.

This is no game, Dornier!

He'd sneak up on you at night and shout 'Boo.' What laughs we had. You're just like him, you know.

I'm your inquisitor, and this is Hell!

Oh yes. I forgot.

This is going to last forever, *Dornier. Forever!*

Oh, surely not. I'm sure I've got an appointment somewhere. . . .

Dornier! Listen to me!

. . . Now was it on Earth, or someplace else? I wish I could remember.

The two Graceland security guards, making their rounds, quailed visibly as Roman loomed out of the darkness. "Halt!" one of them squeaked.

In Roman's shadow was Conchita Sparrow, dressed in a hooded cloak against the night air, and carrying a tray on which rested some pieces of fine porcelain. Roman approached the guards, growling ominously.

He was having a hard time controlling his growl reflex.

One of the guards cleared her throat. "What is your business?"

"I am bringing a pot of restorative tea to the Prince-

Bishop of Nana in the Jungle Meditation Room."

The guards both looked relieved that Roman's answer hadn't been something to the effect of, "I am here to yank your spines out through your necks."

"Pass," one of them said.

Roman passed, growling.

Their wide eyes fixed on Roman, neither guard noticed the slight distortion in the air over their heads that marked the passage of a well-known thief in a darksuit.

Maijstral entered the Jungle Meditation Room and paused for a moment to let his eyes, and his staggered sanity, adjust. He had known that Graceland was renowned for the extravagance of its decor—all the minarets and domes made that clear enough—but he had never seen anything like *this*.

The ferns and the full-sized palm trees that reached toward the domed ceiling, the dome itself covered with an allegorical fresco of Elvis Vanquishing the Blues, its principal figure glittering with sequins, crowned with stars, and with its feet planted on a sunset pink cloud. The animal skins, most with heads attached, that covered the floor in layers. The fall that poured silver water, like a stream of mercury, into a pool lined with lava rocks. The shields, spears, and more exotic weapons that massed on the walls, enough to outfit a barbarian army. The stuffed rhinoceros—at least Maijstral *assumed* it was stuffed. The elephant tusks planted in rows. The furniture covered with hide.

The most normal thing in Maijstral's view was the sight of himself, Drake Maijstral, dressed in ecclesiastical robes and snoring on one of the hide-covered couches.

Maijstral floated toward the couch, dropped to his feet, and turned off the darksuit's holographic camouflage.

"Martin."

The snoring Maijstral awoke with a start.

"Sir!" He jumped to his feet and turned off the hologram that made him look like Maijstral, revealing himself as a small-ish human with a shock of blond hair. "I hadn't expected you."

"Has anything occurred, Martin?"

"Just after I got here one of the Elvii—Elvis XXIII—called to offer you a personal tour of Graceland tomorrow. I thanked him for his kindness but explained that I was not certain my schedule would permit."

"That was well said, Martin. Thank you."

Martin smiled. "It was interesting being a celebrity for a few hours, at least."

"I'm afraid your moment of fame must come to an end." He gestured toward Conchita and Roman, who had silently entered behind him. "I need you to don Miss Sparrow's cloak and leave with Roman."

Martin bowed gracefully. "Very good, sir. Would you like me to instruct you in the workings of the sound effects and video?"

This statement was sufficiently intriguing that Maijstral, though pressed for time, agreed. Martin led Maijstral to a service plate and touched the ideogram for "sound." Immediately the dome began to echo with howling monkeys, bird-calls, and the distant roars of hunting beasts.

"A bit overwhelming, I'm afraid," Martin explained. "They were interfering with my, ah, meditations, so I shut them off."

"Please do so again."

"Yes, sir."

"And the video?"

"There are a great many projectors under the dome, so you can watch several videos at once."

"What videos are they?"

"Oh—a wide selection, sir. You reach the catalogue by

touching this ideogram. There are several of Elvis himself—gathered from primitive media, one gathers—but I'm afraid I'm somewhat Elvis-deaf, if I may coin a phrase, so I haven't sampled them."

"Very good. Thank you, Martin."

Maijstral passed Martin the agreed-upon sum, plus a bonus. Martin smiled, pocketed the cash, and offered, first, his thanks, and second, his congé.

Maijstral turned to Roman. "Return Martin to Miss Tvar's, then stand by with the vehicle. If I find my father, I'll probably need help in getting him away."

"Yes, sir," Roman said.

Martin and Roman took their leave, Martin looking nervously over his shoulder at the continual sound of Roman's growling. Maijstral looked at Conchita.

"Are we ready?"

She grinned. Beneath the cloak she'd been wearing a silver-grey darksuit, and now she triggered the holographic camouflage.

"Fingo all right, boss," she said.

As he flew off into the darkness, Maijstral made a note to himself to find an opportunity to ask Conchita just what that piece of cant actually meant.

"Pardon me, sir," said the Baron Sancho Sandoval Cabeza de Vaca, "but is there a Mangula Arish here?"

Graceland glowed on the near horizon, astonishing, fabulous, and perfectly at one with itself. Outside the gates clustered the vigilant and faithful media, hoping for a glimpse of Maijstral, though an earthquake or a bloody riot would have worked just as well. One of the reporters nodded.

"The lady over there," he said, pointing. "With the high-impact hairstyle."

"Thank you, sir."

Baron Sancho squared his shoulders and marched toward his target. Mangula was preoccupied with controlling the media globes she'd deployed around the Graceland perimeter, and paid little attention to the approach of the erect, elderly figure until the Baron, who was too gentlemanly to use his cane on a woman, slapped her neatly across the face with a silk-lined glove.

"Call me a coward, will you?" he demanded. "I demand satisfaction!"

Mangula stared at him for a moment, and then, both to his surprise and hers, turned and fled into the night.

No luck. No luck at all.

There was no sign of Maijstral's father in the apartment that Major Song kept here, and no sign of Major Song either. There was no apartment assigned to Alice Manderley, but she could have been hiding or using a pseudonym, or hiding Maijstral's father in the apartment of an unknown confederate, so Maijstral and Conchita were faced with the tedious prospect of checking every single apartment in the blocks assigned to visitors. And with the Memphis Olympiad coming up in a few days, the greatest orgy of Elvis impersonation in all civilization, the apartments were almost all full.

"Did Elvis actually *live* amid all this?" Maijstral asked. "Legend would have us believe he was a simple country lad."

"Oh no," Conchita said. "The original Graceland wasn't very large—well, it was small compared to Tvar's place anyway—but it was destroyed in the New Madrid Earthquake centuries ago. Since then Elvis's admirers have built what I believe are termed 'creative reinterpretations' of the original."

"I wish they had been less lavish," Maijstral said.

Conchita looked glum. "I wish they had been less numerous."

Fortunately there were few places in any given apartment

where something the size of a cold-coffin could be hidden, so each apartment could be checked fairly quickly. But even so the eastern horizon had turned pale by the time Maijstral and Conchita had finished.

"There's only one set of apartments we haven't checked," Maijstral said, speaking over their coded communications link. "The Elvii themselves."

"Oh no." Behind her holographic camouflage, Conchita sounded shocked. "They wouldn't, would they?"

"All it takes is one fanatic."

"I suppose." She sighed. "But the place is so *huge.*"

"Let's do it quick, the sun will be up in a minute."

"Right."

They soared off to the extravagant Pavilion of the Elvii, the nerve center of Graceland, where the Clones of Elvis, all reconstituted from the original's remains and genetically identical to the King Himself, administered the huge empire that was in their charge.

There was the cult center, with its priests and temples. (Elvis had not yet been added to the official Khosali pantheon, but there were hopes.) There was the vast acreage of Graceland itself, a giant center for tourism. There were concert halls and auditoriums. There was the Memphis Olympiad, where Elvis impersonators from all over the galaxy competed for the prize of the Championship Belt. And there were royalties to collect, licenses to grant, and concessions to administer.

No one in Graceland was in danger of going broke.

The security was formidable around the area: guards marching in pairs, and the place was studded with detectors that required the full complement of Conchita's black boxes to overcome. Peering in the windows with their detectors deployed, Maijstral and Conchita observed the Elvii—old Elvii, young Elvii, fat Elvii, and thin Elvii, Elvii sleeping and Elvii meditating, Elvii eating and Elvii fasting . . . Elvii, Elvii everywhere . . . but no coffin could be found.

"Thagger," Maijstral swore. "I've had it. The sun's up, let's get out of here."

He was sweating, but not as a result of heat from the rising sun. The distortion caused by their darksuits was much more apparent in full daylight than at night, and there were more people about to observe them. Detection was an ever-increasing possibility.

"There's an Elvis coming," Conchita warned. "Better wait."

The Elvis in question was an elderly one, with thinning white hair. He was mounted on an imitation panhead Harley (training wheels extended) that gave a gentle electric whirr as it coasted up to the gate of the Residence. The Elvis parked the bike, then walked to the gates (ornamented with old human-style musical notes covered in gold leaf) which parted silently in his path.

Maijstral's mind snapped to attention.

"Wait a moment," he said. "How did the gates know to let him in?"

The elderly Elvis ambled up the path (huge slabs of emerald and ruby cut from asteroid material) and toward the doors (trefoil wood from Canther, carved with reliefs of Elvis Healing the Deaf), which likewise parted without a challenge.

"He's got to have some kind of identification that takes him through security," Conchita said.

"If we can get one, we can enter anywhere."

"Especially if we look like Elvis."

"Let's steal one."

"Right, boss."

As they reached this decision, the elderly Elvis became visible again, rising to the top of one of the Pavilion's towers (sheathed in green jade and carved with dragons) in one of the

Pavilion's exterior glass elevators (in the boxy form of an antique microphone). Maijstral and Conchita flew to the top of the tower (carved in the shape of a giant lotus), where they watched through window glass (inscribed with an image of Elvis Negotiating a Peace with the Aborigine Geronimo) as the Elvis yawned, removed his vestments, and headed for the shower. Maijstral swiftly neutralized the tower room's various alarms—easily spotted because they were in the shape of grimacing demon masks—opened a window, and flew in to pass his detectors over the Elvis's discarded clothing. A diamond-studded pin in the shape of an ancient Cadillac ground vehicle responded with a complicated energy pattern, and Maijstral removed it.

"Are you certain that's it?" Conchita asked, as he closed the window behind him.

"No. We'd better test it."

He flew down to one of the Pavilion's doors and dropped the pin onto the stoop. No alarms rang. The doors silently opened. Maijstral dropped to retrieve the pin and then made a careful, zigzag flight back to the Jungle Meditation Room.

"I want you to analyze this pin and duplicate it," he instructed as he pulled on his clerical vestments over his dark-suit. "If that Elvis has the seniority I suspect he does, it should get us in anywhere."

"We'd have to move fast, boss," Conchita said. "Once the Elvii find out this pin is missing, they'll reprogram their computers to call security instead of open doors."

"I suspect the old fellow just got off duty and is heading for bed. So we'll have some hours, anyway."

"I hope he's due for a long rest." She took the pin, looked at it for a moment, and then put it in a pocket. "Well," she said, "I'll fly out of here."

"Thank you, Conchita. You've done very well."

"Yeah." She grinned. "I usually create a catastrophe by this point, but I haven't embarrassed myself yet, have I?"

"No, you haven't."

"I'll try to keep it up, then."

She turned on her camouflage and flew toward the doors, which opened at her touch. She gave a yelp, and then the doors closed and Conchita reappeared.

"Guards, boss! Hundreds of them!"

Maijstral's heart crashed in his chest as he hastened to the doors. He opened them a crack and peered out. Uniformed guards were, in fact, pouring into the open square outside. But they were forming ranks and facing to Maijstral's right, not assuming assault positions, and they were dressed in fatigue uniforms, not armed and armored for battle. He closed the doors and turned to Conchita.

"It looks like a morning formation," he said. "They'll probably disperse after receiving their instructions."

Relief flooded Conchita's face. "For a minute I thought I'd done something horribly wrong again."

"Wait until they disperse before you leave. All it takes is for one of them to look in your direction as you fly out, and the jig's up."

"Right, boss."

He sat on the meditation couch and looked at the tea that Conchita had brought earlier. "Is there real tea in here?"

"Sure. Shall I tell the pot to warm it up again?"

"By all means."

Conchita sat next to Maijstral on the couch and gave the pot its instructions. Maijstral stretched and yawned.

"I wonder how long it's been since I've slept."

"You look tense, boss. Why don't I give you a massage? It'll perk you up."

"That would be nice. Thank you." Maijstral offered her his back. Conchita's small hands proved surprisingly strong and effective in finding the knots in Maijstral's muscles and dispersing them. He straightened, his back tingling with pleasure.

"Thank you," he said. "That was very considerate."

He glanced up, saw her looking at him.

"Oh," he said. After a moment's thought, he put his arms around her.

"It's about time you noticed," Conchita said. "I haven't been hanging around in your air ducts just for the fun of it."

"Sorry," Maijstral said. "But I've been distracted."

"I'll forgive you," she said, "if you'll kiss me right this second."

"Very well," Maijstral said, and did so.

In the matter of being captain of his fate, he thought, perhaps he could just leave the tiller unattended for a while.

SIXTEEN

✳ ✳ ✳

Let us review your sins, Dornier.

Excuse me?

Your sins, Dornier, your sins!

Oh for gracious sake. Why do you keep repeating yourself?

Because you don't seem to comprehend your position!

Oh, I understand it perfectly well. I'm in this, ummm, Hell place, and I'm supposed to, to . . . oh, what is that word again?

Atone, Dornier! Atone!

Oh yes. That's it.

I call to your attention the League for Imperial Youth.

Ah yes. We had the most jolly meetings.

An attempt to corrupt the children of the Constellation with alien ideas!

Oh, what rot. You talk the most amazing brand of stuff, do you know? Stuff and . . . what's the other word?

I'm here to force you to confront your past! To admit that you conspired against the Constellation by corrupting its children.

We had sing-alongs at our meetings. And nice little cakes that Miss Ginko sent up from the bakery.

You conspired, Dornier! Conspired!

Lovely little cakes with strawberries on them. And those creamy sort of buns that have that, you know, filling. And then the kind with the little nuts on them. I wish I could have a taste of them now. . . .

Confess your crimes, Dornier!

. . . What are those nuts called again?

Never mind the nuts, Dornier! You must confront the reality of your crimes and confess!

I can almost taste those buns . . . You wouldn't have one or two in the pantry, would you?

No! You're dead and in Hell! There'll be no more buns for you!

No buns? What a pity. Perhaps a little biscuit with jam, then?

You're dead! You're dead! You can't have a biscuit!

Oh that's right. Sorry.

Now, Dornier. We'll begin again. And pay attention this time.

If you just keep repeating yourself, my dear fellow, I don't see why I should.

I'm not your dear fellow!

Well, yes. That's obvious enough, I should think. But there's no reason not to be polite, even in Hell.

"The guards are dispersing. You'll be able to leave in another moment."

"Fingo all right, boss."

"I'll call Roman and have him bring me out in the flier. It looks as if he and I will have a busy morning. But I want you to get started on breaking the code of the Elvii right away."

"It'll be a piece of cake."

Beat.

"Conchita?"

"Yes?"

"You wouldn't mind answering a question, would you?"

"Only too, boss."

"You're not planning on marrying me, are you?"

"Why? Are you about to pop the question?"

"Frankly, no."

"Well, that's only sensible. You should get to know me first. Besides, I think I'm a little young for all that."

A smile. "Ah. Thank you."

"No prob, boss."

"No, as you say, prob."

Darkness loomed. It was a darkness that yearned to be broken by a flash of lightning, or perhaps by a stabbing organ chord, but instead it was broken by a voice.

Not, one must admit, a *nice* voice either.

"Drexler, you may as well admit you're awake. The neuromonitors make that clear enough."

Drexler's eyes, which had been determinedly shut, now shifted to determinedly open. "I want a doctor," he said. "I've been injured."

"What makes you think I'm *not* a doctor? You find yourself on a standard surgical table, with all the appropriate restraining straps, blood gutters, and so forth. You will observe I am wearing a doctor's apron—a bit spattered, unfortunately, from the last operation, but it's still perfectly functional."

"If you're a doctor, why are you wearing a mask and electronically altering your voice?"

"Because if you refuse to cooperate with me, I may be

compelled to commence a surgical procedure that the Medical Association might not sanction. You will observe that I have my instruments sharpened and ready."

Drexler's body gave a leap within its restraints. *"Aagh! What are those?"*

"Custom instruments. *My* instruments. *Nice* instruments."

Drexler stared. *"Nice?"*

"This is my favorite—you will observe that it is a pair of scissors designed to cut *outward,* not in toward the center. And *this* instrument, originally designed for pulling teeth, but which has been found perfectly suitable for extracting, well, just about *anything . . .*"

"Let me up! Let me up!"

The masked figure put out a calming hand. "Not until you've had your *operation,* Mr. Drexler."

"What operation? I don't need an operation!"

"It's best to let doctor decide, don't you think? I believe we need to *extract* something. Either information, or *something else. . . .*"

"What do you want to know? I'll tell you!"

"Why are you conspiring with Alice Manderley against your employer?"

"Because I was *paid,* of course! It more than made up for the money that Maijstral cost me!"

"Cost you? How did Maijstral cost you money?"

"On Silverside, I was working for Geoff Fu George. Chalice and I had a bet against Gregor and Roman about whether Fu George or Maijstral would steal the Shard first. I bet all I had, all my savings, and I lost. I wanted to start my own career as a burglar whenever Fu George retired, and I couldn't. *Now let me up!*"

"I don't believe your operation is quite over yet."

"Put that thing down!"

"Doctor knows best, Mr. Drexler."

"Just put it down! I'll tell you what you want to know!"

"Very well. Who was it that contacted you?"

"A human named Commander Hood. He's a free-lance leg-breaker, works the circuit."

"When did he first contact you?"

"About three months ago, just after I'd started working for Maijstral. On Kobayashi."

"Who did he say he was working for?"

"He didn't."

"I'm not certain I believe you, Mr. Drexler. . . ."

"Put that down!"

"But if you won't let me extract the *truth,* I'll have to extract . . ."

"I'm telling the truth! Put it down!"

"I think I'll just leave the instrument right here where you can see it. Now what exactly did this Commander Hood tell you to do . . . ?"

"Drake! Welcome back."

"Thank you." Sniffing Roberta's wrist. "I hope your Aunt Batty is well?"

"Oh, she's fine, thank you. Just tired. The hospital will be releasing her later this morning."

"Splendid. Any news?"

"Well, that short person—the one with the hair—flew in about an hour ago, demanded a room, and has been at work ever since."

"Very good."

"And I just finished watching Tvar's interrogation of Drexler on a video link."

"And . . . ?"

"Drake, it was most uncanny thing I've ever seen. She put on Savage Simon's apron and became *another person.* She was terrifying."

"She got results, I take it?"

Roberta shuddered. "Yes, but . . . you know, I think she's been around all these macabre objects far too long. They've gone to her head."

"I recall her remarking to the effect that when Khosali go bad, they go *really* bad. I'll have to take care never to get on her wrong side. What did Drexler say?"

"He says he was hired by someone named Commander Hood."

"Hood? I've met him—he got into a scandal years ago and was thrown out of the navy. Since then he's been making a living as a thug for hire. No style at all—couldn't ever get into a sanctioned form of larceny."

"Drexler claims he doesn't know who Hood was working for."

"Fortunately we do, so that doesn't matter."

"Drexler admits that it was he who put Joseph Bob's pistol in the air duct, but otherwise he just transmitted intelligence to the other side, telling them where you were going to be, and what defenses you'd installed. He gave us the number he'd called to report, and it *is* registered to a Mr. Hood."

"Does Drexler know where they took my father?"

"He said not. I am inclined to believe he was telling the truth."

"Well." Maijstral's heavy-lidded eyes closed to slits. "I have a pair of tasks remaining for Drexler—perhaps I had better ask Tvar to keep wearing Savage Simon's apron so that he will perform them willingly."

"What do you have in mind for him?"

"First, I want him to call Commander Hood and tell him that I've decided to flee to Tasmania and go into hiding."

"To allay their suspicions."

"Exactly."

"And the other is to transfer his—sixty novae?"

"Sixty. Yes."

"Transfer it into my account. There's no reason why he

should be allowed to profit from all this. And anything else in his account should go as well."

"I commend your sense of justice."

"Thank you."

A door banged open. Roberta jumped.

"Boss!"

"Conchita. You have met Her Grace of Benn, have you not?"

Conchita barely spared Roberta a glance. "Last night, yeah. I just wanted to tell you that I've broken the code and we can get into Graceland anytime. How many coded badges will you need?"

"One for me, one for Roman, one for yourself . . ."

"And for me."

"Thank you, Roberta. It's not necessary, of course."

"I think I would enjoy being in on the kill, so to speak. And Kuusinen will come, too."

"Five copies, then, Conchita."

"Right, boss."

"And then go into Memphis and purchase five holographic Elvis disguises."

"You bet, boss. Is that all you need?"

"For the present, yes."

"Right, then. Bye."

The door banged again. Roberta frowned.

"Roberta. You seem puzzled."

"I am marvelling at the breadth of your acquaintance, Drake. I was barely aware of the existence of people such as Miss Sparrow, and now it would seem I am involved in an adventure with her."

"You should broaden your circle, Roberta. After all, there are far many more of Conchita's sort than of yours, or mine. I hope you will consider the experience an enriching one."

"I am dubious as to the nutritive value of this brand of enrichment. Why are you smiling?"

"A private thought, regarding enrichment. Nothing with which to concern yourself."

An image flickered to life. A shifting image, difficult of aspect.

"Miss Manderley?"

"Who's that? I can't see. Are you wearing a darksuit?"

"Let me adjust the angle of the camera. There. Is that better?"

"*Ahh!* No! What is he doing to Kenny?"

"Dangling him upside down over the Grand Canyon, Miss Manderley."

"Tell him to stop! I'll pay anything!"

"I'm afraid I can't tell him to stop just yet, Miss Manderley."

Alice Manderley shrank back into her seat. "Why is that Khosalikh bald? Why has he painted himself all red like that? He must be mad!"

"He's just a bad molter, Miss Manderley."

"*Nobody* is that bad a molter!"

"Kenny will not be harmed if you agree to our demands."

"Anything!"

"Within the next minute, I want you to step into the flier that just landed on your front lawn. You will not carry any arms, communications equipment, or locator beacons."

"Yes! Yes! Just don't hurt him!"

"Miss Arish?"

"Yes."

"My name is Copac. The Prince of Quintana Roo has sent me to—wait! Come back!"

*   *   *

The flier's door hissed closed. Earth spiraled below as the machine took flight.

"Take me to Kenny!" Alice demanded.

"Not just yet."

"Drake!"

"Now, now, Alice," Maijstral pointed out from behind the controls. "I am wearing a darksuit and am camouflaged. You don't know who I am, nor do you know my companion, likewise disguised, who is pointing a pistol at you."

"Who was that freak who was dangling Kenny off the canyon wall?"

"An acquaintance of mine who can be trusted to fling Kenny to the gravitational constant if you should disobey my instructions in the least iota."

"Well." Muttering. "You've obviously got the goods on me."

"Exactly. And what I require is the absolute, perfect truth."

"Fine. Just don't hurt Kenny!"

Behind his camouflage, Maijstral smiled. "Firstly, how long have you been engaged in this conspiracy?"

"With those fanatics? Virtues, it seems forever—but they first contacted me a few days ago, after I got off the liner from Qwarism. By that point Kenny had acquainted me with the results of his financial speculation, and I desperately needed the money they were offering."

"Who contacted you?"

"Major Song. What an *unpleasant* woman."

"That has been my impression."

"She just ranted on about the Empire and some conspiracy of which you were supposed to be a part. I didn't take any of that seriously, of course, but her money was good, and—well, I didn't have any choice. I was desperate. I tried to keep Kenny away from her, though, when he suggested having her finance one of his productions."

"I recall that."

"Her fiancé, that Captain Whatsisname, isn't a part of the plot, by the way. I was told never to mention it in front of him."

"So when he challenged me, he was doing it all on his own?"

"Absolutely. Song was appalled."

"Where did you take my father?"

"They ordered me to take him to Graceland."

"What did they do with him then?"

"I have no idea. They paid me off, took possession of the coffin, and then I called for a flier and left."

Maijstral thoughtfully twisted his diamond ring. "So you didn't even try to keep the coffin in your possession until midnight tonight? It will never be yours legally, and you can be prosecuted for the theft at any time?"

"Well—yes."

"That's awfully careless of you."

"You weren't supposed to find out I'd done it."

"Ah. Sorry not to have been killed in a duel as planned."

"I'm sorry, Drake. I truly found this job distasteful, and my employers appalling. I've been motivated by fiscal desperation, not by any personal animus toward you."

"Ah. And I suppose it never occurred to you that once I'm out of the way, you'll have a better shot at being rated number one?"

Silence.

"Do you have any idea what they intend to do with my father?"

"No, not really. Major Song babbled about a vengeance that would last an eternity, but she talks like that all the time, so it's hard to say whether or not it was hyperbole. She's truly insane, you know. It's lucky someone else was planning all this, I don't think she's capable."

"Wait a minute. *This wasn't all Major Song's idea?*"

"No. Not at all. She's following someone else's orders. She has it all written down for her—otherwise she'd forget something." Alice shuddered. "She's not a very rational person, Drake."

"*Who's behind this?*"

"I don't know. I didn't *want* to know. But whoever it is, he hates you with the most perfect hate of all time."

"Mr. Maijstral."

Maijstral looked up from the table where he'd placed his gear. Pistols, knives, restraints . . .

"Mr. Kuusinen," he said. "Please sit down."

Kuusinen did so. "I've been thinking. I think your father is still, ah, intact, and still at Graceland."

"I'm pleased to hear you say so. May I ask your reasons?"

"If Major Song and her cohorts intended to destroy the coffin and its contents, there was no need to take it to Graceland in the first place. They could much more easily have built a bonfire out in the countryside somewhere, and destroyed the coffin in perfect privacy. I imagine it would be difficult to find a place even in such a large place as Graceland where a burning coffin would not go remarked."

"Yes, I follow."

"So they took your father to Graceland for a *reason.* I must admit I have not discerned what that reason may be, but possibly it is related to the upcoming Memphis Olympiad. Perhaps Major Song wishes to use the coffin in her act—I've never known Elvis impersonators to use anything so eccentric as a coffin in a performance, but I gather she is an eccentric person."

"An understatement if ever I've heard one. Do you have any further thoughts?"

"Somewhat, sir. Though we cannot know the reason the

coffin was taken to Graceland, we can know that whatever it was that Major Song intended to do with it, she may have done it by now. In which case the coffin and your father may be shipped out and destroyed."

"Time is of the essence, then."

"I fear so, sir. With this in mind, then, I have called up from computer files all the available architectural plans of Graceland, and I have asked my computer to perform an analysis of the data in order to determine all the places in Graceland where something the size of your father's coffin may have been hidden."

"I imagine there must have been a very great many."

"The resultant number was dismayingly large. Somewhere in excess of fifty thousand. But the *probability* of a coffin being hidden in many of these places was not very large—one could hardly put it anywhere public—and so I have further analyzed the data and come up with something in the neighborhood of three thousand possible—sir?"

"Yes?"

"You look startled."

Maijstral's green eyes glittered, and he smiled thinly. "An inspiration, Mr. Kuusinen. I just realized where the coffin is hidden. I believe we may go ahead and rescue my father now."

"Ah—very good, Mr. Maijstral."

"But keep your architectural plans in reserve. I may be wrong. And—do you have a few moments?"

"Yes."

"I wish to employ you in your legal capacity, if I may. Would you mind accompanying me to my room?"

"Mangula Arish, I've tracked you down! *Stop! Come back!*"

SEVENTEEN

❋ ❋ ❋

*T*orment, Dornier! Eternal torment!
Eh? Eh? You were saying?
Long have I planned my vengeance, Dornier! Years have passed while my plans grew to fruition!
What are you going on about?
And now our minds have been wired together. You can't escape me—you're at my mercy! My mercy, Dornier!
Are you . . . Quigley?
Who is Quigley? Is Quigley a spy?
A spy? Oh, Virtues, no. Quigley is an old school chum.
Enough of your school chums, *Dornier!* You're in Hell now!
Hell. Oh, yes. I remember now.
Contemplate your sins, Dornier. . . .
Quigley's cook used to make the most perfect little omelettes. You couldn't have her make me one now, could you, Quigley?
I'm not Quigley!

You're not?

Get this through your head, Dornier! You're dead, you're in Hell, and I am not Quigley! *Can't you get it straight?*

Oh, of course. I'm being so silly. Of course *you're not Quigley.*

Just remember that, Dornier!

You're Jacko. I remember now.

I'm not Jacko!

Of course you are. You're Jacko, and this is one of your jolly little pranks.

I'm not Jacko!

Ha ha ha! I've found you out at last!

Aaaaah! I give up! I can't stand it!

Most amusing, Jacko. Your best yet, as far as I'm concerned.

Your brainlessness! Your endless drivelling! I refuse *to spend eternity with the likes of you! I'm cancelling Hell, and I'm cancelling it* now!

No need to get upset, old man. After all, I was bound to guess your identity sooner or later.

It's over! I'm going to call Major Song and have you disconnected!

Oh . . . I say, tell the Major to bring tea and cakes. I've worked up quite an appetite.

"Roman?"

"Sir? You called?"

"Please sit down. I have something to say."

The red-eyed, fiery-skinned giant seemed uncomfortable as he sat in Maijstral's presence. In addition to the obvious reason for his discomfort, Roman wasn't used to being seated in the presence of his social betters.

Maijstral frowned down at the table before him, where his genealogy, so carefully assembled by Roman, had been unrolled. He looked at his ancestors running back thousands of years, and thought of Roman's own genealogy, which went back even farther.

He cleared his throat. He wanted to be able to pick the right words for this.

"Roman," he said, "before we go off to rescue my father, I thought I would acquaint you with some of the contents of my will."

"Sir!" Roman barked. "Not necessary!"

This was hardly Roman's usual form, Maijstral knew, but then he reminded himself that this was hardly the usual Roman.

"I am certain," Roman added, more in his usual style, "that any dispensation which you have chosen to make is more than adequate."

"Well. There's a little more to it than endowments and so forth. Something special."

"Sir?"

"Your family has been in service to mine for hundreds of years. Never in all that time has there been a single instance in which your family has failed to give its utmost for mine."

Maijstral was startled as Roman gave a brief roar, but it proved not to be anger, but rather something more in the nature of clearing the throat.

What Roman said, finally, was, "We endeavor to gratify, sir."

"And you have. You have. And in recognition of that, I placed in my will the intention that, on my death, the City of Seven Bright Rings be petitioned that one of my titles—that of Baron Drago—be given to you, or your heir. I also made provision for the transfer of sufficient funds to support any reasonable pretensions to which a member of the nobility might aspire."

"Sir!" The arm of the chair came loose in Roman's hand.

His reddened eyes almost leaped from his head.

"But *then*," Maijstral added, "I reconsidered."

A twitch danced across Roman's countenance. "I understand, sir," he said. "It is hardly fitting that I—"

Maijstral tried to repress a smile. "Roman," he said, "please let me finish."

"Very good, sir."

Roman observed the chair arm in his hand, and looked at it in surprise, not knowing how it got there.

Maijstral cleared his throat. "I reconsidered," he repeated. "I thought, why should all this wait till I'm *dead*, when by all rights you should have your reward *now*. So I have just now instructed Mr. Kuusinen to draft a petition to the City of Seven Bright Rings, and as soon as the Imperial Recorder in the next room copies it with his jade pen, and I sign it, the petition will be sent by the Very Private Letter service to the Emperor. And since we did the Empire that service on Peleng, as I'm sure you remember, I have every reason to believe that my petition will be granted. . . ."

His voice trailed off as he saw that Roman was simply staring off into space, the chair arm in his hand, his mouth fallen open and his tongue lolling.

"Well," Maijstral said. "Soon you'll be Lord Drago, so I thought you'd better be prepared. That's all, Roman—you may go."

"Sir—"

Maijstral rose and held out his hand. "Thank you, Roman. You have always given complete satisfaction."

Slowly Roman rose from his chair. He held out his hand, recollected the chair arm was still in it, switched the chair arm to the other hand, then took Maijstral's hand and clasped it. Maijstral winced as bones took the strain.

"Thank you, sir!" Roman bellowed.

Maijstral winced a second time at Roman's astounding volume.

"You'd best go and prepare," he said. "We'll be leaving in a few minutes."

"Very good, sir!" Roman roared, turned on his heel in formal military fashion, and marched out, the chair arm still in one hand.

Maijstral massaged his wounded hand, looked down at the genealogy, and smiled.

He had always thought that Roman would make a good lord. Every so often he and Roman were compelled to travel incognito, and Roman had on occasion operated under the name of Lord Graves, a perfectly genuine person who happened to be Maijstral's distant cousin. Roman had been so splendid at being Lord Graves, at adopting the proper mix of lordliness, condescension, and noblesse oblige, that Maijstral had often found it very odd of the universe that he, Maijstral, was the lord, whereas Roman, who was so much better at it, was the servant.

Of course Roman also *believed* in lords, and emperors, and so on, and Maijstral didn't. Perhaps conviction added something to Roman's performance that Maijstral, for all his birth and training, lacked.

There was a knock on the door, and then Tvar entered. Maijstral sniffed her ears.

"How fare our guests?"

"Drexler, Manderley, and Chang have been safely locked in Savage Simon's dungeon. Drexler has also been persuaded to forfeit his sixty novae and change."

"Very good." Maijstral would make the sixty novae part of Roman's—Lord Drago's—endowment.

It wasn't enough to support a lord for *very* long, but it would make a good start, and Roman could always steal some more. And it was more than Maijstral had to his name when he joined the nobility at his father's death.

"We'll leave as soon as Conchita gets back," he began.

"Right here, boss."

The camouflage holograms dissolved and Conchita floated down from the ceiling.

"Conchita," Maijstral said, "you must some day allow me to introduce you to the concept of a *door,* and of the *doorframe,* on which you may *knock.*"

"Sorry," Conchita said, "but the window was open, so I just flew up and came in. It seemed quicker than going the long way."

"Do you have our disguises?"

"Well—mostly."

"Mostly?"

"You asked for five, boss, but I could only find four."

Maijstral raised his eyebrows. "You could find only four Elvis holograms in all of Memphis?"

Conchita looked apologetic. "There's a high demand, boss, with the Memphis Olympiad coming up next week. And there's some kind of big ceremony going on right now, pre-Olympiad, with pilgrims from all over. You know how much Elvis's admirers like to dress up like him, right? Well, I called all over Memphis and I only got four holograms."

"Well," Maijstral sighed. "Can't be helped, I suppose."

Conchita brightened. "But I got a fifth hologram. It was the last one the store had."

"What does it look like?"

"Ronnie Romper."

"*Ronnie Romper?*"

"Yeah. The puppet from the children's videos. I really liked him when I was little."

Tvar lolled a Khosalikh smile. "I *adore* Ronnie Romper!" she said. "I used to visit the Magic Planet of Adventure every week."

Maijstral, it is apropos to remark, did *not* adore Ronnie Romper. He believed that the little puppet, viewed by everyone else as a harmless vehicle for juvenile delight, was in fact a horrid omen of doom.

This was not precisely superstition, but rather a product of some dubious inductive reasoning: a maniac assassin had once tried to cut Maijstral in half while wearing a Ronnie Romper disguise; and therefore Maijstral always viewed any close association with Ronnie Romper as an invitation to homicide.

If not precisely logical, the view has a certain consistency. That's inductive reasoning for you: it's sneaky, but at least it's based on data.

"How are we going to sneak Ronnie Romper into Graceland?" Maijstral demanded.

Conchita gave it some thought. "Well," she said, "if Ronnie's with *us* . . ."

Maijstral surrendered. Obviously it was his fate to take Ronnie Romper into battle.

"Very well," he said. "But let's leave at once, before I think better of it."

The main gates of Graceland were jammed: pilgrims, both human, Khosali, and otherwise, a great many of them either dressed as Elvis, wearing Elvis masks, or disguised by Elvis holograms, were swarming up against the stanchions, trying to get into the festival. Music boomed indistinctly in the distance, all bass notes and rhythm. The far-off roar of an audience rose and fell.

"Why you are Ronnie Romper disguising?" asked one Troxan. The tiny alien, who normally would have stood about as far from the ground as Maijstral's navel, was floating through the crowd on an a-grav harness ornamented with rhinestones, a cape, and a standing collar.

Maijstral found himself devoutly wishing he'd given the Ronnie Romper disguise to someone other than Roman, who by virtue of his height was far from inconspicuous.

It occurred to him that, insofar as Roman's answer to the alien's question might be to remove the Troxan's head from his shoulders, he should answer the question himself, and quickly.

"We're coming from a party," he said.

"I am climaxing this system my unbusiness journey," the Troxan said. "Most event making, friend finding grand tour."

To his horror, Maijstral realized that he *knew* this particular alien—his name was Count Quik, and Maijstral had met him on Peleng.

It really wasn't Maijstral's fault that he hadn't identified the Troxan immediately. Identification of Troxans is one of the minor arts, as they all have the same bodies, multilayered onion heads, and more or less fixed expressions. Sound resonates between the various cartilaginous layers of their heads and gives Troxans the most acute and discriminating hearing in the galaxy.

Maijstral cleared his throat and lowered his voice, afraid that his speech would prove fatally recognizable to the Troxan.

"I'm afraid we've run out of time," he growled. "So sorry. Good-bye." He began to elbow his way back to the rear of the crowd.

"Farewells, Mr. Maijstral," the Troxan said politely.

Maijstral clenched his teeth and continued his progress to the rear of the crowd, the others in his party following.

"Was that Count Quik?" Kuusinen asked.

"Yes."

"Do you think he will give us away?"

"He didn't last time."

"Last time he didn't catch us in the act of breaking and entering."

"Either way we've got to act swiftly, and crowding in

front of the main gates is the least expedient way I can think to deal with the situation. We'll find a side entrance, and our identification codes should get us in. Once past the perimeter, we'll go straight to our destination. Very likely we'll get the business over with before Count Quik even gets to the main gate."

"Very good."

Out of the blue, a woman marked by a stiff, distinctive hairstyle charged right through the midst of them, knocking Roberta to the ground in her haste before she disappeared into the crowd. Media globes circling the woman's head marked her position in the crowd as she ran on. Kuusinen and Maijstral bent to pick Roberta up.

"Are you all right?" Maijstral asked.

"I'm fine. Wasn't that Mangula Arish who just knocked me down?"

"I don't know," Maijstral blinked. "Was it?"

The party scattered before a flying wedge of Mayans, who likewise disappeared into the crowd at a run.

"What's going *on?*" Roberta demanded.

"I haven't the vaguest . . ." Maijstral began, and then his blood froze at the sight of the Baron Sancho Sandoval Cabeza de Vaca bearing down on him, waving his cane.

"Are you sure my holograph is functioning?" Maybe, he thought, all these people were *recognizing* him.

"You look fine," Roberta said.

"Let's get out of here anyway."

They made their escape before the elderly Baron Sancho could hobble up to them, then circled around Graceland's perimeter until they discovered a gate, the entrance that led to Love Me Tender Street.

"If we'd had time to develop a plan," Maijstral pointed out, "we would have come here at the start."

Assuming the dignified mien of the Elvii, Maijstral led

his group toward the gate, which obligingly rolled open at his approach. Two guards stationed behind the gate snapped to attention, and a third presented a portable log-in scanner and pen.

"Please sign in, sir."

Nothing for it but to continue, Maijstral decided. He reached for the pen and signed "Elvis Presley" in what he hoped was a bold hand.

The guard looked at Roman. "Why the Ronnie Romper disguise?" he asked, then turned pale at the sound of Roman's answering growl. His hand automatically rose to the pistol at his belt.

"We've been to a party," Maijstral said, in what he hoped was the voice of an old man. "My friend has a bad case of indigestion."

"Hrrrr," Roman agreed.

The guard's suspicion dwindled, but didn't vanish entirely. "And why are *you* disguised?" he said. "You're one of the Elvii—you *already* look like Elvis."

Inspiration struck Maijstral. "Ahhhhhh," he said, drawing out a world-weary sigh. "Even I sometimes yearn to be young again."

"Oh," the guard said. "Gotcher."

Maijstral led his group through the gate. The guard looked after Roman as he passed.

"By the way," he added, "my kids love your show."

Maijstral discovered, once inside, that Love Me Tender Street was crowded. Several concerts were going on at once in the various auditoriums and open-air concert venues, and more visitors were entering every second. The sound of music and the roar of the crowds were much louder. Maijstral's group found it slow going, but they made steady progress until a group of children spotted Ronnie Romper and ran up to join the party.

"Do your Pumpkin Dance!" one of them demanded.

"Take us to the Magic Planet of Adventure!" said another.

"The Pumpkin Dance!"

"Where's Cap'n Bob?"

"Sing the Pangalactic Friendship Song!"

Graceland, Maijstral realized, was a tourist mecca; and the tourists, seeing a holographic video character, were assuming that this was part of the *entertainment*.

Maijstral was on the brink of explaining that Ronnie was very busy now, in the midst of an adventure that was taking him from the Magic Planet of Adventure on a mission to Graceland to rescue Elvis from danger, but he found his explanation preempted by Roman himself.

Roman leaned over the children, raised his arms, and bellowed *"Buzz off!"* in a voice that froze the entire crowd in their tracks.

The children turned pale and fled, all except for the youngest, who wet himself, sat down, and began to cry. The child's mother rushed up to the child and picked him up in her arms.

"Beast!" she shouted at Roman's retreating back.

"Perhaps we'd better fly," Maijstral said. "We'll be more conspicuous, but we'll make better time."

They triggered their a-grav harnesses and rose into the air. Maijstral led them onto shade-lined Big Hunk O' Love Boulevard toward the center of Graceland, triggering as he flew his darksuit's sensory enhancements that increased his range of hearing and vision. An unforeseen consequence of this decision was that he could hear with unusual clarity the comments of the crowd below.

"What's this on my shoe?"

"Look! It's Ronnie Romper!"

"Hi, Ronnie!"

"Hrrrr!"

"My kids love your show!"

"I didn't know Ronnie was so *huge*. He's so little on vid!"

"Hey, Ronnie! Where's Auntie June and Uncle Amos?"

"Sing the Pangalactic Friendship Song!"

"What's this on my shoe?"

And then, lurching down the avenue, came a sight that Maijstral scarcely required enhanced vision in order to detect. It was a frightening figure, horribly disfigured, as tall as Roman and as powerful as a colossus.

It was Milo Hay, the fiancé of Major Ruth Song. After the double thrashing he'd received from Prince Hunac's bodyguard and then from Roman, he'd been strapped into an exoskeleton to enable him to heal while moving about normally—if, that is, being strapped into a humanoid-shaped collection of gleaming, articulated metal can be called "moving normally."

Hay marched onto the boulevard with a hiss of hydraulics and a clank of metal. His face was covered by the semilife patches that were sopping up his bruises. Despite all his injuries, he had a strange, dreamy smile on his face, doubtless a side effect of overeffective painkillers.

Hay turned and began clanking down Big Hunk O' Love Boulevard in the same direction as Maijstral's party. Maijstral's blood turned cold.

"Faster," he said, and increased speed.

Hay looked up as Maijstral's group passed over his head. His dreamy smile widened. He waved.

"Ronnie Romper!" he said. "I love your show!"

At the geographical center of Graceland, surrounded by a company of guards in full dress uniform, stands the monument known as the Heart of Graceland. The huge gold-sheathed obelisk, in the shape of a giant torch, is by far the tallest freestanding structure in Tennessee, and on clear nights the Eternal Flame surmounting the structure can supposedly be seen from Pikes Peak. Long reflecting pools stretch from the monument in each of the four cardinal directions.

Maijstral dropped to the ground and his entourage followed suit. Moving with the dignity of authority and old age, he approached the main gate. A guard captain pointed a detector at him, read the display, and promptly saluted.

"How may I be of service to the Elvii?"

Behind his holographic camouflage, Maijstral smiled.

"Could you check the directory and remind me of the location of the resting place of Fleet Admiral Song?"

"Right away, sir."

The captain went to a service plate, consulted it for a moment, and then returned.

"Level Three, Row 300, number 341. He has a freestanding monument that will make the location plain. Do you wish me to escort you to the vault?"

"No, thank you. That won't be necessary." Maijstral nodded regally and led his group through the entrance.

"It is my constant joy to serve the Elvii!" the captain said fervently, and saluted again.

Maijstral entered and found himself in a huge room panelled in marble and draped in red velour. As he walked toward the center, the flagstones under his feet lit up one by one as he stepped on them, and an invisible organ began to sigh "Are You Lonesome To-night?"

The Heart of Graceland loomed ahead, a huge slab of polished black marble beneath which lay the mortal remains of Elvis Aron Presley, lying forever with members of his family.

"Of *course!*" Kuusinen said. "I don't know why I didn't see it."

"I feel the same way," Roberta added. "Now it seems perfectly obvious."

"Beg pardon?" Conchita said. "It's not that obvious to *me*."

The party approached the King's final resting place and came to a stop against the polished brass rail that circled the monument.

"Alice Manderley said that Major Song was just following orders," Maijstral said, "Which means she isn't behind the scheme. And Mr. Kuusinen was right when he suggested that there had to be a reason why my father's coffin was taken to Graceland, and not somewhere else."

"He was taken here to meet his chief adversary," Kuusinen said, "the man who headed the plot against him. It was *necessary* that Gustav Maijstral be brought here, because otherwise the meeting couldn't take place."

"Who is it?" Conchita demanded. "One of the Elvii?"

"Fleet Admiral Song," Kuusinen said.

"Admiral *Song?*" Roman roared. "But he's *dead!*"

"So is my father," Maijstral said. "But my father retains a kind of tenuous existence in his cryocoffin, and I suspect the same is true of Admiral Song."

Roberta nodded. "The late Duke—I hope this observation does not cause offense—is not always in a rational state. I suspect the same is true of Admiral Song."

"Long freezes rarely benefit the rational faculty," Kuusinen pointed out.

"Admiral Song was one of the Constellation's greatest heroes," Maijstral said, "and I suspect his granddaughter obeys his slightest wish without question. My grandfather caused the death of the Admiral's first wife, and he's been hungering for revenge ever since. Since his death, I suspect his vengeful desires have overwhelmed his reason."

Conchita whistled. "That Admiral's a sad case."

"Yes," Maijstral said. "And it's high time we deprived him of his prize. To the vaults!"

The elevator was lined with mirrors shot with gold veins,

large enough to carry any number of cryocoffins without crowding, and played a cheerful arrangement of "Bossa Nova Baby" as it rose with a certain deliberate grandeur to the third level of the structure.

As soon as the doors opened, Maijstral's amplified senses began to hear a high-pitched, hectoring voice that rose and fell over the cheerful elevator music. He used the proximity wire in his darksuit to open his private communications channel, and subvocalized as he gave his instructions, inaudible to any eavesdroppers but clear enough to his own party.

"Something's up," he said. "Quiet now . . . and let's be certain to find the right vault. And if you have to talk, remember to subvocalize."

The others, silent, nodded.

The entire level consisted of the long, solemn marble rows of those who lay for eternity in the Arms of Elvis. An invisible chorus of angel voices sang a dirgelike, minor key version of "Mystery Train." Tasteful gold flashing neon signs directed Maijstral to Row 300.

The hectoring voice grew louder.

"*Ridiculous drivelling fool!*" it said. "*All my years of planning, and for this?*"

"Now, now, Bertie. Don't get upset—it will injure your digestion."

Maijstral stiffened as he recognized the voice of his father.

"*I'm not Bertie, you maniac!*"

"Admiral—don't get upset." Major Song's voice, a female baritone.

Maijstral drew his spitfire from its holster and set the charge to maximum.

"Why shouldn't I get upset?" said the first voice. "My vengeance is ruined! This fool is too thick-witted to appreciate the Hell I had in store for him, and you've bungled the other part of your assignment!"

"Sir—"

"When will Maijstral die in a duel, that's what I want to know!"

"He's still supposed to fight Hunac, sir," Major Song said weakly. "We just don't know when."

"Robert the Butcher's offspring must die! That's what my vengeance demands!"

"Yes, Admiral."

Maijstral reached Row 299, just before Admiral Song's resting place. He looked at the others—with his enhanced vision, he could do it without turning his head—and subvocalized.

"Roman, take Mr. Kuusinen down this aisle. Prepare to fly over the row of vaults and aid us on my signal."

"Hrrrrr, sir!"

"All of you, be careful when it comes to shooting. I don't want my father's coffin hit."

Roman's party drifted down the aisle and positioned themselves.

"I'm tired of waiting for Hunac to do the job," the Admiral ranted. "Go out and have Maijstral killed!"

Maijstral's blood froze. His pistol trembled in his hand.

"Have Hood do it," ranting on, "or have him hire someone. Just blow the monster's head off!"

"Yes, sir."

The Admiral's voice turned smug. "There is no guilt," he said, "in extinguishing vermin."

"I say, Bertie," ex-Dornier said reproachfully, "this prank is going a little far, don't'ee think? What if someone takes you seriously with this killing business?"

"*Shut up, you—you—*"

While the late Admiral spluttered in search of an appropriate epithet, Maijstral heard Roman's voice subvocalizing on his communications channel.

"These people intend to assassinate you, sir! We should eradicate them!"

Maijstral reflected how cheerful it might be to simply order *Roman! Kill!* and then sit back until it was all over.

But no. Something in him cringed from ordering a cold-blooded murder, even with all the provocation in the world.

His heart thrashed in his throat, making it difficult to subvocalize.

"Save my father first," he said. "If they resist, that's one thing—but if they don't, it's another. We have plenty of witnesses to their plan—we can have them arrested later. A crazy man in a coffin and a woman surgically altered to look like Elvis won't get very far."

"Hrrrrr!" Roman replied, his tone resentful. And then, "Very good, sir."

Maijstral turned to face the others in his party. (He could have seen them without turning, but they wouldn't have known he was talking to them.)

"Keep large intervals," he said. "If we clump up, we're just one large target. Keep your weapons ready, but no shooting unless I shoot first."

Where, he suddenly wondered, were these phrases coming from? He'd never been in the military, and he'd done his best to run away from any dangerous situations in his life; but now here he was lecturing the others on tactics like some wizened Death Commando sergeant in an action vid.

Probably it was all bubbling up from his subconscious. Maybe he'd watched too many Westerns.

He holstered his pistol, wiped sweat from his palms, took his pistol in hand again.

"I say, Bertie!" ex-Dornier said cheerfully. "You wouldn't have any of the bubbly about, would you?"

"Shut up! Shut up, shut up, shut up!"

For some reason the sound of the deranged corpse shouting at his father set Maijstral's blood boiling, and the anger set him marching around the corner and down Row 300 without conscious thought. And immediately he knew this business was going to be a lot more difficult than he'd expected.

There wasn't just Song in the aisle, for one thing. She had three companions disguised as Elvis. Maijstral recognized one of them as Commander Hood, the ex–naval officer turned bully, whose burly form was unmistakable even in a wig and paste-on sideburns. The two others looked like hired muscle. And a fourth companion, unless Maijstral missed his guess, was one of the Elvii himself, a sullen-looking youth in black leather vestments.

A pedestal bust of Admiral Song had been moved aside to permit access to his vault. The marble front of the vault, with his name and a patriotic inscription, had been removed. Two coffins were visible, both for the moment suspended in the grappler beams of a kind of cartlike lifting apparatus that itself hovered on its repellers a few inches above the ground. One of Song's henchmen was sitting in the cart's seat, operating the controls. Apparently both coffins had been jammed into the same vault, and it was necessary to remove both at once in order to sort them out.

That was the one piece of luck that Maijstral could see. He had brought straps and a grav repellers to help carry his father's coffin from Graceland, but instead, if he worked things right, he could just commandeer the cart and drive it off.

Maijstral tried to summon authority and dignity as he marched toward the group. He held his pistol behind him, because he wasn't certain if the commercial hologram would conceal it or not. His enhanced vision showed Roberta and Conchita marching out behind him, spreading out as per instructions. One by one, Song's party noticed his approach and stared at him nervously while the late Admiral raved on.

"Do we have a problem here?" Maijstral's voice sounded faint over the crashing of his own heart.

"Who the hell is *that?*" Admiral Song snarled.

"I am of the Elvii," Maijstral said. "I heard a disturbance."

Maijstral was terrified that someone would simply ask, *Why's he wearing a hologram?* but it didn't happen. The young Elvis—the genuine one—stepped forward. Sweat glazed his brow. "There is no problem, sibling," he said. "Two of the deceased have been arguing, and we've decided to move one of them to a different vault. There's no reason for you to concern yourself."

Maijstral affected to consider this as he peered down his nose at the young Elvis. "I do not believe you are authorized to make these decisions," he said, making a hopeful guess.

The Elivs looked abashed and mumbled something. Song and Hood exchanged glances. Maijstral looked at the vault, at the two coffins.

"Two coffins in a single vault?" he said. "This is quite irregular."

Major Song stepped forward. "Sir? If you will permit—"

Maijstral looked at her. She was devout, supposedly, and perhaps would be disinclined to harm or question one of the Elvii.

"I do not recall that I gave you permission to speak," he said, and Major Song fell back in confusion. Maijstral cleared his throat. "I believe I will have to take the coffins downstairs and sort this all out with the proper authorities. Follow me, please."

For a moment he thought they'd actually do it—he could see the inclination in their eyes, the automatic impulse to obey the voice of authority when they had no plan of their own. But then the worst thing possible happened.

Maijstral's father spoke.

"Drake?" he said. "That's you, isn't it, Drake?"

There was a long moment of horrified paralysis. Maijstral could see calculations running behind all the others' eyes. Then Hood went for his gun and without thought Maijstral raised his spitfire and fired. "*Yaaaaaah!*" he shouted, the Yell of Hate coming to his lips unbidden. Flame fountained off Hood's shields, which apparently he'd managed to trigger in time. Slugs from Hood's chugger whanged off Maijstral's shields.

"What's that noise?" asked Maijstral's father. "Is it fireworks?"

And then things got confusing.

In a surge of terror Maijstral realized he was not accomplishing anything standing there and yelling, and that furthermore he was in the line of fire. He flung himself to the ground. Hood and one of Song's henchmen dived behind the coffins and began shooting from behind cover. Gunfire roared in the enclosed marble space. Spitfire charges fountained bright fire. Alarms began to ring, and purple fire-retardant foam began to pour from hidden reservoirs in the ceiling.

The Elvis, caught in the middle of it all, patted the pockets of his leather jacket frantically, looking for a weapon that wasn't there.

"I'm not shielded!" he shouted as bullets cracked by his ear. "Help!"

"*Cease fire!*" the late Admiral roared in a voice of thunder. "*Cease firing, you fools! You could hit me, and I'm not shielded!*"

The shooting dwindled away as this line of reasoning penetrated the startled combatants. Each side wanted at least *one* of the coffins to survive.

"Fireworks!" exclaimed Maijstral's father. "Is it the Emperor's birthday?"

At this instant two figures appeared, silhouetted against

the ceiling—the flying holographic Elvis that was Paavo Kuusinen, and a giant roaring Ronnie Romper, both stooping on the villains like falcons on their prey.

Roman went for the burly Commander Hood, recognizing a fellow professional when he saw one, but on his way clotheslined the henchman who was sitting on the cart and knocked him into Song and the other henchman. Hit hard, Hood went down but dragged Roman with him into the growing river of purple foam. Kuusinen, acting with perfect logic, dropped into the cart's seat and seized the controls. As the cart spun on its heel, the coffins knocked the bust of Admiral Song to the floor and revealed Major Song and one of her henchmen, deprived of cover, struggling to their feet in the froth. Maijstral fired at the targets while he had the chance, his spitfire charges bouncing off shields but raising a huge purple cloud of steam.

Kuusinen got the cart pointed in the right direction and accelerated, running smash into the back of the leather-clad Elvis, who was flung forward into the foam, sliding along on his stomach until he cracked heads with Maijstral. Seeing stars, Maijstral grabbed the Elvis's collar, prepared to beat him senseless with the butt of his spitfire, but observed that the Elvis was already unconscious.

Maijstral looked up just in time to see the cart careening toward him at top speed. His heart lurched. He dropped his face into the foam as the cart, supported by its a-grav repellers, passed harmlessly over his head.

He looked up again. Dimly visible through a haze of purple mist, he saw Hood and Roman locked in combat. Hood's wig was badly askew. Roman aimed a kick at Hood, slipped in the foam, and crashed to the ground. Hood tried to stomp Roman while Roman was prone, but his support leg slid out from under him and he crashed to the ground as well. Both combatants rose, dripping foam, lunged for one another again, grappled, and fell.

"What's going on?" the Admiral shouted. *"What's happening?"*

Song rose from the foam, looking frantic, but promptly slipped and dropped into the purple with a mighty splash.

It looked as if Maijstral's side was winning. And winning, to Maijstral, had always meant getting while the getting was good.

"Follow the coffins!" Maijstral ordered, forgetting to subvocalize, and then he triggered his own flying harness and zoomed into the air after the retreating cart, flying backward and navigating through his enhanced, expanded vision. As he passed, Roberta and Conchita triggered their repellers and rose out of the foam themselves.

From behind the curtain of mist came roars and meaty thwacks as Roman and Hood pummeled each other. Major Song staggered upward and gaped after her disappearing grandfather. Her two henchmen likewise rose unsteadily to their feet.

"They're getting away!" she said. "After them!" But as they started to run they tripped over the bust of Admiral Song, hidden deep in the foam, and they tangled and crashed heavily to the ground.

Kuusinen's cart reached the end of the row and he tried frantically to make the abrupt right-angle turn demanded by the room's configuration. He failed and ran both coffins straight into the wall. Maijstral hadn't anticipated Kuusinen's abrupt stop and he sailed backward into the cart, sweeping Kuusinen off and slamming him against the far wall.

"Ouch!" said Maijstral's dad. *"What just happened?"*

Maijstral came to a halt, the breath hammered from his lungs by the collision, stars flashing in his eyes. He looked up dazedly just in time to see Roberta flying straight for him.

The impact bent a few ribs. And then Conchita crashed into the pile, making a surprising impact for someone her size.

"I believe we were supposed to turn," Roberta remarked.

Major Song and her henchmen slowly rose from the pile again. "They're helpless!" she called, pointing. "Get them!"

They began loping toward the stalled cart, foam splashing at every step. Maijstral and his group tried to get untangled. As the pack loosened, Kuusinen fell unconscious into the foam. Maijstral wondered where his spitfire had got to. If it was in the froth, he'd never find it.

And then Roman, who had finally choked Commander Hood into submission, rose from the foam and took flight, arms outstretched.

He rammed Major Song with his head, and his extended arms clipped the others as he passed. All three dropped, landing hard. Roman floated to where Maijstral's party were still trying to sort themselves out, picked up the unconscious Kuusinen, and set him at the cart's controls.

"Shall I drive, sir?" Roman said.

"By all means," Maijstral mumbled.

"Don't take the elevator," Conchita said. "Guards will be responding to the alarms by now."

They took the stairs, the cart thudding down the risers on its repellers. Turning the cart on the landings took time, and Ruth Song and her henchmen were closing on them by the time the cart crashed through some door and began moving down a long tunnel.

"Where does this go?" Roberta asked.

"I don't know," Maijstral said. "Kuusinen has the maps, and he's out of action."

"What's that *noise?*" Conchita wondered. There was a distant, powerful sound, a roaring like a distant ocean. It was coming from dead ahead.

The cart smashed through another pair of doors into a large, dark place, and the noise was suddenly much louder.

Startled people darted from out of the way of the cart. And then the darkness fell away, and to Maijstral's horror he realized what was making the roaring sound.

Thousands of people . . .

Garvikh really had them rocking. He had the audience in the palm of his furry hand.

He had heard it said that he was the finest Elvis ever to be born Khosalikh. Certainly he was among the best Elvises now alive. As part of his apprenticeship he had mastered the difficult, antique Earth dialect, a dead language no longer spoken anywhere, in which the King had recorded his masterpieces. Garvikh had devoted thousands of hours to a series of special exercises designed to limber his sturdy Khosali hips and torso, never intended to move with the fluidity more natural to the human form, so that he could perform the demanding, difficult hip thrusts, the stilted, pigeon-toed walking style, the sudden knee drops and whirling assaults on the microphone that characterized the rigidly defined Elvis repertoire. This was High Custom, and High Custom performances required the utmost in precision. Each step, each gesture, each twitch of the hips or twist of the upper lip, was performed with the utmost classical perfection, the most rigid attention to form. There was no room for accident, for spontaneity. All was performed with utmost care to assure that every nuance was subtly shaded and subtly controlled, in the tradition of the great Elvis Masters of the past.

And now all the work, all the dedication was paying off. Garvikh was performing live in front of an audience of thousands, and he was wowing them. A Memphis audience was said to be the most knowledgeable, the most demanding; but if you could win them to your side, you had a place in their hearts forever.

He had opened with "All Shook Up" and "Jailhouse

Rock" to get the audience on its feet. He'd made them swoon with "Surrender" and "One Broken Heart for Sale." Then he'd jumped into "Good Rockin' Tonight," to which he had choreographed jets of water from the fountains in the ornamental pond at the foot of the stage, the leaping water turned into a fantasy of color by spotlights. Now he was ready to wail on his best song, "Heartbreak Hotel." He had worked on the refrain for months, to get precisely the right tone to the mumble of the "I'll be so lonely" section.

But before he started, he wanted to drive the audience into a frenzy of anticipation. He carefully assumed the Sixth Posture of Elvis, cocking his head at a precise sixteen-degree angle and looking at the audience slightly sidelong. "Well..." he drawled, and the audience roared. He shifted to the Seventh Posture, the provocative "Undereyed Stance," difficult for a Khosalikh to pull off because it required him to look at the audience in a challenging way, as if from under his brows— but of course the Khosali have no projecting forehead the way humans do, and the whole movement had to depend on careful effect and illusion.

"Well..." he said again, and seven thousand hypercritical Elvis fanatics roared with approval.

He waited the prescribed six seconds for suspense to build. "Well..." he began again, and then perceived a movement off to his right. Not daring to change his posture, he turned his eyes in that direction, and almost immediately wished he hadn't.

Three flying holographic Elvises, trailing purple foam, were zooming onto the stage at high speed, accompanied by a hovercart that carried two long metal boxes covered with purple goo. A fifth Elvis lolled on the cart, drunk or unconscious, while a sixth figure—a preposterous red-haired giant with a fixed grin—sat behind the controls.

Ronnie *Romper?* Garvikh thought, but discipline demanded he not move a muscle, that he stand in the "Undereyed Stance" for the five to eight seconds necessary to provoke the audience to an ecstasy of anticipation.

The cart bore down on him, showing no sign of stopping. Garvikh was struck with the full horror of his dilemma. If he stepped out of the cart's path he would be making an unscripted move, defying thousands of years of performing tradition and probably ending his career on the spot. And if he didn't move out of the way, he would be run over by the cart, its cargo, and its redheaded occupant.

Garvikh decided to tough it out. He held the Seventh Posture, clenching his teeth in a snarl. The audience held its breath. Then the impact came, and Garvikh felt himself cartwheeling across the stage . . . and as stars exploded before his eyes and the stage came up to meet him, he heard the roar of audience approval.

Garvikh had not trained all his life in order to cave in easily to misfortune. He staggered upright, his hand still triumphantly clutching the microphone, and automatically assumed the Eleventh Posture, the one called "The King in Glory."

"I—" he began, the world swimming around him, and then through his confusion observed that three more Elvises—and wasn't one of them Ruth Song?—had just charged onto the stage and were engaging the first set of Elvises in battle. Fists flew. One of the first group of Elvises was knocked down.

The fans could hardly blame him for *this*, he concluded. Trying not to break character, he stalked forward and tapped one of the Elvises on the shoulder. "What's going on here?" he demanded, unconsciously speaking in the dead language he'd been performing all night.

The other Elvis whirled, punched him on the muzzle, and dropped him to the stage. The audience roared.

Garvikh decided to crawl to safety, but this proved more

difficult than he anticipated, because first one, then another of the Elvises tripped over him and crashed to the stage.

Garvikh shook the stars from his head and rose cautiously to his feet again. Someone new had joined the fray—a ghastly-looking human in a clanking mechanical suit, trailing water as he climbed to the stage. Apparently he had crossed the ornamental pond in front of the stage. "Ruth!" the human shouted. Despite his apparent desperation, his face bore an odd, unfocused grin.

"Milo!" cried one of the Elvises. "Help!" It *was* Ruth Song, Garvikh saw, being held down and pummeled by a pair of Elvises.

Garvikh concluded that he should come to her aid—at least *she* was an Elvis he recognized. But as he ran to Ruth Song's assistance, Milo seized him from behind by his standing collar.

"Rat!" Milo yelled. Garvikh's teeth rattled as Milo shook him back and forth. Hydraulics hissed as Garvikh was flung across the stage.

The lights went out for Garvikh for a while, but when he cleared the cobwebs from his head the battle was still going on. Elvises were battling back and forth, but Milo held center stage, engaged with Ronnie Romper. Roars, thumps, hydraulic hisses, and clangs marked the blows of fists, feet, stage equipment, and Milo's armored shell.

One of the Elvises hit another Elvis so hard that he knocked his wig off. Another Elvis smashed an Elvis with the microphone stand. Yet another Elvis was trying to strangle a different Elvis.

A youngish human female with rocklike hair dashed across the stage, artfully weaving among the battling Elvises. Media globes orbited her head. Then a group of short, copper-skinned humans ran across the stage as well, scattering Elvises but exiting after the female.

The short humans were followed by an elderly human who hit several of the Elvises with his cane as he made his way across the stage.

The audience was going mad.

Milo's forearm thudded into Ronnie Romper, knocking him back into the cart. But Ronnie was undeterred—roaring like a demon, he picked up one of the boxes from the cart—was it a *coffin?*—and then used it as a ram to smash Milo in the chest. Milo staggered back. Ronnie pursued his advantage, hammering Milo again and again. Milo's arms windmilled as his heels stopped at the edge of the stage.

"Kill them all!" screamed one of the coffins.

Roaring, Ronnie apparently intended to do just that. He thrust one last time, and Milo gave a despairing wail as he went off the stage. A giant splash rose as the man struck the ornamental pond. And then Ronnie raised the box above his head, roared once more, a terrible sound, and flung the box down after Milo. There was a horrid clanging noise followed by a bright flare, as if some electronics had just short-circuited, and then Ronnie stepped back, his posture one of satisfaction.

Four Elvises were sprawled on stage, incapacitated. One of them, Garvikh perceived, was Ruth Song.

The Elvis still on his feet, plus Ronnie Romper, picked up two of the unconscious Elvises, then flew from the stage, followed by Ronnie Romper and the cart. Three wounded Elvises were left behind. The audience screamed for more.

Dimly, Garvikh realized that this was his cue. He dragged himself to his feet, staggered downstage, and found the microphone. He picked it up and assumed the Seventh Posture again.

"*Wellllll . . .*" he repeated, and the crowd went wild. He held his pose for ten seconds, then for another six, then for another six. The audience's excitement knew no bounds. Garvikh had probably achieved some sort of record. Finally he waved his arm, signalling the downbeat for "Heartbreak Hotel," then stepped back into the powerful "Wailing Stance" to cry the opening lines. Unfortunately his foot landed on a pile of the purple foam that seemed, unaccountably, to have been smeared around the stage.

While the opening bars to "Heartbreak Hotel" rang out Garvikh performed a crazed, whirling dance for a few brief seconds, then fell to the stage.

From his prone position, he heard the roaring sound of audience approval. *Immortality at last,* he thought, and then he surrendered his hold on consciousness.

Maijstral and his party made their way to the stage door, which parted automatically for Maijstral's coded badge. As the doors rolled open, Maijstral gazed out into the combat-ready eyes of a platoon of well-armed guards, led by the same officer who had admitted them to the Heart of Graceland.

Oh dear, he thought, and prepared to surrender.

In his imagination, dungeon gates yawned.

The officer looked up from his portable scanner. "Are there any instructions, sir?" he asked.

Maijstral's thoughts brightened. "Why, yes," he said. "Some false Elvii have just disturbed the concert. Take your men to the stage and put them in custody."

The man saluted. "It is my constant joy to serve the Elvii!" he proclaimed.

Maijstral's stunned party left the amphitheater, trailing purple ooze, and the guards filed in to do their duty.

"Are we having a good time, Drake?" ex-Dornier asked. *"I can't really tell."*

EIGHTEEN

✾ ✾ ✾

Colonel-General Vandergilt walked into Tvar's north-west drawing room, and Maijstral observed that she looked different from those occasions on which she was swooping down on miscreants, her eyes alight with fanaticism and hatred for all that was unEarthly. At the moment, having made her way past the pack of reporters at the gates of Tvar's estate, and having had to request admittance from the servants instead of stalking through the door with a uniformed group of bullyboys at her back, she seemed quite altered.

Even her hair was less threatening, with more disobedient strands than usual sabotaging her dignity.

Maijstral couldn't help but be pleased with the change.

"General Vandergilt," he said, "the butler told me you had news?"

Vandergilt's voice was a carefully pitched monotone, concerned only with the facts. "Major Song has confessed her part in the plot to have you killed by provoking a series of duels, and she has also confessed her scheme to steal your father's coffin."

Maijstral nodded. "I should congratulate you on your interrogative technique," he said. "I had thought she would prove sterner stuff."

Vandergilt reached a hand up to twine a strand of hair around her finger, then realized what she was doing and disciplined the hand promptly. "I had little to do with it," she said. "The Elvii ordered her to confess."

"Ah. Very good of them."

"The Elvis involved in the plot—Elvis XIV, by the way—has also confessed. I gather the other Elvii will formally expel him."

"The Elvii," Maijstral smiled, "are surely the reservoir of wisdom."

Vandergilt flushed slightly. "As for the instigator of the plot—" she began.

Maijstral's smile, like Vandergilt's flush, expanded. "You mean Fleet Admiral Song?" he asked. "The Nelson of Neerwinden? The Hero of the Human Constellation? Vigilant defender of the human race from all wickedness and alien contamination?"

Vandergilt cleared her throat. "Yes," she mumbled. "Admiral Song. As someone already declared legally dead, he is immune from any legal penalty, but it appears the matter is moot. There was some damage to his coffin, apparently due either to collision or to stray gunfire, and when he fell into the water he, ah, short-circuited."

Maijstral had wondered what that flare of energy implied. "Admiral Song is no more?" he said.

"Such existence as remained to him has been terminated, yes."

"Such a shameful end for a great man," Maijstral smiled. "Involved in a mean, sordid little conspiracy of theft and murder." He successfully resisted an impulse to snap his fingers and laugh out loud.

Maijstral directed her attention toward her boots. She cleared her throat again. "It appears that Captain Hay had no part in the conspiracy," she said, "and was acting in order to defend his fiancée from assault. He was severely damaged by the discharge of energy from Admiral Song's coffin, and is currently in hospital."

"What a shame," Maijstral grinned.

"Of course," Vandergilt said, and a bit of steel entered her glance once more, "there remains the problem of who entered Graceland illegally in order to liberate your father, and engaged in illegal gunplay within the sacred precincts." She looked hopeful. "These people, if discovered, could almost certainly be arrested."

"I'd love to help you, General," Maijstral said, "but I'm afraid I have no idea who these individuals might be. All I know is that my father reappeared in his room. If I were you," he suggested, "I might inquire among the Elvii. Perhaps they discovered the plot and acted to quell it on their own."

Vandergilt's look darkened. She tossed her head to get hair out of her eyes. "I will investigate the possibility," she said.

"Of course," Maijstral lied, "my information suggests that the Elvii were so appalled by the goings-on within their sacred precincts that they would never prosecute anyone who acted to expose malfeasance within their ranks."

Vandergilt's expression was sour. "Your information suggests that, does it?"

"Alas for justice," Maijstral said, "it does."

"The question remains," Vandergilt said, "of your intent to prosecute. If Major Song is to undergo a trial, of course it would require you to alter your schedule and remain on Earth for an indefinite period, with enormous inconvenience to yourself and your career." There was a subdued but hopeful glint in her eye as she spoke.

"And there would be such enormous publicity," Maijstral said.

"Yes." Leaping at her chance. "Very troublesome for you, I'm sure."

"And of course much of the publicity would be aimed at exposing the moral bankruptcy of the pro-Human movement, with unforeseen consequence for the Security and Sedition Act, which would legalize forms of discrimination against nonhumans and vastly increase the power of, among others, the Special Services Corps, to which you belong."

Vandergilt's face was a mask. "I'm sure I couldn't make those judgments, sir."

Amusement glowed behind Maijstral's lazy eyes. "I don't see why I should be inconvenienced by a trial at all," he said. "My presence probably won't even be required, not with Major Song's confession. And, of course," smiling thinly, "an abstract consideration for justice requires me to prosecute."

"As you say, sir." Stonily.

"Do I have to sign anything?"

"Right here, sir."

Maijstral signed with a flourish. "Very well, then, General Vandergilt," he said. "I leave you to your job."

"Yes, sir."

Maijstral waved a hand commandingly. "Go forth and arrest the miscreants, officer!"

"Yes, sir."

Colonel-General Vandergilt marched out, furiously stuffing loose strands of hair back under her cap.

Maijstral, pleased with this little scene, made his way from the northwest drawing room into the southwest drawing room adjacent.

Nichole looked up from the documents she was reading—information concerning the very best place to eat Fleth à la Normandie at Luna City, her next destination.

"Did it go well, Drake?" she asked.

"I believe it did, yes."

He sat next to her on the sofa. "It is in large part thanks to your researches that everything has gone as well as it has," he said.

"It was my pleasure. Those people were absolute *poison.*"

"Indeed they were. And now they've not only been thwarted, they've been exposed and humiliated."

She looked at him with her famous blue eyes. "You lead a surprisingly dangerous life, Drake."

"Perhaps. But at least I'm lucky." He took her hand. "Most of all, I am lucky in my friends," he said.

"Thank you."

"I will always be grateful for our friendship."

She cocked her head and regarded him. "I sense a *but* somewhere in this stretch of conversation."

"I regret it, Nichole."

"So do I." She blinked and looked thoughtful. "You are the only man ever to turn me down, Drake, do you know that? And now you've done it twice."

"Even with these disappointments factored in, I think your percentage of conquests remains admirably high."

She gave a smile. "Perhaps so."

"I hope this won't stop you from asking at regular intervals. I may yet change my mind."

"Well." She disengaged her hand and rose from the sofa. "Perhaps it was a foolish notion, anyway."

"I trust not, my lady." He stood, escorted her to the door, sniffed her ears.

"Next time you're in mortal danger," Nichole said, "I hope you won't forget to call."

"I won't. Thank you for everything."

"Give my love to Roman."

"I will. Thank you again."

A pang of regret touched his heart as he watched her leave. If only, he considered, there were two of him, or perhaps three, so that he could explore all the choices available to him.

He'd managed to duplicate himself in his magic act, he thought. Pity it had been a trick, and hadn't lasted.

Prince Hunac's unblinking dark eyes were still a bit unsettling. Maijstral was brought to mind of obsidian knives and bloody altars.

"I called as soon as I heard," Hunac said.

"That is very good of you."

Hunac blinked. Finally. "It is my part to apologize, isn't it? I misinterpreted events."

"Some highly intelligent people took very good care that you should."

"It is good of you to say so. Still, I should have seen that there was something wrong."

"You allowed Her Grace of Benn to persuade you to delay, and that enabled me to deal with the situation. For that delay I should thank you."

The obsidian knives flashed again in Hunac's eyes. "It strikes me that those responsible for the situation should be compelled to atone for their crimes. I have sent out emissaries in quest of Major Song and Alice Manderley, who so abused my hospitality."

Alice Manderley, Kenny Chang, and Drexler had been released as soon as Maijstral and his party returned from Graceland. Maijstral suspected that Alice and Kenny would book passage on the first liner leaving Earth.

Drexler, deprived of funds, would have to steal something in order to make an escape, a task made difficult by the fact that Maijstral had kept all Drexler's burglar equipment in his own possession. Maijstral was certain that Drexler would never be employed by any high-ranking burglar again, not once Drexler's treachery had been thoroughly aired by the media.

"Would you happen to know," Hunac inquired, "where Miss Manderley might be?"

"If she's not at home, I'm afraid I have no idea." Thoughtfully, Maijstral fingered his diamond ring. "I would appreciate it, by the way, if you postponed any encounter with Major Song until after her trial. I would very much like to make certain that her cause is publicly and thoroughly discredited."

Hunac nodded. "I will take your request under serious consideration."

"Thank you."

"My emissaries have had no luck with Mangula Arish—she keeps running away the second they appear."

Maijstral repressed a smile. "That is unfortunate indeed, Your Highness."

"Now I learn that she has resigned her post and fled outsystem."

"Perhaps this is a victory in itself."

"I will have to consider it so—after I give her flight the maximum possible publicity."

"I hope other journalists will bear it in mind."

Hunac permitted himself a flintlike smile. "So do I." The smile warmed a bit. "I hope you will accept my hospitality in the Underwater Palace again. I think I can promise you that you will have a much better time."

Maijstral nodded. "I will accept, if I can. My plans are a bit uncertain at present."

"Good-bye, then. Thank you for being so understanding."

"Farewell. Give my best to the toadfish."

"I will."

The Prince's image faded, leaving Maijstral with an after-taste of pure satisfaction.

Things had worked out well.

"Dad?"

"Drake? Is that you, Drake?"

"Yes, it is."

Maijstral sat on a chair and signalled to his father's guards to leave the room.

He wasn't about to let his father become the hostage of yet another political lunatic. He had hired a squad of well-armed, well-equipped bodyguards—well, *coffin*guards—simply to sit in the room with him and keep him safe from any further adventures until ex-Dornier could be shipped back to the family crypt on Nana.

If the guards had to spend their time listening to the corpse's prattle, at least they were well compensated for their efforts.

"How are you doing, Dad?" Maijstral asked.

"Well," the late Duke remarked, "I seem to be dead."

"Yes." Trying not to smile. "I had noticed. I meant, you're not suffering any ill effects from your adventure?"

"With Bertie? Oh no. I had a *splendid* time!"

"Bertie?"

"Oh yes, my old school chum. He had this most elabo-rate *prank* worked out. It had to do with, oh, metaphysics and things."

Maijstral worked for a moment at understanding, then gave up.

"I'm glad you enjoyed yourself," he said. "Is there any-thing you'd like now."

"A cup of cocoa and a biscuit would be nice."

Maijstral sighed. "Well," he said, "I'll see what I can do."

* * *

"Nichole sends her love."

"Thank you, sir."

"Is there anything you need?"

"Thank you, sir, no. I am provided with all the necessities."

Maijstral smiled as he left Roman's hospital room.

Roman was recovering swiftly. His flesh had lost its alarming scarlet color and was approaching the normal, healthy grey. Black stubble covered his skin where his fur was growing back. The new age-ring had healed.

Roman's molt, thank the Twelve Passive Virtues, was over.

It wasn't the molt that had put Roman in the hospital, however. When he raised Admiral Song's coffin above his head and flung it down on Milo Hay, Roman had strained his back.

It was the part of a lord, Maijstral thought, to retire to bed when his back pained him. Roman might as well get used to such privileges while he could.

He walked down the hall to Roberta's room, knocked, and entered. Roberta was propped up in bed, smiling and chatting with Will, the Bubber, who had come to pay a visit.

Roberta had broken some ribs in the fight at Graceland. She had committed herself to the hospital less because her medical condition required it than because the rest of her household, Batty and Paavo Kuusinen, were already inmates, and she thought she might as well make a party of it.

"Hello, Roberta. Hello, Will."

The Bubber rose from his chair. "Hello, Drake."

"It's good to see you, Will." Maijstral sniffed Roberta's ears and kissed her cheek.

"How are the ribs?" he asked.

"Well enough."

"And Mr. Kuusinen?"

"Well, he *was* knocked unconscious. The doctors want him under observation. But so far no serious damage has surfaced."

"Very good."

The Bubber shifted his feet awkwardly. "I should push off. But first—" He smiled. "Drake, would you like to see a card trick?"

"By all means."

Will's trick was a complex one, involving a force, a shift, and a back palm. When he produced at length the three of rovers, Maijstral and Roberta both affected amazement and offered congratulations.

"Very well done," Maijstral said.

"Thank you." The Bubber beamed. "Is there any room for improvement?"

"Well, your patter could use a little work. And I could see the little finger break from this angle."

The Bubber's face fell slightly. "Oh."

"I'd advise working the trick in a mirror."

"I will. Thanks." He looked thoughtful. "You know, Drake, I'd like to ask your advice in another sphere, if I might."

"Certainly."

"Joseph Bob is wondering if he should challenge Alice Manderley and Major Song for their part in misleading him."

Maijstral gave the thought his consideration. "Well, it was Drexler who stole the pistol, not Alice."

"J.B. wouldn't challenge a servant."

"I shouldn't think so. And Major Song is about to undergo a trial that will discredit her forever, I expect."

The Bubber nodded soberly. "True."

"And—just between the two of us—" Maijstral touched the Bubber's arm and smiled. "Duelling is a perfectly silly custom, don't you think?"

The Bubber looked surprised. "Uh—if you say so. I suppose it is." He shuffled his feet. "I've taken up enough of your time. Good-bye, Drake, and thanks. See you later, Roberta."

Roberta waved from her bed. "Good-bye, Will."

The Bubber left. Maijstral sat on Roberta's bed. "I suspect I have not thanked you enough," he said. "You kept me out of Hunac's clutches, and you risked yourself in my behalf yesterday. You've performed superbly, and I'm thankful you suffered no more than some cracked ribs."

Her violet eyes warmed. "I'm glad it's over."

"So am I." He smiled, took her hand. "I've had time to think."

"At last." Her look turned serious. "And your conclusions?"

"You've made the most attractive offer—"

Roberta's face hardened. "But you're not going to take it."

"My life is too unsettled at the moment for me to consider marriage. If you'd made the offer at another time—"

"It can't wait." Shortly.

"Or if it were possible for us to spend time together normally, to get to know one another before making any decision—"

She sighed. "I had a feeling this would happen. Ever since our night together."

Maijstral's ears cocked forward in surprise. "Beg pardon?"

"Well. That night wasn't—well—it wasn't what I'd expected. Perfectly *pleasant,* you understand, you were very nice, but somehow—I don't know—the whole experience was somehow lacking."

Maijstral was surprised. "It was our first night together," he said. "A certain amount of awkwardness is to be expected in the early stages."

She waved a hand. "Oh, it wasn't that. Just—well, I'd

been thinking about being with you for *years,* understand. And it wasn't what I had anticipated."

Maijstral felt a touch of annoyance. He could hardly be blamed, he thought, for any failure to live up to Roberta's lush schoolgirl fantasies.

"Perhaps," he ventured, "your expectations were a trifle unrealistic."

"What do you think of Will?"

Maijstral's eyes lifted. "Sorry?"

"Do you think I should marry Will?"

"Er—"

"If I'm not going to marry *you,*" tartly, "I've got to marry *somebody.* And I've spent a lot of time with Will in the last days, and he seems suitable enough."

Maijstral gave it thought. "Speaking dynastically, it would be a good match."

Fire flashed from her violet eyes. "He's a little green," she judged, "but I reckon I'll be able to make a man of him."

Maijstral found himself thoroughly glad he had not consented to the engagement. The result might be admirable enough in the abstract, he thought, but hard to live with in the long run.

"If I may be permitted to make an observation," he said, "it would be that men are not *made,* but make themselves. A partner can make the task easier, but cannot drive a person to it."

Roberta frowned.

"Will's problem," Maijstral added, "insofar as he has one, is that he has nothing to do that his brother, or someone in his circle, has not done before him. If you marry him, you should encourage him to be something other than a consort."

Roberta seemed a little amused. "You think I should give him a hobby?"

"You are a very well-known racer," Maijstral pointed

out. "And I think you'd be a lesser person without *your* hobby, no?"

"Hm," Roberta said, and frowned.

As Maijstral left, he cast his mind back to the night he spent with Roberta, and felt a cold little anxiety gnawing at the back of his mind. She had seemed enthusiastic enough at the *time,* he thought. He had thought he had behaved rather well.

And then he wondered if the whole comment had been some small attempt at revenge. Very possibly, he thought.

He dropped into Kuusinen's room and found him asleep. He would thank Kuusinen later.

The next room was Aunt Batty's. He dropped in, spoke generally of his admiration for Roberta, and then mentioned he had decided with regret to decline her offer of marriage.

"Indeed," Batty said, and her ears flicked forward in disapproval. "This will not improve my standing with the family. Most of them thought Bobbie's schemes highly unorthodox, and I supported her. When recriminations are handed out, I will receive more than my share."

"If it is any consolation, I believe she has replaced me already. With Will, the Bubber."

Batty considered this. "Well," she said, "she could have done worse."

"I hope this will not prejudice your biography."

Batty looked down her muzzle, her face severe. "Some in the family might consider this rejection an insult, though I suppose I should take a more charitable view. I will try to do my historian's duty and avoid any reflections—on your character, say, or your valor—which may seem to me unwarranted."

Valor? Maijstral thought, a taste of panic fluttering in his throat.

He really *would* have to get a look at that manuscript.

*   *   *

The last room was that of Conchita. She, like Kuusinen, had been knocked unconscious in the fight, and likewise was being kept for observation. He opened the door, peered inside, and saw Conchita watching a video.

"Hello," he said, and knocked.

She brightened. "Hi! I was just watching the vid."

Maijstral looked at the screen and saw people in Stetsons racing across the prairie on horseback. "Are you fond of Westerns?" he said.

"Only too. They're my favorite."

Better and better, Maijstral thought.

Conchita smiled and patted the bed beside her. Maijstral closed the door behind him, stretched out next to her, and put an arm around her.

Their kiss was very long and very pleasant.

"Why don't you stay awhile?" Conchita said when it was over.

"I have no other plans." He contemplated the situation for the moment. "Perhaps," he said, "I should lock the door."

"Can you lock a door in a hospital?"

"If the top-ranked burglar in the galaxy can't figure out a way to rig a door," Maijstral observed, "then he isn't worth his title."

Some time later, Conchita curled up next to Maijstral, pillowed her head upon his shoulder, and closed her eyes. Maijstral gave thought to the situation.

"You haven't experienced any disappointment, have you?" he asked.

"Disappointment? Why should I be disappointed?"

"No feelings that, say, your fantasies haven't been in some slight way, ah, completely fulfilled? Your expectations haven't been in any way disappointed?"

"Don't be silly," she said, and yawned. "You don't mind if I take a nap, do you?"

Roberta, Maijstral concluded, was simply *wrong*.
Experience told in these matters.

"There is only one thing I have to request," he said.

"Mm?"

"The hair," he said. "You'll have to change it."

"The fin? It makes me look taller!"

"I think your height is perfection itself."

"Well. Thank you for saying so."

"The fin goes, yes?"

"Oh." Sleepily. "If you insist."

As Conchita drifted off to sleep, Maijstral noticed that the video was still on. He looked for the service plate to shut it off and saw that it was too far to reach without disturbing Conchita.

He looked at the image. The Western had ended, and instead Maijstral saw a red-haired puppet with a fixed smile.

Ronnie Romper, Maijstral thought. *Oh no.*

He looked in despair at the service plate, still out of reach.

"Gosh, Uncle Amos," the puppet was saying. "I sure was scared. My knees were knocking together like anything!"

"Those dinosaurs were intimidating, that's for sure," Uncle Amos said, puffing his pipe. "I was getting pretty anxious myself."

"I was so afraid I almost ran away."

"But you didn't," Uncle Amos said. "That's the important thing."

Ronnie batted his eyes. "I don't understand, Uncle Amos."

Uncle Amos gazed at Ronnie from beneath his wizened white eyebrows. "Bravery doesn't mean that you don't feel fear," he said. "A fellow about to be run over by a herd of dinosaurs would have to be pretty stupid not to feel fear, now wouldn't he?"

"Gosh. I guess so."

"A brave person is one who feels fear, but who overcomes it and goes on to do what he has to do."

"Wow, Uncle Amos," the puppet said, "I never thought of that."

Maijstral stared at the screen. *I never thought of that, either,* he thought.

A sense of wonder overcame him. He lay back and reviewed his life. Based on a conclusion he'd drawn at sixteen, when he'd fought his first duel, he'd always assumed he was a coward.

But he *had* fought the duel, and another just a few days ago, and in between he'd been in a number of situations in which either he was shooting at people, or they were shooting at him, or both were happening at once. And yesterday, during the raid on the Heart of Graceland, he'd been giving orders as if he were an experienced warrior instead of a sneak thief with a sinking heart.

It wasn't as if he hadn't been afraid the whole time. But, just like Ronnie Romper, he'd done what he'd come to do, and not run away. Or rather, he hadn't run away until it was *time* to run away.

And of course his profession involved breaking into other people's homes. Preferably when no one was there, of course, but maybe that was merely common sense rather than a reflection on his bravery.

Perhaps, he thought, his sixteen-year-old assessment of himself had been overharsh.

He looked at the screen and blinked. *Thank you, Ronnie,* he thought.

The puppet had his uses, after all.

He lay back, Conchita peacefully sleeping on his shoulder, and gazed upward, past the hospital ceiling, into a universe of expanding possibility.

* * *

Some months later, when she and Roberta had returned to the Empire, Aunt Batty went in search of her notes and failed to find them.

They were missing—all the information she'd gleaned from Roman's genealogy, from her interviews with Joseph Bob, from her long conversations with Maijstral's father. All gone.

She had packed them most carefully, she knew. And now the entire package was gone.

She considered this for a long moment. *Most foolish,* she concluded. Her memory was perfectly good, and of course she could draw on the pages of notes and manuscript that had never left the Empire. Most of the second volume was completed. It was only the third that would be delayed.

It was never wise to annoy a biographer, she thought. They—*we*—have ways of getting our revenge.

If there was anyone who was an expert in the matter of interpretation, in the slight distortions of the facts necessary to cast aspersions on a person's character or ability, on an individual's motivations or worthiness—well, that person was a biographer.

She would take *very good care,* she thought severely, with her study of Maijstral.

And if he regretted the outcome—well, Aunt Batty thought, whose fault was it anyway?